# after the rain

aisling smith

# after the rain

hachette
AUSTRALIA

Quote on page 263 is from 'Things I'll Not Do' by Allen Ginsberg, copyright © 1956, 1961, Allen Ginsberg, used by permission of The Wylie Agency (UK), Limited.

Quote on page 274 is from 'Do Not Go Gentle into that Good Night', *The Collected Poems of Dylan Thomas: The Centenary Edition*, London, Weidenfeld & Nicolson, 2014, reproduced with permission.

hachette AUSTRALIA

Published in Australia and New Zealand in 2023
by Hachette Australia
(an imprint of Hachette Australia Pty Limited)
Gadigal Country, Level 17, 207 Kent Street, Sydney, NSW 2000
www.hachette.com.au

Hachette Australia acknowledges and pays our respects to the past, present and future Traditional Owners and Custodians of Country throughout Australia and recognises the continuation of cultural, spiritual and educational practices of Aboriginal and Torres Strait Islander peoples. Our head office is located on the lands of the Gadigal people of the Eora Nation.

A catalogue record for this book is available from the National Library of Australia

ISBN: 978 0 7336 4879 3 (paperback)

Cover design by Grace West
Cover image courtesy Stocksy
Author photo courtesy Andrew Ferdinands, Ferdi Photography
Typeset in 12.25/19 pt Adobe Garamond Pro by Bookhouse, Sydney
Printed and bound in Great Britain by Clays Ltd, Elcograf S.p.A.

*For my mother, who has always lived her life with grace*

# part 1

# 1987

# chapter one

WHAT HAS HAPPENED to Benjamin?

Malti feels the question in her body. Not in the once-mysterious triangle of her womb—where she now knows that their baby grows—but somewhere higher up, behind her ribcage. She has not yet told Benjamin that she is pregnant. Settlement is tomorrow and they will take possession of the beachside house. All these new things make Malti shivery: excitement or nervousness, she cannot tell. She has cut her hair to shoulder length, thrown away six and a half boxes of old novels (mostly classics from her high school book list—sorry, George Eliot and Katherine Mansfield) and is counting down the days on the kitchen calendar as they speed towards their inevitable conclusion.

But Benjamin is working late at the office. He kisses her when he comes home but his mind has not followed him through the door. They have always lived together in a world of words, but he has now become taciturn. Where have the words gone? He no longer tells her about what he is researching, and when she recounts the details of her cases, she can see that he is not really listening. He nods and makes noises in the right places, but his eyes are only meeting hers in the shallows.

Their new home waits for them to arrive, perched on its graceful hill overlooking Port Phillip Bay. It's a far cry from their first rental eight years ago, a granny flat out the back of an Armadale mansion, with no heating in winter and no cash for it anyway. Although both she and Benjamin are making good money now, this new place on Beach Road represents years of hard work and cold noses every July in the name of their savings account and the abstraction of Future Opportunity.

But when Malti drives out there the evening before they move and sits across the road in her Fiat, watching the dark windows of the empty house, she wonders if it was all worth it. The house they're renting in Oakleigh is as uninhabited as this one tonight: it's 9 pm and Ben is still at work. And, right now, all she can see of the dream home are dark rooms and empty light fixtures.

---

Sometimes Malti wonders if she brought a curse down upon them. She grew up with stories and superstitions and these die hard. She knows the seeds of folklore and how they blossom with retelling. She remembers her father in the front seat of the car, hands spaced on the steering wheel (at ten and two o'clock) telling her about Ratu Udre Udre in his BBC accent—a time warp from the 1930s, when he'd been a kid learning English off the radio. She remembers the cold flush on her skin, even though three of the car windows were halfway down, letting in the thick blanket of tropical heat. Udre Udre, the island's most famous cannibal. The ancient tales promised that eating the flesh of a thousand bodies would bring immortality and Udre Udre had believed. It was the cultural convention of a time and place. Consume the bodies of your enemies to transcend your own physicality. Her father had recounted the horror story with precision and adult indifference, his mind was preoccupied by electricity bills and the 8 pm news broadcast, but in the back seat Malti was wide-eyed, totally awake to magic. The mysticism of the doubled name had got under her skin; *Udre Udre*, she repeated to herself, and her skin prickled. The power of its sound never has lessened for her. Even now, if she thinks about the story, she'll squirm in discomfort and Ben will raise his eyebrows at her. 'Did someone walk over your grave?'

Udre Udre. He was the cautionary tale in their households, the coconut-scented bogeyman—*Be careful, child, or Udre Udre will get you*—but more powerful than the West's amorphous creature under the bed. Udre Udre had history on his side: he was real. They had driven past his grave, way out in Rakiraki, as they made their way home to Nadi. Malti had felt caterpillar chills—something about the clotted overhang of trees and the way the roads crossed there, but it was also more than that: the air here was marked. From the window, Malti stared as her father pointed out the grave. Somehow the act of looking would keep her safe; if she wasn't looking, who knew what would happen? The grave itself was whitewashed, now stained and dirty-looking, with Udre Udre's name etched in capital letters on the side. Long after their little blue car had passed it, Malti had twisted around and glanced uneasily out the back window. But all she saw was the dust conjured by their car's wheels and a dirt road bordered by greenery. There was no figure trailing after the car. Still, she had to make sure. Udre Udre—shadow man, ghost man—he must not follow them home.

Even now, Malti doesn't see herself as superstitious. She calls it being open-minded. It's just that some things are worth paying attention to. From nine to five, she's logical and lawyerly—and yet she owns three separate decks of tarot cards and practises creative visualisation every other night. She'll toss the salt over her shoulder if no-one is watching.

'Hedging your bets,' Benjamin teases her. 'Believing everything, just in case something is true.'

He does the same thing, of course—goes to church once a year on Christmas Eve, just in case there's really a God who happens to be watching and taking attendance. Malti knows that he will want their child baptised.

They're not always on the same page with things.

For their wedding anniversary eighteen months ago, Benjamin gave her a knife set and she couldn't quite hide her apprehension. It had been 8 pm on a Tuesday and their specially chosen French restaurant was almost deserted. There had been far too many staff for the three couples on dinner dates. Waiters walked around aimlessly, and Malti saw them sneaking forlorn glances at their wristwatches. Both Malti and Benjamin had come straight from work. Malti arrived first and adjusted her streak of Chanel plum lipstick at the table with a two-dollar compact mirror. Its glass was scuffed from the wilderness of her handbag and she had to squint to make out her reflection in its tiny circle. When she caught sight of Benjamin in her peripheral vision, she snapped the compact shut—hurriedly, sheepishly. Which was weird; she woke up beside him bare-faced every morning, he saw her brushing her teeth. This, the act of touching up her make-up, shouldn't have been any different, but it somehow made her feel so much more vulnerable to be seen putting on her face.

Benjamin was carrying an immaculately wrapped gift in his hands. Red cellophane and a curling gold ribbon, just as Malti wore a red blouse and gold jewellery tonight—it was a wink to the sari she'd worn at their wedding. He had bent over to kiss her lips and then sat down at the table.

He whistled. 'You're a knockout,' he said, heat in his blue eyes.

He handed the gift over awkwardly, one-handed, and received Malti's own present in much the same way. Some people always treat gifts like bombs. But Malti and Benjamin both knew what was in the velvet box she passed to him, so he went first. Cufflinks. Although he smiled, he didn't bother to feign surprise. It was her go-to gift. She'd been working in the CBD too long: this was a present for a lawyer rather than a linguist. Benjamin smiled anyway, leaned across the table to kiss her again and promised to wear them the next day, even though most shirts buttoned at the wrist nowadays so he'd have to wear a formal one, which would be a nuisance. Once, he'd have done it without thinking, simply to see her smile when she saw him wearing her present. Now he looked like he was thinking about how uncomfortable he would be all day.

But if he had been expecting her present, his gift to Malti took her by surprise. When she peeled the wrapping away and saw the photographs on the cardboard box, she bit her lip.

'*Wüsthof knives. Form, function and quality. Guaranteed precision*,' she read aloud. 'These are . . . great.'

'I remember you saying we need some good knives.'

'Yeah, I do. We do. That's so sweet . . . but do you think it's a good idea to give me these?'

'What do you mean?'

'Sharp presents sever relationships.'

'Huh?'

'You're not supposed to give someone you love something sharp. It's a bad omen.'

'That old wives' tale?'

'Yes!'

'Oh, for God's sake.' And now the heat had crept out of his eyes and into his voice.

'Symbolism,' she murmured.

'That's ridiculous.'

'Yeah, I guess. I mean, thank you. They're lovely.' She picked up a bread roll and then put it down again. 'I know what we can do,' she said. 'Why don't I give you a silver coin for them—a token payment. That way, technically, I've bought them from you.'

Benjamin didn't look at her; his face was tilted down as he re-read the wine list.

'Fine. Whatever.'

Malti pulled her wallet out, there at the table, and just before Benjamin took the fifty-cent coin she held out, she realised how hard-edged it felt in her palm. His face was carefully neutral, but she knew her insistence was walking a fine line between endearing and annoying.

They ate their meals and drank the wine Ben chose, smiling softly at each other and striving for cordiality, and neither of them mentioned their presents again.

Back home that evening, Malti put the new knives into their pinewood block. She had to admit that they were impressive, their handles buffed black, with a little red logo down the bottom. In the following weeks, she found she quite liked them—both looking at them and using them. They felt good in her hand and fitted as gently as a pen. She tried not to think about the messy start she'd had with them. Some gifts are hard to receive graciously, but when she thought about it in hindsight, it was with a jolt of regret. She sometimes wondered what Benjamin had done with the fifty-cent piece. And then, inevitably, would follow the question: Had fifty cents been enough?

---

The next morning Malti waits alone to greet the movers. This is the day the new house becomes theirs! She collects the keys from the real estate agent first thing in the morning and hooks hers onto the Waikiki keychain she bought years ago. The old house is all packed up and triaged. She has already loaded her car with boxes and now waits in the scrappy front yard for the removalists to arrive. The day is warm and the light is bright and glary in a way that she has always felt is quintessentially Australian. As she waits in the front yard, she closes her eyes and lets the sun bathe her face.

The road outside the house is quiet and it's easy to hear the hum of the removal truck as it arrives. It's still only January and the year is off to its usual sleepy start as people dawdle home from their summer holidays. The two bearded movers deftly manoeuvre the truck into the driveway with a spatial awareness that Malti can only admire. They work rapidly, dismantling the queen bed and the bookshelves, loading them onto the truck.

'Sorry we didn't take those apart for you,' she says.

'This is the easy bit,' one of them calls back. 'It's moving all those boxes of books that we're dreading!'

Malti laughs. 'Yes, buying books is an addiction.'

'Where are the new digs?' the other one asks her.

'Brighton.'

'Moving up in the world, huh?'

'Moving into a mortgage actually.'

They laugh, though she isn't joking.

'We'll follow you, love,' they tell her when the truck is full.

It takes about twenty minutes to get to the new house. Malti jumps out to pull the heavy front gates open—the metal scrapes jarringly across the driveway—then drives through them. The truck comes in after her, trailing a slight plume of black. It's incredible having a driveway that is big enough to fit both vehicles. The road outside the house is busier here. As the removalists turn off the ignition, Malti watches the traffic and the handful of pedestrians carrying beach towels, heading down the hill towards the water.

She puts her key in the front door and feels it swing open. It's wooden and heavy—the kind of door that could be slammed shut with a real sound effect. And then she is standing inside their house.

One of the movers whistles through his teeth as he comes in behind her. 'Nice place.'

They ask her where she wants things. She feels like she is directing a play as she points to the rooms where the furniture should go. Malti is fishing through boxes for the bed linen to carry upstairs. Around her, the movers unpack at high speed. They resurrect the table and the bed within minutes it seems.

'Why so fast?' she asks them.

'If we're not done in the next twenty minutes, you'll be charged for another hour.'

Malti stares. 'Isn't that more money for you?'

'Yeah. But, you know, you're on your own here and all.'

'Your hubby's a bit of a slacker,' the other one agrees.

'It's fine,' Malti says firmly. 'You can take your time. And he'll be here later.'

Although they nod, they continue to dash around and finish seventeen minutes later.

'Cup of tea?' she asks them. But they decline. Malti stands in the cluttered entrance hall and watches their truck drive away, slipping into the stream of traffic just beyond the gates.

—

Even the endless spray of cars up and down Beach Road night and day cannot dampen the loveliness of number 112. It has a little balcony on the second storey, a French-looking thing with a filigree of wrought iron. It's perhaps too noisy outside for them to ever really use it, but she pictures them eating breakfast there, the gentle curve of the bay spread out ahead and the gleaming sunlit city rising from the far shore. Every night there will be orange and pink sunsets, brighter than anything she has ever seen in neon, before darkness turns the city into their own personal light show. Dream home. People who grow up next to the water can never really do without it. Its osmotic power easily crosses the membranes of the skin, and Malti thinks that without water she would simply dry out to a husk. She spent the first seventeen years of her life on an island in the Pacific and she's hopelessly under the spell of the sea. She never misses that island home—doesn't even think of that place as home—but she needs the ocean, as though salt water rather than haem runs in her veins.

Despite what she told the movers, it *is* kind of strange that Benjamin isn't here. Most years, he has been even less busy than her in January, as university doesn't start up again for two months, but this summer he is using the student-free period to get on top of his own research. He has undertaken extensive field work in the outback and presented at numerous conferences; he has barely had a chance to relax at all. It's okay—Malti doesn't mind picking up the slack. This is a partnership. She will spend the day getting the house in order and the two of them will celebrate tonight.

Malti cajoled both the greengrocer and the pharmacist into giving her their spare boxes and, weeks ago, began the sacred process of packing the books she planned to keep. The remaining hardback anthologies of Shakespeare and her old textbooks from law school sit side by side against cardboard that still smells like nashi pears, kiwi fruit and cantaloupe. Meanwhile, Benjamin's thick biographies and science fiction had remained in the bookcase for several more weeks. He had been coming home from work far too tired to pack boxes.

She spends the day sorting out as much as she can, but doesn't seem to make tangible progress. She has co-opted the box with the encyclopaedias to serve as a makeshift perch as she looks around what is now their dining area in the large open-plan space. Thank goodness the removalists took care of the heavy items—the stocky Arthurian dining table sits squarely in the middle of the room and all the floor-to-ceiling bookshelves have been assembled too. Benjamin has many talents, but he is not handy; hammering a nail into a wall stretches his capacity to the limit. Between the two of them, they can just about hang a picture frame.

Malti has been glancing at her watch constantly for the past hour. Benjamin should have been here by now, but she shouldn't be surprised that he isn't. Despite promising when he leaves for work each day that he will be home on time, she inevitably ends up watching the clock. Except tonight she won't pick a fight over it.

Malti is rehearsing sentences in her mind, trying out the right words and auditioning synonyms. Words have power—she and Benjamin have always known this. Both their careers are predicated on this very concept: Malti thumbs through common law and legislation, scours the language for the ratio decidendi or that one clause that matters, while Benjamin draws syntax trees, researches etymology and knows his phonology.

Malti wants to get her words right tonight.

Benjamin's new keys are waiting on the kitchen bench, so she has left the front door ajar for him to enter. And soon enough, she hears the sound of his car in the driveway. The metallic moaning of the gates opening is not familiar, but his engine certainly is. So is his gait—her ears know the way he moves. She hears him walk to the end of the unfamiliar corridor then cross into the room where she sits, hands neatly folded and eyes swivelling between the door and her watch. He is forty-five minutes late. She makes a note of this and files it away to consider later.

'Oh, hello,' Benjamin says and flashes that evergreen smile which makes anger impossible.

'Welcome home,' she says, for the sheer novelty of saying it.

'Home sweet home,' he agrees with a laugh.

She wonders if they will talk in clichés all evening.

'How was work?' she asks, getting to her feet and peering at the labels on the boxes.

'Good, good. Sorry I'm late.'

Nothing else is forthcoming and she doesn't press him.

'The place is looking good,' he says, wandering around the ground-floor rooms and poking his head into the laundry. 'The towels and cleaning products don't seem to have made their way out of the boxes. But I'm assuming the books are all unpacked, of course?'

'And the record player,' she agrees. She moves into the kitchen. 'We should have a toast.'

There's champagne in the fridge for him and cloudy apple juice for her, which she'll drink from one of their crystal flutes all the same. He joins her, rummaging through the boxes. It takes three goes to locate the one with the glasses. When they do, Benjamin slits the masking tape with a Stanley knife and Malti unwraps the glasses from the newspaper. She frowns at the smudgy residue of ink smeared inside and out. She puts them in the sink and starts fishing around through the boxes again, trying to find the one with the kitchen detergent. Benjamin shakes his head and flicks his eyes upwards to the ceiling.

'Just rinse 'em!'

And so she does (though later, when she lifts the glass to her lips, she can still smell newsprint on the rim). Benjamin hunts in the fridge and pulls out the champagne with surprise that turns into a smile.

'You would've been a great boy scout,' he tells her over his shoulder. He pops the cork and fills one glass, but when he goes to pour the second, Malti shakes her head.

'Not for me. I'll have some of the apple juice in the fridge.'

'Why?' He frowns, the bottle suspended over the second glass; realisation has not yet crashed down on him. 'Aren't you feeling well? This is good stuff!'

She pauses, poised on the precipice of what she knows is one of Those Moments.

'Benjamin,' she says, 'we're going to have a baby.'

The bottle, still almost full, thuds heavily when he places it on the bench. The excruciating fragility of this moment makes her want to wince—breathe wrong and it could be destroyed.

The next moment he has moved around the counter, his hands springing up to grip her elbows, then her upper arms. He leans forwards, staring into her eyes. 'Are you sure?'

How can he be so taken aback? They've been trying for eighteen months, after all.

'Yes.'

'Well . . .' He's still looking at her, the seam of a frown stitched in place between his eyebrows. He doesn't say anything else.

'Aren't you . . . aren't you *happy*?'

His smile is instantly back in place.

'Well, of *course* I am!' He pulls her closer now, wrapping his arms right around her, and kisses her. 'You just caught me off guard, that's all. And we'll have to watch our spending a bit more this year. But we're going to be parents? That's incredible.' He places his hand on her abdomen, spanning its flatness with his big palm. 'How far along are you?'

'Five weeks.'

He laughs, throwing that golden head right back, and she can suddenly see real wonderment awakening in his face.

'Five weeks,' he repeats, and the shell-shocked excitement now entering his voice is what she'd expected to hear from the first.

Benjamin moves back to the champagne flutes and now fills hers right to the brim with apple juice. They stand in their empty kitchen, surrounded by their cardboard boxes, and raise their glasses—his clear, hers opaque.

The flutes clink and they drink a toast to newness.

# chapter two

THEY SPEND THE weekend adjusting to the new house and unpacking the rest of the boxes. The place isn't perfect—one day it will need to be renovated. In fact, if they had the money (which they certainly don't), they would do it now. The two guest bedrooms are minuscule and tucked away on the ground floor, as though the architect believed guests were better kept out of sight and out of mind. The cobbled driveway has moss in its cracks and there is ivy growing on the front fence that will need to be pulled away before it destroys the structure with its pretty creeping ways.

For the first time in a long while, Benjamin stays home with her all weekend. There are no urgent trips to work. Rather than waking up on a Saturday morning to find Benjamin's side of the bed neatly made up again and the sediment of coffee in a cold cup on the sink, Ben is to be found sitting at the table reading a newspaper. The coffee in his mug is hot and fresh. He looks up when she enters and beams—rises to greet her in the doorway then drops to his knees to kiss her stomach.

'Corny,' she tells him, rolling her eyes.

He just laughs. 'How about a cup of tea?'

He boils the kettle and takes out a teapot and loose leaves, rather than simply reaching for the Twinings, gathering a jug of milk and a teacup to accompany it. He's been fussing over her since the night before, scolding her whenever she lifts something heavy. Now he insists she should drink more milk with her English breakfast.

'You need to make sure you're getting enough calcium,' he says bossily.

'You know you're a PhD, not a medical doctor, right?' she counters.

The newspaper he put down to say good morning stays folded; he does not bury his face behind it this morning. Instead of silence, the kitchen is full of the whistling kettle and Ben's chatter.

'Tell me about your cases,' he says, setting the timer on the steeping tea-leaves. His eyes are bright and fixed intently on hers. She feels a rush of relief. Benjamin is back!

'Well,' she begins, and chooses a few juicy facts from one of her current cases. She recounts it expressively and Benjamin is a good audience, laughing, sighing and frowning in all the right places.

It's true what they say, she thinks. A baby is miraculous.

They only leave the house for a short walk along the beachfront on Saturday—all that buttery sand is now sixty seconds from their front door—and to go to the shops on Sunday. They buy croissants from the little French bakery in Church Street and carry them home to spill crumbs all over their new kitchen benches.

It's a bit strange having this block of time together—somehow disconcerting to see Ben in the other room in bare feet and a t-shirt, Malti has become so used to him in work shirts. He moves efficiently around the house, always another cardboard box of things-to-be-unpacked in his arms. Does the distracted expression that she has become accustomed to seeing still lurk in the hidden corners of his face? Well, he's chirpy and engaged. And home.

That evening, Benjamin looks out the window at the bright sunset over the water. 'We haven't done too badly for ourselves, have we?'

---

On Monday, it only takes Malti twenty-five minutes to get to work, catching one of the bloated, vermicular trains to the CBD. It took upwards of an hour from the rented place in Wheelers Hill and not much less from Oakleigh. Benjamin has to go forty minutes into the eastern suburbs, but he gets the comfort of his Toyota and the cassettes which they keep in the glove compartment. His musical taste got stuck in the sixties and he fills the car with Bob Dylan, Leonard Cohen and Phil Ochs. He never bothered to go to the protests and rallies, but he loves a good folk song.

Malti wears a pencil skirt and lightweight shirt with lace at the throat. It's not time to buy the maternity clothes or make the announcements yet. It will be her secret under her corporate outfits.

But she cannot help smiling at absolutely nothing and people look at her curiously.

'You seem unusually happy,' one of the secretaries tells her dubiously as Malti walks from the communal bookshelf back to her chambers.

Malti raises an eyebrow (she's good at it). 'I am usually so sour-faced?' she stops to ask, balancing an armful of documents on her hip.

The secretary takes the question seriously and thinks for a moment.

'No,' she says at last, 'not sour, but normally you look stressed out. Or just sad or something. I dunno. You don't really smile that much.'

'That's barrister life for you,' Malti says lightly. 'But I did have a good weekend.'

She makes a point of smiling at the secretary now, but as she turns to walk back to her room the smile fades. The other woman's words are finding fertile soil in a dark corner of her mind. Stressed out . . . sad. Benjamin had hurled something similar at her in a fight six months ago: *You're like a ghost haunting the house. A grey ghost.* His face had been red and contorted that night. He'd arrived home four hours later than he had promised and she had confronted him, hands on hips in her grey flannelette dressing-gown. He had risen to meet her in anger and together they had ignited. Malti has not thought much about his description since—she tries to discount words uttered in anger—but it returns to her now in a sudden rush.

Still, she's too happy to dwell on painful memories of the past few months. The weekend had felt just like old times. They've been together for eleven years and married for six. Happily married. They do things other people mostly just talk about after the first couple of years have passed. They visit wineries and have weekends away. They still go on weekly dates in the city, and Benjamin brings her hyacinths and gerberas even when it isn't her birthday. Malti knits him jumpers to wear in winter, agonising over which pattern he might like best. In summer, they go on picnics and Benjamin makes Pimms (the alcohol settles on the bottom of the jug and makes them drunk in a late burst). They are the sort of couple you do not see in real life. They are perpetual—the couple everybody looks to for continuity. It's only in the past eighteen months or so that things have been different—that all their efforts have fallen away and left them with something suddenly changed.

But Malti is determined to focus on the new things: home and baby.

Back in her chambers, Malti sits in her ergonomic chair and reads the brief she has been given. The solicitor, Ernst Krause, is due in her rooms at 11 am, so she has a milky coffee at her desk instead of going out for one, and does not take off her high heels even though she would like to. She is gazing around the room aimlessly when she realises that she hasn't told Erik her news yet.

Her fingers tap out his phone number—she has known it off by heart for years—and waits for the familiar voice at the other end.

'Erik speaking.'

'Guess what?' She doesn't bother to announce herself. They have known each other since law school and her voice is its own announcement by now.

'I hate guessing games.' He has one of those voices that sounds stern even when it isn't—something about its deepness and his slow way of speaking.

She hesitates, thinking about drawing it out, but the excitement has reached its pinnacle. She feels the geyser of words rising within her, the urge to tell. To share.

'I'm pregnant.'

For the second time in three days, there's a long pause on the other end.

'Erik?'

'Oh, Malti, that's wonderful,' comes the immediate reply. 'Sorry, I was just surprised—but I'm so happy for you and Benjamin. Congratulations.'

'Surprised?'

'I forgot that we're old enough to be having children.'

Malti laughs, because she feels the same way every single day. Impending motherhood? The sulky teenager still lurking somewhere inside thinks that this is a disaster. And that's Erik: disarming and honest. They met in a contracts class in first year. Bonded over Williams v Roffey—and were instantly friends. Some people just connect.

'It's early still,' she warns him, because she knows that she is supposed to give this disclaimer. 'You're the only one who knows other than Benjamin. I'm not even telling my parents until after the first trimester.'

'Can I tell Clara?' he asks.

'Of course,' she replies. Erik and his wife have a five-year plan and children don't figure in it yet.

'And how's Ben?'

'Oh, he's so excited.'

'As he should be.'

They chat for a little longer. But Erik is at a big commercial law firm in Sydney and has to worry about billable hours. He rings off with the promise of a trip to Melbourne soon and Malti is left staring a bit wistfully at the phone. She usually tries not to talk only about herself, but this is one of those subjects it's very hard not to rhapsodise about.

She turns back to her own work and is jotting down notes for the Belleville matter when Ernst Krause knocks on her door. When he enters, he walks over to Malti and actually kisses her hand. He has always been like this. He is in his sixties, with a Mitteleuropa accent, a genuine love of tie clips (and cufflinks too, no doubt), a tailor-made three-piece and a squarish head, dusted salt and pepper. He sinks down into the seat across from Malti's desk and begins to brief her on the case while she takes notes. It's a property case—boring as hell.

When they finish, they chitchat for a bit about the weather, the new Melbourne Theatre Company season and Krause's children. Malti feels a sudden urge to confess her secret, but she remembers her doctor's warning and bites her tongue. Krause has gone quiet himself; his eyes have caught on the tiny framed photograph on her bench: she and Benjamin barefoot on the sand of Taveuni. She is wearing a white sarong and he has discarded his shirt; they were swimming in the sea about sixty seconds after the shot was taken.

'My honeymoon,' Malti explains. 'Six years ago.'

But Krause doesn't smile. 'I didn't realise you were married to Benjamin Fortune,' he says, his eyes still on the photo.

'Oh, you know him?' she asks.

Krause doesn't respond at first, then says, 'I consulted with him on a couple of cases last year. I went into the university several times.'

'That's a coincidence,' Malti laughs. 'Ben never mentioned it; what a small world.'

Krause nods. 'There was some ambiguity in a transcript and we were told he might be able to help. He's an excellent linguist, I'll say that for him.'

'I'll tell him you said so.'

Malti is smiling, but Krause is not. The air feels like milk past its use-by date. That's what things left unsaid always feel like to her: curdled. She would know that feeling anywhere. She has felt it too often at home this past year. Krause looks distracted and Malti feels as though she has strayed into murky waters.

'Is something the matter?' she asks him.

But Krause shakes his head and hitches up what she recognises as a professional smile. 'No, not at all.'

---

She brings it up with Benjamin later that evening as they sit together over grilled chicken breast—a change from her curries.

He learned the meat-and-three-veg quartet from his mother. He had it sizzling in the pan barely a minute after she walked in the door.

'Krause?' he repeats, piling carrots onto his plate. 'Yeah, met him last year.'

'He said you were a good linguist . . .'

'That's very kind of him,' Benjamin says, eyes on his cutlery.

'He got a bit weird after that, though.'

'Oh?' Benjamin looks up now.

'He went kind of . . . quiet . . . when I said we were married.'

Benjamin regards her for a second and then shrugs. 'Probably keen on you himself.'

Malti shakes her head. 'It's not that.'

Benjamin frowns. 'Then I don't know what was going on. I liked the guy, and I'm glad to know he found my input helpful.' He gestures with his fork. 'Could you please pass the sprouts?'

It's been a long time since he cooked, and when he bites into the chicken he frowns.

'Does this taste right to you?'

She nibbles her fillet. 'Yes.'

They eat some more, and then Benjamin puts down his fork.

'Nope,' he says. 'Tastes weird.'

'It's fine. It just isn't spicy,' she tells him.

Realisation dawns on his face. 'No chilli,' he says wonderingly.

She has infected his palate.

He disappears from the table and returns with the pepper grinder. 'It's chilli's poor cousin, but it'll do.'

Their cupboard is full of spices, most of which she gets at the Indian shop in Dandenong: ground ginger, garish turmeric, cardamom pods like teardrops and coriander seeds. Malti still buys most of the spices whole and uses the mortar and pestle where she can, all the while thinking of her mother and aunts. Once a year, the ladies would gather to grind the spices by hand and fill jars to hand around to the rest of the family. When Malti's father came home from work, the women would still be in a flow of chatter and elbow deep in turmeric, so he would join them—and so too, gradually, would the other menfolk. As a child, Malti had watched them from the edge of the room, and now she cannot bring herself to purchase the shiny little sachets she is beginning to see hanging in supermarket aisles. Not when she knows the taste of freshly ground *elaichi*—cardamom—and remembers its sweetness on the air. Of course, that was a long time ago now. But it lingers on, imprinted on her tastebuds and her mind.

Just as now there is something scenting the air. But what is it? Something hangs, heavy and unspoken. Malti knows a pivot when she sees one; Benjamin has changed the subject. If she was cross-examining him, she could pin him down—she controls the words in that space. Except they are not in court. The food might be a little bland, but the walls of their new house rise around them and Benjamin winks as he twists the pepper grinder.

'Ah,' he says, taking a fresh bite of the chicken and closing his eyes in relief. 'That's much better.'

She laughs. 'I'll make an Indian of you yet.'

# chapter three

FOR THE NEXT fortnight, Malti arrives home at six each day to find Benjamin either already there or walking in the door right behind her. When she checks the answering machine on the phone, she finds only messages from her old friend Maeve, Amanda from Ben's work and his parents rather than the familiar: *Sorry, babe, I won't be home till late.*

He buys a new cookbook and prepares spicy kumara soup. The chilli scalds her tongue, but she ignores it.

'Your new speciality,' she announces as she takes a second helping.

He tells her that the Renoir poster they bought from the National Gallery of Victoria five years ago would look better in the hallway than the living room. And Malti tries not to stare at her husband as he washes the dishes and weeds the front garden. It's the phantom of the old Benjamin—the Ben she married—haunting their new house, except she doesn't know which forbidden word will make him disappear again. She finds herself half-preparing for that moment: she won't become cold and distant this time. *Sure, honey, see you when you're back*, she'll say, glib and unconcerned. The perfect wife. Or maybe just the 1950s wife. The fights they had in recent months are still sharp enough to prick her when she thinks about them; that mustn't happen again. It's all different now, she tries to remind herself as she waits for Ben to walk in the door. But her hands are fluttering like moths, too afraid to stay still. When he bounces into the kitchen after work, kissing the nape of her neck where her hair is drawn upwards, she recognises the warm flare she feels as not just gladness but relief.

He has started talking about child language acquisition.

'We were meant to have language. The human vocal tract has features suggesting that we have evolved to facilitate speech: muscular lips, teeth, agile tongue, streamlined voice box. Amazing!'

He chats away about the lateralisation of the brain and the critical learning period. The babbling stage, the holophrastic stage and the telegraphic stage are all thoroughly explained to her over dinner.

'Watch your couscous,' she warns as he brandishes his fork. But it's nice, actually, to hear him talk about linguistics again.

'We'll get to watch our baby experience language,' he says, and his eyes are full of wonder.

They turn their attention to baby names, too—though they are rarely on the same page. Malti goes for unusual names, while Benjamin is stuck in Victorian England. Naming is power and responsibility. A terrible responsibility. If words matter, then names certainly do. Malti's name was chosen for its sound: its mulled feel in the mouth and the echo of the pretty diminutive syllables in the ears. Benjamin's name was stolen from a dead man—a friend of his parents who had died.

'It was a tribute,' Ben told her in the early days.

'A theft,' she had teased.

But all their stories have long since been shared. Their first names are now commonplace to one another and they share a surname. Talking about names again is a strange reminiscence—even if, this time, it's for their baby.

---

At fourteen, Malti had declared she would never have children. Babies were unformed lumps: drooling, crying, screaming. Everything so wet and messy. She hated mothers' invitations to cuddle a new baby—the inexplicable assumption that she, as a girl, must want to hold the thing. She'd take the bundled creature awkwardly and pass it back as soon as possible. If I drop it accidentally, will it bounce? She had bigger things on her mind.

The change in mindset crept up slowly and took her by surprise. At eighteen she found babies cute rather than unnerving. At twenty-two she was vaguely pleased to get to hold a newborn. At twenty-four she started to notice babies when she was out and about and felt a seeping protectiveness over their small faces and tiny toes. At twenty-five, Malti held Maeve's hand in the waiting room when her friend went in for a termination. Maeve's face was streaked with exhaustion, dark smudges under her eyes and desperation colouring her irises. Malti drove her friend home after the procedure and wondered what she and Benjamin would do in the same position. She'd finished law school, but neither of them had the time or money for children. And yet . . .

It crept up slowly, the desire for kids. And now, at thirty, she is pregnant.

She will tell their baby stories. Wrap the little one in a warm blanket of words and give its mind the gift of magic. She doesn't want a lawyer's baby—some beige dreamless child. She has not forgotten her roots. She will pass the lore and magic onwards, beguiling the infant with the thick branches of folklore, the stories you hear that forever stay with you. The ones which thread strongly enough through you to become part of you, all twisted up in your essence. Malti's child will learn about the goddess Durga, fearsomely mounted on her tiger. The valiant warrior Karna and his tragic death at the hands of his brother. Although these stories are Indian, Fiji was actually the birthplace for generations of her ancestors and herself. Her baby will need to understand its own complex heritage. And Udre Udre—will she tell her baby about him?

There is so much to consider. What kind of mother does she want to be? She knows that Benjamin will be a wonderful father—warm and loving—and their kids will love him. There is a pirate's gleam in his eye that promises adventure; he'll build their children box kites and read them stories each night. Some people are cut out for parenthood more than marriage—brilliant fathers who never got the hang of being husbands and mothers who didn't really want to be wives. But she can't help feeling that her own capacity for motherhood is more open to doubt.

The prospect still doesn't feel quite real. She is more tired than usual, even lightheaded at times, but her stomach remains flat—only her breasts are slowly swelling. She is not sure how she feels about the changes ahead. She is not used to this idea that her body is no longer entirely her own. That her *life* is no longer entirely her own. Of course, she will have to take maternity leave. But the idea of not working is alien and not entirely appealing. She loves her job; she had wanted to be a lawyer since she was a child—since, as a twelve-year-old, she had first read a dog-eared copy of *To Kill a Mockingbird* she found on her father's bookshelf. Harper Lee had done her job too well—created too great a hero in Atticus Finch. When she saw the movie two years later she had loved that as well. She still re-reads the novel each year, except now she pictures Gregory Peck as Atticus.

Her parents had hoped that she would become a doctor, but she didn't have the stomach for medicine—even a clinical description of a wound in a novel made her squirm and close her eyes tight, skimming those pages until it was over. Words always affected her. Words were her territory. She would defend, she would speak and she would be heard.

But being heard is far more difficult for an adult woman than she expected—this has been a painful lesson to learn. And even being loved isn't the same thing as being listened to.

---

One Thursday in early March, Benjamin arrives home late for the first time in over a month. Malti has cooked a shepherd's pie, timing it for his arrival. She watches as the cheese she grated onto the top turns from golden to bronze before taking it out of the oven, glancing towards the driveway from time to time in anticipation of Ben's arrival. Except none of the cars speeding down Beach Road slow at their house. As the headlights flash past without pause, the familiar serpentine writhing in the pit of her stomach returns, like a disease which has simply lain dormant—and, following it, comes the numbness.

At 9 pm, an hour and a half later than expected, her husband finally pulls into the driveway, and she quickly retreats from the window so he doesn't see her waiting there. She takes a seat at the table, spreading the pages of a brief in front of her as if she has been reading.

When he enters the room, Ben murmurs an indistinct apology then goes to the kitchen.

'Something smells good!'

'Where were you?' she asks, keeping her tone breezy as her nails bite into her palms under the table.

'At work,' he replies. He's clattering at the stove where she left the casserole dish, serving up. His own tone is perfectly neutral.

'So late?'

'Yeah. A department meeting that ran over. Sorry about that—I meant to let you know but didn't have the chance.'

He sits down at the table with his food and a beer, bringing a plate for her too. She watches him as he eats. Yes, she has seen him working hard—research demands a lot—but surely he could make a phone call?

She can't let it go there, so she simply says, 'Oh.'

She picks up her fork and eats a few bites, but her tastebuds are dull. She can feel Benjamin starting to bristle and can sense a fight in the offing, but can no more stop the words than she can stop her hurt. 'Why were you there so late?'

'Look, I had stuff to do, alright? Not all of us work for ourselves,' he snaps. He is quick to anger and quick to forgive: a flashpoint of white hot rage. Malti boils slowly but holds grudges.

'Who was there? Surely they didn't keep you all back so late.'

'Me, Raj, Artem, Amanda and Frank. All of us.'

'I see.'

'Mmm, this is good,' he says again into the silence that draws out.

'It was even better when it was warm.'

But he just laughs like it's a joke and sips his beer.

---

The next morning, Ben wakes her with a kiss and a cup of tea. She searches his eyes, but not even a fragment of last night's disagreement lingers in the blue. Sleep has washed them clear. Her mouth wants to return to the issue—her treacherous lips want to twist her sentences that way. *Hush*, she tells them. And that evening, he is home on time again, Thai takeaway in his hands.

It was just one night. One aberration.

---

Her clients the following week are irritating. She stands at the bar table, trying to put forward an argument, as Mr Keneally tugs the back of her gown. She can hear him hissing, 'Don't forget to tell them this,' as he brandishes a scrap of paper at her. The judge is frowning and Malti hastily tells Mr Keneally to remain silent.

She turns back to the court and continues, though she can hear Mr Keneally furiously scribbling more notes behind her. When she has finished, and turns around to ask him if there's anything else, he holds out what looks like seven scrawled pages of notes. She skims through them quickly. None of it is remotely relevant, but Mr Keneally is watching her read with fierce satisfaction. She runs her finger down the page, trying to find something. Three-quarters of the way down the fourth page, there are two sentences she can read aloud without sounding like an idiot. Mr Keneally beams when she does so. When she sits back down he nods solemnly.

'Excellent point, that. That'll win it for us, just you watch.'

Malti, thinking back to the hours of research and preparation in her chambers before her presentation to the court just now, rubs her temples and silently counts down the months until her maternity leave.

---

On Saturday morning, she decides she doesn't want to wait any longer to tell her parents.

'Aren't we supposed to wait until after the first trimester?' Ben asks.

'It almost is,' Malti reminds him. 'We won't make any official announcements until April, but we may as well tell the family.'

Benjamin hovers at the table with a stack of crumpets while Malti dials her parents' number.

When her father picks up, they chat for a few minutes.

Her mother shouts from the other room, 'Don't hang up without putting me on.'

'Actually, I wanted to talk to both of you,' Malti says. She uses the same wording she had for Benjamin all those weeks ago, the pre-tested sentence: 'We're going to have a baby.'

'Oho!' her father exclaims. He relays the news to his wife, who gasps and snatches the phone.

There follows a twenty-five minute interrogation of her sleeping habits and whether she's eating enough vegetables. When she hangs up, Benjamin is sniggering.

'Right,' she says firmly. 'You're telling your parents.'

That shuts him up pretty quickly.

But while Benjamin dawdles in the kitchen that afternoon, fussing with corned beef and mustard sandwiches, it's Malti who picks up the phone. To call Erik.

His voice at the other end is tired.

'They're working you too hard,' she tells him.

'It's what they do,' he agrees. 'Their pound of flesh and all that. How are you managing?'

'Oh, pretty well. The baby seems healthy and the doctor is pleased. Work is busy.' She hesitates, thinking of Thursday night, alone in the shiny new house.

'What is it?' Erik asks.

She had never confided in Erik about the troubles of the past eighteen months. She'd thought about it several times—would even go so far as to open her mouth—but somehow the words never came. Maybe it was something to do with the hard plastic of the receiver pressing against her jaw. It just wasn't the same.

'What is it?' Erik repeats.

'I just miss you heaps. When are you and Clara coming down to Melbourne?'

He laughs. 'Soon, I promise.'

'You haven't even seen the new house yet. It's much nicer than the last place.'

'Well, I'll make it a priority. I'm thinking I'll be able to take a week off around Easter.'

'So far away! Oh, well. I suppose it'll have to do.'

'We'd fly down tomorrow if I could spare the time from work,' he assures her. 'Put Easter in the calendar.'

They hang up and, a few minutes later, Ben brings the sandwiches over. They eat in silence; Ben doesn't ask after Erik. When she pauses to sip some water, he reaches across the table and takes her hand. It's sticky from mustard, but he doesn't seem to notice.

'You know what? I'm glad it's the weekend. Let's go for a walk along the beach this afternoon.'

---

Two weeks later, it happens again—though at least this time he calls. It's late Wednesday afternoon and Malti is lying on the sofa, thumbing through the *National Geographic*, when the phone rings. There are so many places I have not been, she is thinking, with something between hopefulness and regret, and she contemplates letting the phone ring out so that she can simply keep looking at pictures of Belize. But after a second or two she rolls off the sofa and jogs to the phone.

'Home already?' says Ben's voice at the other end.

'I left work early,' she admits. 'How's your day been?'

'Actually it's been really busy. I was, ah, just going to leave a message. I'll be home late tonight.'

'Oh, right. How come?'

'Some field work results are in and I've got to check them over. I need to be familiar with the data so I can think about how we frame the write-up.' The project is focusing on the address terms used by teenage girls in a spread of suburbs across regional Victoria. Benjamin is a sociolinguist, with an interest in language change and identity.

'Of course,' Malti says. 'I understand. You'll be home in a few hours?'

'Sure,' says Benjamin, which she doesn't find entirely reassuring. 'Hey,' he says, evidently picking up on her disappointment. 'I did call!'

'Yes, you did.'

She hangs up and returns to the sofa, but she doesn't feel as relaxed anymore. Come on, she tells herself after several minutes staring out the window. Back to Belize. She picks up the magazine and lies back down.

—

The next day she detours past a bookshop on her way to work. Benjamin had got in late and was still resurrecting himself with black coffee when she headed out the door at 8 am. The bookshop is two blocks away from Owen Dixon chambers, and she arrives just as the sales assistant is opening up.

'Can I help you at all?' the woman asks as Malti enters.

'Um, no, thank you.'

She pretends to browse through the new releases as the woman settles herself behind the cash register, taking out a crossword puzzle and chewing on the end of a biro. Then Malti wanders deeper into the store. Non-fiction is up the back and Malti isn't entirely sure what she is looking for. *Smart Women, Foolish Choices*; *Women Men Love, Women Men Leave*; *Women Who Love Too Much*. Dear God. Their titles make her nauseated and she is reluctant to even take them off the shelves. But could they help? Is the answer somewhere in these pages? She thinks of Benjamin's footsteps on the stairs at twenty past eleven the previous night and of how she'd quickly rolled over and pretended to be asleep so he didn't know that she'd waited up for him.

Ugh, she says to herself and grabs one of the books off the shelf. It has a white cover with lilac cursive writing. She carries it, shame-faced, to the register.

She flicks through it on her lunchbreak at work. It says things like: 'Marriage should still surprise you. This keeps the spark alive.' Ugh, she says to herself again.

'Are you okay?' the secretary asks when Malti passes on her way to the bathroom after lunch. 'You look like you're feeling queasy.'

The next day, Malti drops the book in the St Vincent's donation bin.

# chapter four

BEN HAS ALWAYS had air whistling through his veins. He walks mostly on the balls of his feet and has a slightly anxious habit of twirling locks of hair around his finger when he reads. He is reading the paper now, holding it out at arm's length. It's a giant monochrome screen in front of his face.

'Those High Court judges of yours really fancy themselves linguists, though, don't they? The purposive approach indeed.' He shakes his head.

'I thought you always said lawyers were frustrated actors?'

He grins. 'That too.'

It's Tuesday morning and they're sitting on the balcony having breakfast before work, talking in raised voices to be heard over the stream of traffic along Beach Road. Malti tries not to look at the scraggly front garden with its bare trees and dandelion weeds. The house might be unpacked, but the garden needs work. Instead, she shifts her gaze beyond their front gates, where the sand and waves are beckoning. Why must there be briefs to read and journal articles to write?

'I wish it was still the weekend,' she laments.

Benjamin pauses. 'How about we go out on Friday?'

Malti feels an immediate flare of excitement. 'What's brought this on?'

Benjamin shrugs. 'I'm trying to make more time for you. Work got too busy last week.'

Malti smiles. 'That sounds lovely. What were you thinking?'

'Let's do something fun. How about a concert or something?'

'*Tosca* is playing at the Arts Centre,' she suggests, and he makes a face.

'I was thinking a blues gig somewhere, or rock. I wish we could see David Bowie.'

'He's touring in November, isn't he?'

'Yeah,' he says.

'If you see *Tosca* with me, I'll come to Bowie with you.'

'Deal.'

---

The work week is very slow, spent in an endless rotation between court and her chambers. Malti wades through the judicial gossip of obiter dicta and makes notes for her next appearance. She stares out the window of her chambers a fair bit, mind drifting away from the thick volumes spread open on her desk.

It has taken a long time to walk these halls like she belongs. But she'd spent a couple of years as a solicitor before going to the bar, which has given her a few connections and insulated her from some of the more overt cruelty reserved for new barristers. One particular group, all members of a small lunch club, had established a ritual of forcing newcomers to run cases against them unnecessarily. They would refuse to negotiate any settlement, and when the matter went to court they took obvious pleasure in objecting aggressively to every sentence uttered by the new kid, even interrupting during opening statements. Malti had seen it once with her own eyes—an insurance case where the senior barrister kept cutting the new barrister off mid-sentence. Even though most of the objections were ruled out of order, the new barrister—running his first-ever case in the court—had started to shake and stammer. She had left the courtroom in disgust, unable to watch. Soon after, Malti had taken the opportunity to go on the offensive, forcing a member of the group to run a case against her. He'd had to hand back several high-paying briefs that he could've settled before lunch to waste the day running the case. She'd cost him a few thousand dollars and made her point clear: settle with Malti Fortune if you can; she won't hesitate to run you otherwise. The bullies had shown her a grudging kind of respect subsequently—or at least given her a wide berth.

Then again, there was the judge in the equity court who hadn't mocked her when she'd turned up fully robed—incorrectly—to her first-ever brief. She'd just finished the Victorian Bar Readers' course the week before, with about twenty peers, and had been sitting in her mentor's chambers on her very first day as a fully-fledged barrister. Technically, Julian was her master, but the colonial subtext had rankled too much for her ever to feel comfortable using that word. When the phone rang, she had assumed it was for Julian, but he had held the receiver out to her with a grin before going back to his cryptic crossword. It was her clerk on the other end, offering her a brief.

'Malti, I've had a look at the diary and you appear to be free tomorrow. Would you be able to take a brief to hear judgement in the Equity Division? The counsel who was on it fell through and it would be fantastic if you could help out.'

'Oh, no problem,' Malti said, marvelling at the smoothness of her voice as she spoke the words. But when she hung up, she turned to Julian. 'Oh, shit.'

He laughed. 'When the brief arrives, we'll go through it together.'

And so they had, talking through the procedures, possible outcomes and orders. But she'd still been breathless and nauseated the next day, fixing her wig onto her hair and fastening the long black robes for the first time. She'd cradled the brief and her copious handwritten notes in her arms as she located the correct court, somewhere far down in the Supreme Court Annexe. Except when she reached the courtroom, the tipstaff had tilted his head to the side and the court recorder had stifled a laugh. The opposing counsel had walked through the door a few minutes later in trousers and a shirt and, embarrassment crawling over her, Malti had realised her mistake. Then the judge and his associate entered, and they were not robed either. Sitting at the bench, the judge's eyes had swivelled to Malti and he had given her the same kind of grin as Julian the night before. She watched his eyes drop to the appearance sheet to check her name.

'Nice to see you before me again, Ms Fortune. From the manner of your dress, I assume you have another appointment shortly, so I'll be brief.'

They both knew it was the first time she'd ever stood in front of him. But he knew that the most recent Bar Readers' course had finished up and that the new kids were having their first day: he was making sure she felt welcome.

Nowadays she knows what to wear and when. Her pulse doesn't race when her clerk calls. She doesn't take nonsense from bullies. Everything has fallen into place.

---

On Friday night Malti dresses up. She can still fit into her most beloved burgundy evening dress and she is determined to make the most of it. She consults the mirror before she leaves the house, turning sideways. No, she doesn't look pregnant yet. She is waiting for her belly to bulge outwards in announcement—she is eagerly anticipating the time when she looks the part. She has bought a few maternity tops already and hung them in her wardrobe, stroking the floaty chiffon material when she opens the double doors each morning.

Tonight she wears mascara and her lipstick is bright. She drives to the city and parks under the thick canopy of elms on St Kilda

Road. She walks the few hundred metres to the Arts Centre and descends the staircase until she is encased by the wine-coloured velvet walls of the foyer. The bar is open and well-dressed patrons are buying champagne. The liquid glints golden in the light as people tip the flutes towards their lips—it looks even better to Malti now that it's off limits.

'You'd better be worth it,' she tells her stomach.

Everywhere she looks, she can see high heels and glittering necklaces, neatly knotted ties and ironed shirts. Her eyes scan the crowd for golden hair. There he is—unmistakeable. He's sitting on one of the velvet sofas, but he stands when he sees her.

'Thought I'd steal you a seat,' he says, kissing an inch to the side of her lips, and ushering her into the chair that is still warm from the heat of his body.

A night out together! She tries to remember the last time they went on an evening date, but her memory snags on nights spent at home in separate rooms, or by herself reading in bed and listening for the sound of tyres on gravel. She thinks they might've gone to the cinema together a few months ago. She doesn't remember the film, but remembers sharing popcorn with Benjamin in the darkness, her salty fingers brushing his. Or perhaps that was last year. Either way, it's been years since they've seen an opera together.

As the bell sounds to signal that it's time to take their seats, Malti and Benjamin join the others drifting towards the theatre. They are the last ones to enter and the ushers close the doors behind them. They shuffle along the row to their seats, past the drawn-up knees of the other patrons, murmuring apologies. As the room darkens and the conductor ascends the steps to his podium, Malti reaches for Benjamin's hand. The stage is illuminated as Angelotti runs into the chapel. Cavaradossi appears. And, finally, Tosca—who believes false promises . . .

At interval, Ben is unimpressed.

'Isn't Tosca supposed to be young and beautiful? The soprano has to be fifty at least.'

'Shhhh!' Malti makes hushing gestures as an elderly couple nearby give him scandalised looks.

They are back in the foyer, everyone raising their voices to be heard. Malti sees rather than hears Benjamin sigh.

'Well, it confirms that opera is more your thing than mine.' He rolls his eyes. 'Another drink? I feel like I'm going need one to get through the second act.'

When he joins the queue, he looks back towards her over his shoulder. That smile. The Benjamin smile.

The woman standing next to Malti sinks white teeth into her vanilla bean ice cream. A man a few metres away plucks lint from his lapel. And then, a familiar voice at her shoulder, an accent she'd recognise anywhere.

'Malti Fortune out of chambers! This is a sight to see.'

Malti spins around to see Ernst Krause, dressed in a suit and smiling at her.

'Ernst!' It's strange seeing work colleagues out of context. He kisses her hand—his usual custom. 'I didn't know you liked opera.'

'My wife does,' he explains, gesturing to a tall, red-headed woman standing in the long line for the ladies. 'She introduced me to it long ago and I fell in love with it too. Are you here alone?' He looks around her, apparently searching for companions.

'No, I dragged Ben along, as he'll no doubt tell you.' She glances at the bar, where Ben has reached the front of the queue and is giving some cash to a teenager wearing a bow tie.

Ernst follows her gaze. 'I see,' he says. He looks away. 'How's the case going?'

They are discussing precedents when Ben joins them. He hands Malti the orange juice and then, holding his champagne flute in one hand, stretches out the other to shake with Ernst.

'How are you, Ernst?'

'Very well, thank you, Benjamin. Yourself?'

'Good, good. How did last year's case go?'

'We won. Thank you for your assistance with the semantics of the transcript. It was most helpful.'

Benjamin waves the words away. 'My pleasure. Anytime.'

'And how are your colleagues? Raj? Amanda?'

'All fine,' Benjamin says, smiling. 'I'll pass on your regards.'

'Please do.'

The conversation is so polite—the men are inclining their heads towards each other and exchanging their faultless words. Work acquaintances swapping pleasantries. But undercurrents are swirling; there is something below the surface Malti cannot define or read. Something about the conversation makes the muscles of her face ache and twitch.

The bell is sounding, summoning them to the second act, by the time Ernst's wife emerges from the bathroom.

'Ilona and I are going for supper after the show,' he says. 'You would be very welcome to join us.'

Benjamin shakes his head before Malti can reply. 'Thank you, Ernst, that's very kind of you, but we'll need to be getting home.'

'Perhaps next time then. I hope Malti can persuade you to come back to the opera?'

Malti laughs. 'Stranger things have happened,' she says.

'You're a sweet girl,' Ernst says to Malti, but he is looking at Benjamin.

Benjamin kisses Malti's temple. 'She certainly is.'

Back in the darkened theatre, the next two acts unfold with more pathos and tragedy. Ben does not try to check his wristwatch in the dim light this time, but sits with his eyes fixed on the stage.

Tosca is betrayed. She bleeds to death next to the fallen Cavaradossi. How can something so painful be so exquisite? Malti blinks the tears from her eyes and Benjamin squeezes her hand.

After the performance, they make their way upwards to the street with the rest of the glittering crowd, hands clutching the brass banister. The women wear shawls like shimmering insect wings draped over their shoulders and the men are stiff-backed black-and-white penguins. The others are laughing with their companions, but Benjamin and Malti walk in silence. She recognises the newfound urge to hold her palm lightly against her stomach as she walks through the throng.

Walking along the streets she thinks of the city; Melbourne has changed a lot in twelve years.

---

Malti flew into the city in 1975, knowing it was her new home. The idea that the same ocean bordered both Fiji and Australia was almost incomprehensible. Well, they had said it was the same ocean, but it wasn't. They were all lying, every person and every map. Any fool could see that—and Malti was no fool.

She had tried to see the water as the plane approached its destination, but she hadn't been able to make it out. The bird's eye view of the bay was spoiled by the perspex of the window. Something dark, a stain, spread out below; that was all she saw. Still, as he struggled to cram her two suitcases into his boot, the taxi driver promised her 'the scenic route' for five dollars more and while she'd hesitated—thinking of the scholarship fund—she decided this wasn't such an unreasonable indulgence. There would certainly be enough left over to last the week, until the next instalment came, wouldn't there?

The taxi drove her through St Kilda and, at her request, pulled in to park by the water's edge. The water was choppy under the overcast sky and the beach was deserted. Overcast or not, she would later learn that the Sunday strollers would be out in force in a few hours, but for now, at 7 am, the beach was her own.

The water of the bay, technically part of the Pacific Ocean, was deep and dark—a dull, slumbering creature. Back home, this same ocean was a hundred shades of blue: turquoise and cerulean and so many others—colours the fashion industry had since claimed for their own. She looked out across that bay and shivered. There was hardly anything beyond this point, she knew—only the little island of Tasmania (did that count?), and then the wintry nothingness of Antarctica. She was glad to be wearing a cardigan.

Back in the car, Malti felt the salt in her hair, left by the wind. The sea was always sure to leave its mark. The driver was bored, ready to move on.

'Seen what you wanted?' he asked, starting the engine without waiting for her response.

'Yes,' she replied anyway. 'Yes, I have.'

She knew it would be a while before she made it back to the beach, and she watched its retreat in the rear-view mirror. The taxi was going to carry her out to suburbia, to where the city dwindled away and the hills began.

As they drove, Malti's head had flicked back and forwards, taking in cul-de-sacs and rubbish bins. The leaves weren't yet changing colour, but the air was cold with the promise of autumn.

It had been strange to be back in Melbourne as a university student. She hadn't been since she was a child on a family holiday, and she hadn't known then what to expect. They had been met at the airport by a friend of her father's, and her ten-year-old self had sat wide-eyed in the back seat, eyes travelling in every direction. When they had driven past some roadworks, Malti had shrieked. 'There are white men digging the road!'

Her father's friend laughed. 'Yes,' he told her. 'That's how it works here. The white men dig the roads.'

She didn't realise at the time that this was a half-truth: yes, the white men dug the roads—but for other white men. Where were all the brown faces? Where were the people that looked like her? That first trip to Melbourne, she had picked up a new name too: Molly. Her parents had used it to introduce her during the trip—it was the closest English approximation they could find for her own name and they'd already learned that Westerners struggled with Indian pronunciation. But Malti had bristled when other children addressed her this way. 'Molly, will you come and play?' She had glared at them and thought: That isn't my name.

And even in 1975, driving across town to her new university, she had silently asked the same question she'd had in mind when she was ten: How could I ever not feel out of place here?

Her shoulders and face were stiff as the taxi carried her away from the sea, towards an intersection of two gigantic highways, crossing each other in uneasy cooperation. She was gripping the fabric of the back seat and, in that touch, she could feel the moisture of her skin. They had arrived.

This was one of Australia's best universities, and had been her first choice, but she felt an uneasy swooping feeling somewhere between her navel and spine as the taxi began to slow. The driver flicked his indicator and its rapid pulse became her own. The area was barren. All she could see was the campus and the crisscrossing highway. Grey-looking granny flats and unkempt yards. The vibrant university town she had imagined, with greengrocers, cafes, bookshops and small parks with benches and duck ponds, did not in fact exist.

The campus itself was as ugly as its surrounds. It was only fifteen years old, but already dated. Malti stared up at it dubiously as they drove past, her eyes moving over each brown brick. The taxi dropped her at the halls of residence at the bottom of the hill and she watched it drive away, standing on the asphalt with her bulging suitcases.

This had been her choice, she reminded herself now. She had always known that she couldn't stay in Fiji. She had recognised a cage when she saw it. Her parents had known it too, and when she announced she had applied to study overseas, they had nodded without surprise. Home was a small island and there was no escaping that. Every whisper caught in the breeze and was heard. When she was sixteen, the desperation set in and she'd never been able to shake it off. She had attended a birthday party with some school friends where people ended up dancing. She hadn't gone with a boy and had been home by 9 pm. But the next morning everyone had known exactly how many dances she had danced and the length of her hemline.

'Was that a good idea?' her father had asked her at breakfast, spooning lime marmalade onto his toast. He'd travelled the world as a young man and had a taste for English breakfasts. 'You ought to be concentrating on your studies.'

'It was just a birthday party,' she retorted crossly.

Her father scowled. 'And you "just" want to study law. You should focus on that and not allow yourself to be led astray by foolish and frivolous distractions.'

Malti had applied for as many scholarships as she could find throughout the USA, Canada, the UK and Australia. In the end, she had been offered places at quite a few institutions but was only offered a full scholarship to universities in Ontario, Leeds and Melbourne. She had chosen Australia because it was closer to home and therefore felt somehow less alien. But now, looking around, she felt doubt clenching in her solar plexus. Perhaps she had only managed to trade one small island for another.

In the foyer of the residence halls, her paperwork was signed by a bored woman with a broad accent. She was about thirtyish, with massive hoop earrings, and though she didn't quite drum her fingers, irritation rolled off her in giant waves. *This is how I'm spending my Sunday?* her manner seemed to ask.

'Hi, I'm Karen. I'll be your student coordinator. My role is to support you in your residence here.' But the woman's voice was flat and she did not smile.

'Okay.'

She was already fishing around in the drawer of her desk. She passed across a trio of keys. 'Front door, bathroom key, room key. Make sure the doors are closed tightly behind you. Don't let people you don't know follow you inside. No smoking in the rooms—use the balcony. Breakfast is from seven to nine each morning. If you have any questions, you come to me. Do you have any questions.' There was no question mark in her tone.

'No.' Malti took the keys.

She heaved her suitcases up the stairs, encountering a few students emerging from their rooms, yawning. They looked at her curiously as she passed. Oh, she thought. She looked down at her hand on the suitcase, its hue.

Her room was spartan, but not unpleasant. There was a bed, a desk, a small sofa with fabric that had once been striped and walls that were almost cream-coloured. She fished a sari from her suitcase—the only one she'd brought—and tacked it to one of the walls. There it hung, orange, blue and gold silk. The only piece of home.

---

Now, outside the Arts Centre, the interior light flares as Benjamin and Malti open the car doors. It will only take twenty minutes to drive home at this time of night. Ben is at the wheel, but the streets they pass through as the buildings get lower and suburbia takes over are as familiar to Malti as they are to her husband. This is her city too now.

'Nice to see Ernst,' she says as they wait at the lights at the Kings Way junction.

'Funny guy,' Benjamin replies.

'He's lovely!' she protests.

'Lawyerly.'

'Caring,' she parries.

'Carious.'

'I wouldn't have minded going for supper.'

'Soporific.'

She can't help it—she laughs.

When they arrive home, Malti opens the gates for Benjamin to drive through. As she swings her body out of the car, she feels a shiver of misgiving, like the prickle-skinned awareness of being watched. She gazes around the darkened front yard, but there is only the stumpy malformed lemon tree and the straggling leafless carpet rose, foundering as the autumnal crispness of late March sets in. Even the sliver of Beach Road she can see through the front gate is quiet; there's the odd passing car but no pedestrians. Udre Udre, she thinks—foolishly, wildly, compulsively—and as soon as the thought crosses her mind, the shadows around the garden seem to stretch and extend. Don't be so ridiculous, she tells herself in the pragmatic voice she saves for difficult clients. But she chains the gate and hurries to the door, which Ben is unlocking. She does not feel right until she is in the house with the heavy oak closed behind her.

She turns to Ben, who is hanging his coat in the cupboard.

'It's been a wonderful evening. Thank you, my love.'

'My absolute pleasure,' he says, wrapping his arms around her waist and kissing her. Not her temple or her cheek—this time it's her mouth.

# chapter five

IN THE MORNING, Malti surfaces from sleep so gently. She is vapour rising from a pot on gentle boil. She is a dandelion seed blown into the air on a wish. She does not need to look into the mirror to feel that her mouth is curved upwards. When she opens her eyes, she sees that the bed is empty—Benjamin's side is rumpled, but there's no warm body. Strange; he usually slept in on weekends. She contemplates reading in bed for a while—*Anthills of the Savannah* is on her bedside table—but she reads the sentences of the new chapter without taking any of them in and gives up after only a few minutes.

She wraps a dressing-gown around her body and fishes her slippers out from where they've half-slid under the bed. It's just starting to get cool enough that bare feet won't do on the floorboards in the morning. Two months have elapsed since the move, but her toes are still used to the stained carpet of the Oakleigh place and she forgets that there's now a price to pay for letting her feet touch the ground.

She wanders downstairs, hand on the railing—not entirely used to the staircase yet either. She should've known that the feeling of home wouldn't be instantaneous; she has had to learn this lesson before.

Ben is sitting on the sofa with an empty cereal bowl beside him. The new Tom Clancy book is on his lap, but he is looking out the window with a faraway expression. He startles when she greets him, the smile slightly delayed.

'Morning, sweetheart.'

'How did you sleep?' she asks as she pours herself some orange juice.

'Not bad. How about you?'

'Really well. You were up early, though.'

'The birds woke me up at sunrise and then I started thinking.' He lets out a sharp laugh. 'No chance of sleep after that.'

'What were you thinking about?'

'Just work stuff. I've got a few grants to fill out this week.' He looks out the window again.

'Last night was wonderful,' Malti says.

'Yeah. Sure was,' Benjamin agrees without turning.

'Why don't we do it again next week?'

At that, he turns back to her, looking dubious. 'Another opera? It was better than I expected, I'll admit, but I couldn't sit through another one quite so soon.'

She laughs. 'I wouldn't inflict that on you just yet. How about dinner?'

'Okay. Thursday?'

'Why not Friday?'

'I have a work event that night.'

'What kind of event?'

'It's an Easter thing.'

Malti stares. 'But Easter isn't for another two weeks.'

'Yeah, but a few of the crew will be on field work then so we're doing it a bit early. It'll just be a drinks thing in the office, then maybe an early dinner.'

'That sounds nice. Would you like me to come? I haven't been to one of your work things for ages.'

She tries to remember the last time, but its hazy. In fact, now that she thinks about it, it must be over a year. Even eighteen months. That can't be right. Malti frowns, scrabbling for the memory. It was at the university, with tinsel draped around the small amphitheatre and bruised strawberries in the punch.

But Ben is shaking his head.

'No partners,' he says apologetically. 'Artem is still getting over his divorce—it was only finalised a month ago. We don't want to make it awkward for him.'

'Well then, Thursday sounds good.'

'You betcha.'

Ben turns back to the window.

---

The weekend is low-key, passing in a haze of domesticity. Although everything has long since been unpacked, there are still small things to do to make the house feel like home. The weeds in the garden reach out raggedy hands for attention and the curtains in the downstairs bedroom have moth holes. The oven needs a proper scrub. But Malti mostly potters around, making changes to the order of the books on the shelves and moving the ferns to new spots. Benjamin spends a lot of time in the study with his Walkman, but comes out to help chop vegetables in the evenings. When she tells him he looks tired, he makes a face.

'I'd prefer it if you told me I look handsome.'

'Are you sure you're getting enough sleep?' she presses.

'I think that's one of the questions I'm supposed to be asking you.' He raises his eyebrows. 'Are you getting enough sleep?'

'I think so.'

'That's all that matters then.'

He smiles, but he still looks tired.

---

The weekend might have been slow-paced, but there's plenty to do at work when the new week begins. The following week she will be out of town, arguing a case in Shepparton—some special fixture she's been roped into by her clerk. Two and a half hours each way is too long to commute, so she'll be staying over for the five days that the case is running. It's been a while since she argued a case out of Melbourne and she is already regretting agreeing to the favour. It's a building case too—her least favourite kind of law. On the weekend, she'd told Benjamin about it and asked if he wanted to come with her.

'It could be a nice drive down together,' she had suggested.

But he demurred. 'Wish I could, but I've got a lot on here, sweets.'

So Malti sits at her desk, scribbling notes on pads and already counting down until Thursday. Her brain always looks for the next thing to be excited about. Even though she loves her job, she wonders if she'll ever come to terms with the endless twostep between the weekend and the working week—the sheer interminability of it. The constant working towards something that never seems to come any closer. What is that thing, looming out of sight and out of reach—retirement? The holidays? She doesn't even know. It's *Waiting for Godot* all over again. But with the baby on the way, for the first time in her adult life the waiting finally has meaning. She is marking time with a purpose.

At lunchtime she picks up a BLT and an apple juice from the milk bar on the corner. Despite the sunshine, there's the threat of Antarctica in the southerly breeze, so she takes her lunch back to her chambers and eats at her desk. The view out the window is all dappled light and pied beauty, straight out of a Hopkins sonnet. She glances at the brief on the desk—she really should get back to it—but instead takes a seat on the small sofa by the window, usually reserved for clients. She glances at the phone. She has learned that Ben doesn't like to be interrupted at work, but it's been a while since she's spoken to Erik. She dials his office in Sydney and he picks up after the third ring.

'Hey, you. I've been meaning to call. Clara and I will come down after Easter.'

'That's only a couple of weeks away,' she reminds him. 'Better book your plane tickets quickly.' There's no need for small talk with old friends—all the niceties circumvented, straight to the heart of things. 'You're staying with us, of course?'

'If Ben doesn't mind?'

''Course not. We'd love to have you.'

A white lie. Ben finds Erik overly serious (Doesn't the guy ever laugh?) and Clara too intense. Erik knows how Ben feels about them, but leaves it unspoken. And if he has reservations about Ben, he doesn't express them to Malti either.

'How is Ben?' Erik asks.

The glib reply—Oh, he's great—is on her lips, but somehow it doesn't come.

'Seems okay. We had a nice time at the opera on Friday.'

'Lovely,' Erik says. But he's good at subtext. 'Things haven't been easy?'

'I don't know. I wouldn't quite say that. He had to work late a couple of times a few weeks ago, but things seem to have settled down.'

'You're worried about him?'

'Jumping at shadows, I think.'

'It sounds like he's got a lot going on. Academia would have its own pressures, and maybe he's worried about impending fatherhood. Have you actually spoken to him about it?'

'I've tried,' she says automatically and then frowns, trying to remember if she had. There have been countless fights and arguments about him coming home late, but have they ever simply had a conversation about it? Has she ever told him that she's worried? Maybe the words they've been using just haven't been the right ones.

—

Late Thursday morning, Benjamin phones her chambers with an apology.

'There's a grant application that's due tomorrow and it just isn't in the shape it needs to be. I've got to sort it out. I really can't take time for dinner tonight. I'm so sorry.'

'Oh. Not a problem—you do what you need to do. I'll cancel the reservation,' she says. But when she hangs up, she dials Maeve instead. She's had enough of sitting around at home. 'Any chance you're free for dinner?'

—

It all comes out after the entrée. The resolution not to tell anyone about her pregnancy has been harder to keep than she expected—the secret keeps sneaking out of her mouth. Maeve is delighted at the news and forgoes wine in solidarity. She sits sipping mineral water, her necklace glinting in the candlelight and her hair a wild blonde cloud. It's romantic mood lighting, except that Malti is here with Maeve while Benjamin is miles away, bent over a grant application. Maeve is a maths teacher at a private girls school and Malti has never been surprised that the students compare her to Miss Honey from Roald Dahl's *Matilda*.

But it isn't just the pregnancy that Malti wants to talk about. Maeve has a slight crease between her eyes as she listens to Malti speak of late evenings and distracted conversations. Of cancelled plans. Of how it's been eighteen months since she last attended a work function with Ben. Of how she used to know all his colleagues and be included in the Friday drinks, even when it meant driving across the city.

'Aren't we too young for a mid-life crisis?' Malti asks dubiously.

Maeve is swirling her water around in the glass as though it is wine. 'Why didn't you say something?' she says, watching the water slosh. 'I didn't know things had been strained. You and Ben always seem so happy.'

'But we are.'

Maeve presses her teeth into her lower lip and doesn't say anything.

---

When she gets home, Malti can see from the dark street that their bedroom is dimly illuminated. The reading light is on, casting its faint aurora. She knows what awaits her; what has awaited her every night for eleven years—when he is home, that is. Benjamin between the cotton sheets, in the jocks and t-shirt he wears to bed, and probably with reading glasses perched on his nose. She knows the look he'll give her over the rim of his teacup when she walks up the stairs, knows precisely the way and in which order he'll stroke her body whenever they next make love. And yet he had cancelled their plans tonight and she hadn't expected that. Marriage should still surprise you.

As she climbs the stairs, she thinks of the conversation with Erik: *Have you actually spoken to him about it?* But she isn't in the mood for words tonight. She decides to be angry. She reaches for righteous anger—she is the wronged party—but it won't come. She just feels sad and deflated, like a balloon two weeks past its use-by date.

As she expected, Benjamin is sitting up in bed with a book in one hand and a cup of tea in the other. He looks calmer now that the grant has been submitted—relaxed, in fact—and smiles broadly when Malti enters the room, already unclasping her dangly earrings.

'How was your evening?' he asks.

'Fine.' She puts the earrings back in her jewellery box, her movements sharp and disjointed.

'How was work?' she asks, looking pointedly at the book in his hand.

'Oh, good. I got through a bunch of stuff. I'm feeling much more on top of it all after a few solid hours of work.'

Malti mulls this over as she undoes the first couple of buttons on her blouse. Benjamin is watching her carefully.

'I am sorry for cancelling our date night, though.' His face is set in lines of contrition, his big blue eyes serious and his mouth in a downward curve. Malti doesn't believe that he's faking it. Or, at least, she doesn't believe that *he* believes he's faking it.

That's the thing with Ben. Every sentence is uttered with unwavering conviction, but his words are as fleeting as his breath. Featherweight words, tissue paper promises—light, airy and floating away. Pretty little ornaments not to be relied upon. Nothing of substance there at all.

'No problem.' Malti's voice is careful and toneless. She doesn't want to fight tonight.

Ben ignores this. His smile easily reorientates itself upwards. 'I knew you'd understand. Now come here and let me cuddle you both.'

Except that she doesn't understand. Not even a little bit. And how come things have changed so much over eleven years?

---

He was named after a friend of his parents'—a sailor—who had drowned. That's what he told her the first time they met. He was sprawled on her sofa with a teacup of claret in his large hand (Maeve had accidentally shattered the last wineglass when she'd been round the night before) and stories lighting up behind his eyes.

Benjamin the sailor had been on deck with a queasy stomach and a storm raging around his head. He had leaned over the rails to throw up but had lost his footing and tumbled overboard. His shipmates had called for him and turned the ship about, but there was no sign of him in the black waters. Just waves and foam.

When Agnes Fortune heard the news about their friend, she was already nine months pregnant. Her husband Timothy was the one to tell her. Gently and nervously, he held her hands in both of his and murmured in a sickbed voice. This pregnancy thing was a mystery and he wasn't really sure how to behave around his wife anymore. He knew she'd be upset. They had known Benjamin since their high school days. He'd written letters to them from distant locales for two years, and Agnes had stuck each new one to the fridge with magnets until the next one came to take its place. She had liked to read about what Benjamin was doing as she went about the domestic chores, her husband busy with work. He would sign his name at the bottom—*Love, Benjamin*—and Agnes felt a warm rush of gladness each time she saw it. Benjamin was the first person to laugh at a joke that fell flat, the quickest to smile, to comfort or to show kindness. Some people are just good people. And as her husband broke the news in a grave voice, she had thought of a far more enduring way to honour their dear friend than a floral wreath. The name had been an elegy. Only it hadn't worked so well. Ten, twenty years later, they had all but forgotten their old friend. Benjamin meant only one thing—couldn't be two things at once. The tribute was lost and the memory faded, like all the letters Agnes kept, yellowing, in the top drawer of her writing desk. For his part, little Benjamin had been able to appreciate the gesture behind his name, but disliked hearing stories of his namesake. He didn't even like second-hand clothes and got squeamish in op shops, so why would he want a hand-me-down name?

Nineteen years later, Malti listened to the story for the first time. It was the first story Benjamin had ever told her. The seasick sailor. It reminded her of 'It's All Over Now, Baby Blue' and she fished through the small handful of records she had brought with her from home, looking for it. She thought about his story as she rummaged. He spoke about his parents with genuine respect. She liked that.

Finding the record, she put it on the stereo, then settled back into the armchair and reached for her own teacup of wine. Three dollars for a cask—bargain. But it was acidic and each sip nipped her tongue like vinegar.

'Dylan?' Ben shook his head when the song started. 'No, no, no. You ought to be listening to Phil Ochs.'

'Who?'

'Come around to my place tomorrow and I'll play you something that'll blow your mind.'

'Not tomorrow,' she reminded him. 'We've got the party.'

'Ah, yes,' he said. 'The ex-boyfriend.'

Benjamin was a blind date to a birthday party Malti hadn't even wanted to attend. She had been on a series of dates with Ian over three months, but when she couldn't get over virginal indecision (they never went back to his place when the movie finished), he lost interest. She had seen him a couple of times across the quadrangle, always in one of his signature vests with a stack of philosophy texts under one arm. There he is, my first-ever boyfriend, she would think to herself when she saw him pass. I'll never kiss his lips or hear his reflections on Sartre again. She tried very hard to feel sad about this, but a vague nostalgia was the best that she could do. So it came as a surprise when she received a calligraphic party invitation in the mail a few months later. He mustn't have many friends if he's stooping to ask ex-girlfriends, she thought tartly. But a twenty-first birthday was a big deal and the mature option was obviously to attend, so she scribbled back an RSVP and pushed it into the postbox, aware of her own smug smile. So this was adulthood. And she didn't even think about Ian or the party after that. She jotted the date on her calendar and forgot all about it, until she spotted Ian in the dining hall with his arm around another girl. He had a new girlfriend? Well! That settled it. She couldn't very well turn up alone. She needed a date for the evening. Anyone would do, really . . .

A few of her friends suggested guys they knew. Sociology studies was full of likely candidates, Tara assured her, and Jocelyn said there was someone in her archaeology tutorial she would suss out. Even Erik had said he could ask one of his friends from tennis. But it was Maeve who actually came through with the goods.

'There's this guy I'm studying linguistics with,' she said slowly—she'd been taking an arts elective that semester to break up the algebra. They were strolling across the wide campus lawns that were not grass anymore but weren't dirt yet either. 'He's nice. And good-looking. I could ask him if he'd be your handbag for the night?'

'Would you? Oh, Maeve, that would be so great.'

'If he agrees, I'll bring him past your place so you two can meet.'

'That'll work fine,' Malti agreed. 'But, Maeve, tell him it's just for the purposes of the party. I'm not interested in starting anything. I want to focus on my studies.'

'I'll tell him,' Maeve promised, but she raised her eyebrows and looked like she was trying not to smile.

What Malti didn't expect was Benjamin, with the sunlit smile so quick to flare across his face, and the quick mind to match. True to her word, Maeve brought him by halls of residence the day before the party. He wasn't like any boy Malti had ever met. He was clever, but knew how to listen. He didn't cut across, correct or patronise her the way so many of the other uni boys did—as she smiled politely and silently thought, I'm smarter than you and you're too dumb to even know it.

He agreed to come to Ian's party straightaway, cheerily murmuring something about an ex-girlfriend. Malti never gave the cool speech she had prepared. *These are the terms: I'll buy the drinks and you don't flirt with other girls.*

The next evening they walked into Ian's party, which was being held in a hall at the back of an Italian restaurant. It was already crowded when they arrived, twenty minutes after the start time. They didn't hold hands—that would've been too pointed—but Benjamin's palm hovered at the small of her back. Ian seemed pleased to see her; he kissed her cheek and thanked her for coming, shaking hands with Benjamin too. The new girlfriend was serving herself punch from the long table under the window.

'So that was the ex,' Benjamin commented.

'Yeah.'

But, truth be told, her attention wasn't really focused on Ian tonight.

'What are you reading at the moment?' he asked her.

'*Crime and Punishment.* I've been meaning to get around to it for ages. What about you?'

'I'm re-reading *Lord of the Rings*.'

'*Re*-reading it? There are too many books I'll never have time to read in the first place; how could you possibly devote time to reading the same thing again?'

'Yes, but this isn't just any book—*Lord of the Rings* is special.'

'Special, or incomprehensible?'

'No!' He was aghast. 'You didn't like the writing? It's so beautiful!'

She laughed. 'Verbose, you mean.'

And soon enough, she was in a bubble with Benjamin, the pair of them telling each other stories and discussing anything, everything and nothing. She'd never experienced conversation like this before, so seamless and fluid. She never realised discussion itself could be like a work of art: a fine tapestry of ideas and expression, created by two people. Malti and Benjamin found that they could meander from one topic to another and never run out of things to say. He asked her about her studies (*Why on earth would you want to do law?*) and she asked him about his childhood. They shared the same politics, although Benjamin claimed to be more of an activist than she was. Still, while he obviously liked the idea of attending rallies and protests, he never actually seemed to go along to any of the marches. He liked science fiction and she enjoyed literary classics, but they spoke to one another about what they were reading, and discussed music and movies. They solved the world's problems and then joked about cheese, the conversation oscillating from light to serious and back again. She didn't notice Ian or the new girlfriend. In fact, she barely even looked around the room.

The party was unravelling as the alcohol infiltrated people's systems. The noise levels were rising and two glasses had already been accidentally broken. The drunk dancing on the makeshift dance floor had been entertaining, but now it was hard to hold a conversation.

'Let's skedaddle,' Benjamin said.

Malti nodded and even forgot to say goodbye to Ian on the way out.

This time they went to his room. Ben sat cross-legged in front of the stereo, a small stack of records beside him. Malti had caught a glimpse of the one on top: a serious-faced man in an overcoat, sitting on his guitar case and reading a newspaper. Phil Ochs. It was terribly sad music: a less beautiful sadness than Leonard Cohen's, but a more devouring one. Music that was full of dead ends and hopelessness, but which somehow seeped into the crevices of self and you found it had become a part of you. Benjamin was light-hearted, and sadness didn't seem to stick to him, whereas it coated Malti in a fine residue. She closed her eyes and felt the power of the solemnity. She could only listen to it in small doses, but often returned to it and, after a while, forgot that Benjamin had even been the one to introduce her to it. It felt like it had always been hers.

'I hope he writes like this forever,' she said earnestly, and Benjamin had nodded vigorously.

Benjamin was beautiful to look at. He was attractive, without the homogeneity of classical handsomeness. His face had character, Malti decided—the tendency of his skin to freckle and the slight waywardness to the tip of his nose were flaws which enhanced the whole. She liked the way his image felt cast against her cornea, liked looking at him from the first. Irises like irises she thought giddily, when he first showed up at her door. They weren't really—they were just a regular blue—but it was too late; her mind was already carried away with metaphors.

As for her, she'd never seen herself as pretty.

'You've got a face like a papaya,' her father used to tease her. By this he had meant its length—from forehead to jaw, it was long. So very long. And she felt that her eyes were dully black. Looking in the mirror, even she couldn't tell pupil from iris. Still, Benjamin didn't exactly seem to be cataloguing flaws when he smiled at her in greeting. In fact, the look in his eyes made her feel like she was the most beautiful thing on earth.

The next time, they caught up at her place again. This time he looked at the bright silk sari splashed across Malti's wall and his eyes widened.

'Look at that.'

She laughed, half gratified and half uncomfortable—suddenly reminded of difference.

But Benjamin had questions. 'Why did you leave?'

She shrugged. 'Home was an island.'

'So is this,' he reminded her.

'It's different here.'

He nodded. 'Yeah, it's a racist conservative shithole.'

'No! It's bigger. More opportunity. Just . . . more. You know what I mean. Where I grew up was small. Parochial.'

'And beautiful—I've seen pictures.'

'Yes,' she sighed. 'That too.'

'Well? What's it really like?' he probed.

How could she answer that? Images of turquoise water rose easily in her mind. The vibrant coral world underneath, so vivid it almost didn't seem real. The holiday brochure images were true: these were not travel agents' concoctions. She pictured her parents' small, whitewashed home and the whirring fans. Endless aunts, uncles and family friends—and big silver vats of food always simmering away on the stove, with enough for anyone who might conceivably stop by for dinner. But she couldn't see it through a tourist's eyes.

'It's . . . fine.'

Benjamin was still looking at her, waiting.

She sighed again, and tried to describe it in an objective way. 'It's pretty. Tropical. Very green. Not like here,' she added, thinking of the Australian landscape and its brown scrub (she'd seen pictures).

'It sounds like paradise.' Benjamin grinned. He was willing—eager, in fact—to be impressed. He wanted to like it and had expected her to try to sell him on the beauty of her hometown.

'Not really,' Malti told him.

'But it's still home, right?'

Malti opened her mouth and closed it again, and Benjamin, sensing her confusion and discomfort, let that subject drift away and the river tide current of conversation which was ever-present carry them onwards.

Two days after the party, they saw a movie together. The day after that, he bought her a tuna sandwich which they ate on the campus lawn. It was already winter, but they sat on the bare grass anyway, catching the dregs of the white-gold sunlight and talking. They took to waiting for each other after classes and argued over whose discipline had the most merit. She would wait for him in the law library on Thursday when he had a late lecture, and he would be there reading a novel in the corridor when her torts tutorial finished. Benjamin had taken linguistics on a whim and found that he absolutely loved it. The planned major in politics was quickly abandoned and a whole new trajectory mapped out.

He was being initiated. The first thing they gave him was new words which, one by one, crept into his vocabulary—no, no: his lexicon. He frowned now when people said dismissively, 'That's just semantics.' He knew the rules of grammar and Malti watched him fight not to become schoolmarmish when people said 'prefix' but meant 'suffix'. They taught him to map out sentences as trees. (Oak trees? Willow trees? Malti wondered.) He got to write exam essays with words Malti was sure his mother would smack him for using. One thousand words on the etymology of 'cunt' and its implications for language across time. Go!

But the most precious of all this new secret knowledge was the IPA. The linguistics department actually bequeathed its students a whole new alphabet: International Phonetic Alphabet. It was similar enough to the Latin alphabet for laymen to be able to guess at words, but it was also different. Especially the vowels—good luck trying to figure them out without a chart at hand. Who needed French? Six weeks after they met, Benjamin wrote Malti a love letter in IPA, which she read with the IPA dictionary close at hand. She had to do this alone in her room, sounding out each letter just to be sure. It was worth it, though, and she was rewarded in the end when the word welded itself together in the air—composite parts deconstructed on Benjamin's end, restored on Malti's. She would write back in plain English—not mean enough to set him the same challenge with Hindi or Tamil (she spoke both).

'Linguistics is all about stories,' he liked to say.

'So is law,' she would retort.

'Law!' he had scoffed. 'Law is about facts. It's prosaic; don't try to pretend it isn't.'

'No,' she argued, 'I mean it. Law is also about stories—each case is a story with two sides.'

Mali was learning her own secret language too, with Latin words and legalese, and finding a whole new bunch of heroes to supplement Atticus Finch. Lord Denning! Wow: Che Guevara in robes.

She liked the way Ben kissed her, always bringing one hand up to cradle the nape of her neck. She sensed that he was less experienced than Ian, less smooth, and yet she felt no hesitation. He crossed the threshold of her bedroom with a sweet hesitancy, Malti pulling him onwards with her own hands. She felt a desire to be close to him, a need to touch, which she'd never felt before. And as they fell into the bed, she could perceive that they were moving out of a world of words and into a world of touch too.

———

Except those early days seem like a long time ago to Malti now. Lying in their comfortable bed, with Benjamin's arms encircling her and his breathing deep and rhythmic, her mind is whirling. Be present, she tells herself. Right now, in this moment, what is there to worry about? She tries to concentrate on the press of his chest against her back and the warmth of his breath on her neck. I am lying in bed with my husband and unborn child. Everything I've wanted is here with me now. And the thought comes unbidden that there is also a lot to lose.

# chapter six

MONDAY IS THE first day of the property case in Shepparton. It's a two and a half hour drive in the morning—she leaves Beach Road before daybreak, kissing the cheek of a sleeping Benjamin, who murmurs and rolls onto his stomach. The roads are empty and the sky is an inky shade between black and blue. The enormous brief is next to her on the passenger seat and *Pleasures of the Harbor* is in the cassette player. In the enclosed acoustics of the Fiat, Malti sings. Loud.

This turns out to be the highlight of her day, though that isn't unexpected—property cases are notoriously dull. She is appearing on behalf of the plaintiffs, a young couple who hired a builder to construct their dream home and have been bitterly disappointed by the result. They are claiming that the workmanship was shoddy and are suing the builder for the cost of the building defects—a list that has about a hundred items on it.

The courtroom clocks are enchanted and operate at their own speeds. When the court is running an interesting matter, they spin around like tops. But mentions, call-overs and ATO prosecutions cause them to slow to glacial speeds. Outside the sun has risen, but the sky is grey and marbled. In the courtroom, the light is fluorescent. Everyone's face has taken on an ashen pallor.

A couple of hours into the first hearing, Malti is stifling yawns. She isn't alone; the magistrate is also surreptitiously checking his watch and even the opposing counsel looks tired as he cross-examines the expert building surveyor who has submitted a report. And they're only half a day in. Her mind is trying to float away to other things—to Ben back home, to faraway memories, to the baby—but she squares her shoulders and takes her pen in hand once more.

---

She has booked a little motel just around the corner from the courthouse. When the case wraps up in the late afternoon, she wanders back to the room and lies down on the quilt with its brown and yellow flowers. It'll be a quick meal in the local pub and then back to the room to do some preparation for tomorrow's hearing. But first, she reaches for the phone and dials home, twirling the curly cord in her fingers as she waits for the familiar voice at the other end. Except the phone rings out with no answer. The little alarm clock next to the bed is green and glaring: it's 6.30 pm. Benjamin obviously isn't home from work yet.

Since arriving here, she has been able to feel the flutters of movement in her belly. The quickening, the nurses have told her this is called. Their baby is awakening. She rests her hands on her stomach, feeling a quivering she has never known before. She wants Benjamin's big hands on her belly to feel it too. Or, at the very least, she wants to describe it to him on the phone. But when she gets home from her steak and chips a couple of hours later, there is still no answer.

---

The cross-examination of the building expert is still underway when they break for morning tea the next day. Malti drinks two cups of black tea and eats a crumbly jam biscuit from a little plastic sachet, but already she is counting down until lunch. The opposing counsel is only up to item twenty-two; there are eighty-three more defects to interrogate. Three and a half more days of this? At this point, the hearing is likely to be extended; things need to move along. Sometimes the haze of boredom creates its own rashness. When the opposing counsel stops to consult his notes, Malti interjects.

'Your Honour, perhaps a viewing of the property might expedite this hearing?'

The room swivels to look at her.

Malti has never seen the house they're fighting over; neither has her opponent, but he does not object to the outing. The magistrate raises his eyebrows, though he agrees that an excursion might be helpful. Everyone, it seems, is keen to break the boredom. The magistrate adjourns the court and everyone heads out to find their cars and reconvene at the house on Rea Street. As she drives,

Malti perceives the risk: what if the place is perfect? But it's too late now—she has thrown the dice.

They walk up the concrete pathway to the house, and all boredom evaporates as they cross the threshold. The floors creak under their shoes from the misaligned floorboards and slivers of light are visible where the crooked window frames do not sit flush to the walls. The magistrate flicks the light switch in the entry hall. His face darkens as only two of the three lights overhead flare to life. In the dim light, he takes out his reading glasses as he consults the list of defects from the expert hired by Malti's clients. She sees his eyes scan the list and swivel around the room to the exposed wiring, the cracks, the power boards hanging loose. He wanders through the house, trailed by Malti and a rather clammy-looking opposing counsel. At the back door, there is a ruptured pipe and raw sewage stagnating in a puddle—explaining the pervasive stench. Malti wonders if this is the first time the smell of sewage has felt like a victory.

'We should get back to the courthouse,' the magistrate says, rolling up the list and hitting it against his thigh as he strides to his car.

Back in the courtroom, the opposing counsel wraps up his cross-examination within fifteen minutes and Malti stands to cross-examine the defendant's expert witness. It doesn't seem likely that the expert has ever set foot in the tumbledown house—the defects must've appeared in the months since the preparation of the report, he insists, at which the magistrate snorts and Malti hides her smile. The magistrate announces that he will give an ex tempore judgement after a brief period of adjournment. On her feet as the magistrate disappears into his chambers, Malti reminds herself not to count her chickens. But an hour later, the magistrate is back and awarding damages of fifty thousand dollars (the jurisdictional limit of the court) plus costs to her clients. Every disputed rectification item has been won. It's a triumph. Her clients wring her hand and the opposing counsel gives her a grudging nod. The five-day case has been wrapped up in two days. When she gets into her car to drive back to the motel, Malti no longer has to hide her smile.

The motel is kind enough to refund her money, so she leaves late in the afternoon—singing along to the cassette again and itching to recount the story to Benjamin. When she glances at her face in the rear-view mirror, she looks smug. Ah well, she thinks. Sometimes you just get lucky.

But pulling into the driveway on Beach Road two and a half hours later, she finds that Benjamin's car is missing from the driveway, and two days' worth of newspapers are sitting on the doorstep.

Inside, the house has a cold and unlived-in feel. It's not that there's dust or mustiness; the light in the hallway is as bright as ever. No, it's the feeling of emptiness. Not even Udre Udre haunts the house tonight; there is a total lack of presence, an absence that imprints itself on the air, as still as a coffin. She shivers, pulling her blazer closer around her.

The only message on the answering machine is from Benjamin's colleague Amanda, her voice stilted, asking Benjamin to come to campus. Malti dials Benjamin's office and, to her surprise, he answers.

'Are you calling from Shep?' he asks.

'The case wrapped up quickly—I'm home.'

'Wow, that must be a record!' There's pride in his voice.

'It was quite a success, actually,' she agrees. She wants to tell the story—the gamble that paid off through sheer dumb luck—but only face to face. 'Have you been away? There's a pile of papers at the door.'

'Field work,' he replies.

'You didn't mention it to me.'

'It was last minute—Artem had set up some interviews in East Gippsland but couldn't get there to do them. I tried to get one of the postdoctoral researchers to help, but they couldn't make it, so I took over.'

'You should've called me,' she tells him, but Benjamin just laughs.

'Didn't want to distract you from the case. Thought I'd take the chance while you were out of town. And didn't you say that Erik is coming after Easter? I wanted to get it done before that.'

'Right. So when are you coming home? You're obviously back in the office now.'

'I'll be there in a few hours,' he promises. 'Have some dinner and put your feet up—you've earned it.'

That's true, she thinks when she hangs up. But it isn't the same celebrating a win in an empty house.

---

She does not say anything when he walks in the door a few hours later, but she can feel the unsaid words in her mouth as she watches him from the sofa. He fishes in the fridge for the leftovers from dinner and makes himself up a plate. He brings the food to the living room to eat beside her as Malti holds a book in her hands and pretends to read it, watching him sideways. She keeps her face relaxed; so relaxed she wonders if the bones of her face will shatter from the strain of it: her zygoma and mandible ache and feel as fractured as fine porcelain stuffed into a dishwasher. This time she will approach the subject—but carefully.

Ben finishes his food and takes the plate to the sink to wash up.

'Let's go to bed,' she says.

He winks at her.

---

The next morning, there is bright sunshine outside and enough space to broach the subject.

'Ben,' she begins, 'can I talk to you about something?'

They're standing in the kitchen, toasting bread. Malti has laid out the spreads—marmalades, Vegemite and peanut butter.

'Sure,' he says. But a moment later he picks up the carton of orange juice, frowning at its label. '*Our juice is one hundred per cent fresher*,' he reads aloud.

'So?' she says, impatient.

'Fresher than what? Than it was before? Fresher than lemons? Or in comparison to other juices? Typical advertising, of course—always using language to embellish, obscure and say nothing at all.'

'Huh?'

'It flouts both the cooperative principle and the maxim of quality, see.' He shakes his head. 'Sometimes all language does is get in the way.'

'Exactly. So can you not be a linguist for one minute?'

'Oh, sure. Sorry. What's up?'

'How come you didn't tell me you had field work lined up?'

'Yeah, sorry about that. Didn't mean to make you worry. It was very last minute. You know what it's like—now that I'm supervising, it's on me to step in if the team can't make it.' He rolls his eyes. 'But I thought you had enough to worry about with that stupid property case. You'll have to tell me more about your win.' He smiles encouragingly.

She resists the invitation.

'You've been very caught up at work lately,' she persists. 'You've seemed distracted or stressed. Is everything okay? Do you want to talk about anything?'

Softly, softly. Gentle like honey, like chiffon, like rosé. Everything sharp and accusatory has been bleached from her tone.

But Ben's voice is curt. 'It's fine.' He takes a piece of toast and butters it.

'But is it really? Please, Ben, I'd like to understand.'

'It's a busy time at work.'

He takes the orange juice and his toast and walks to the dining table. Malti watches his back. Deliberate evasiveness is his hallmark these days, she thinks.

—

Malti touches her growing belly and tries not to rekindle the flames of past fears. She has nurtured them well, these dark thoughts. From seedlings they have grown into creeping vines with minds of their own. In the night her tiny baby pummels the walls of her womb with its half-formed hands—and her fears prick and needle her from the unswept corners of her mind. What does she have to be scared of? No danger here: safe houses and streets all around her. She has a good job. Their names are on the deed to this beachside home and their child is now conceived. All is calm, all is bright.

Wayward husband. Gypsy husband, wandering away from her.

And yet he once quite literally climbed a mountain to bring her a flower. This was on their honeymoon on Taveuni.

Benjamin had made plans to climb Des Voeux Peak to the crater lake. He had risen early to dress in shorts and a t-shirt that morning. There was latent heat in the air already: a threat of sweat and discomfort. Malti sat up in bed, one foot reluctantly peeping from the sheets to find the floor.

'You don't have to come,' Benjamin assured her. She watched as he put a water bottle into his backpack and headed to the door. 'I'll be fine on my own.'

'Are you sure? I don't mind coming with you . . .'

'No, really, you should just stay and relax.'

And with that he was out the door. Malti watched his retreating form through the window—the rapid steps and the furtive way he glanced back at their suite. She knew what he had gone to do: he had gone to find Tagimoucia. *Medinilla waterhousei* was its scientific name, but nobody called it that. It was the reason people climbed to the volcanic crater—Lake Tagimoucia was the only place on the planet where this native flower grew. She had told him the story herself and, as she had spoken, Malti had once again heard her father's voice in her mind, slow and measured. Another one of his stories, this one as sweetly and sadly lovely as the Udre Udre story was horrifying.

'So, forbidden from marrying her true love, the young princess flees her home. She ascends the mountain, faster and faster, until she reaches the lake. She lies down beside it, weeping, and her tears fall to the ground. And they say that the Tagimoucia flower bloomed on the ground where those salted drops were shed.'

'Nice,' Benjamin had said.

'They're Fijian stories,' she'd admitted. 'Not Indian ones.'

'Does that make a difference?' he'd asked.

'Well, they don't really belong to me. They're the stories of my heritage geographically, but not culturally. I guess I should be telling you something from the Mahabharata. *In that only place* . . .' she intoned. 'That's how the Tamil stories begin.'

'Like *Once upon a time*, you mean?' he had asked. 'And what's the phrasing for *happily ever after*?'

She laughed. 'I don't remember actually, but I think we're going to live it.'

Benjamin returned that afternoon, sweating and grimy, but there was victory in his eyes. He walked straight to the bed where she was reclining, reading in front of the fan. He carried nothing in his hands, but shrugged off his backpack with an inordinate amount of gentleness—no casual slinging. He placed it on the floor and unzipped it, his hands emerging with a trio of hanging flowers.

'Oh my God, Ben!'

She had never seen it in real life before, only in pictures (as the national flower of the country, it was in plenty of pictures). But it was different seeing it with her own eyes. It was lovely: a white centre, cased in waxen-looking red—soft white petticoats under a stiff red skirt. She held the flowers as tenderly as she could by their stems and cradled their hanging forms in her palm. Benjamin had often bought her flowers over the years, and she was always delighted, but she'd never before received flowers with all the weight and magic of folklore behind them.

He was standing at the edge of the bed, smiling as he watched her reaction. His hair was sticking up and his neck was slick with perspiration, but his eyes didn't leave her face. She opened her mouth to say thank you, but he kissed her before she could. And then the words got lost in touch and—a strange anomaly—for once, they didn't seem to matter at all.

---

In the semi-dark of their bedroom, Malti trails her fingers down Benjamin's chest, curling them into the fine dusting of hair there.

He has once again stopped reaching for her in the night. His cuddles are perfunctory, his hands polite rather than passionate. When she pushes him down one night and crawls on top of him, he squirms away awkwardly.

'Don't want to hurt the baby,' he mutters.

'It'll be fine—really.' She pulls him close and continues her downwards trail of kisses. He lets her, but there is tension in his thighs and toes. 'Forget it.' She rolls onto her back and stares at the ceiling.

---

At the dinner table, she chats away about her cases as Benjamin eats pumpkin curry with a roti in his hand. He eats the way she does—even from the beginning he'd been happy to dispense with the cutlery and be shown how to use his fingers. His eyes are on his plate.

'Honey?' she prompts him, when an anecdote about a recent court appearance is greeted only by silence.

'Huh?' he says.

She can still engage his interest by talking about language. She knows she should steer them back towards these safe harbours—get him talking about the Great Vowel Shift or Lev Vygotsky. Or even just throw out an unusual word for them to play with. Discussing the idiosyncrasies of English never gets old, and her eyes stray to *Mrs Byrne's Dictionary of Unusual, Obscure and Preposterous Words* on the bookshelf. Maybe she should take it down? But sitting at the table, all that occurs to her are the words she hates: *gelatinous*, *pulchritude* and *fetid* float across her mind. All the ugly-sounding words.

She can't help thinking of the little things—like how it rained the day that Benjamin submitted his thesis. One hundred thousand words, each sentence lovingly crafted. It was a verbal sculpture, turned into a physical object. They took turns to hold the bound form in their hands and marvel at it. The hours slumped over a desk were remembered, sure, but the pain and tedium were swept away by euphoria and relief. When they dropped it off at the submissions office, he touched the tip of her nose playfully.

'Now I have a PhD. That's an even higher degree than yours.'

Did that actually matter to him?

'You'll have to change the title on your credit cards,' she said. She graduated three years before him and wangled a job with a decent salary at a sleek law firm. She was the breadwinner after she graduated, but now Benjamin had secured a good job of his own, straight out of his PhD into an academic role. He would be earning quite well himself now and she felt like she could see some awareness of this in his eyes. Would that shift the dynamic? The rain was only becoming heavier, so they'd scrapped their dinner plans in favour of wine at home—but it wasn't quite the celebration she'd hoped to give him.

These memories from the early days all look different in hindsight. Some are far more golden than she'd realised at the time, while others are strangely rough-edged. Lately, her mind has been spinning helplessly to the past to make sense of the present. But the answers still elude her.

# chapter seven

AS SHE HAD expected to be in Shepparton all week, Malti takes a couple of days off work and puddles around the house, getting the spare room ready for Erik's arrival.

When she returns to the chambers, her clerk calls almost immediately.

'Bloody well done! You must have a knack for property.'

'I wouldn't say that,' she mutters, but he isn't listening.

Later that day, she runs into Ernst Krause outside the elevator.

'I heard you had a big property win.'

'How'd you know that?'

'Word travels fast around here. You can expect to be flooded with property cases for the next couple of months.' He laughs at her grimace. 'Sometimes it's better to fly under the radar.'

'Perhaps you're right.'

'Will we be seeing you on Saturday?' he asks as they step into the elevator.

'Saturday?'

'It's the next opera.'

'So soon? Wasn't the last one only a few weeks ago?'

'Yes, it's a short season.'

'No, we've got friends staying this weekend. Plus, I don't think I'll be able to coax Ben back quite so soon.'

Ernst Krause nods, seeming unsurprised.

'You're welcome to join Ilona and me. I'd hate for you to miss out.'

'Thanks, Ernst.' She waves as she gets out at her floor.

As he had predicted, by the end of the day she has been contacted by three solicitors asking her to appear in property matters. She flashes on something her mentor used to say: *You don't have to be crazy to practise at the bar, but it does help.*

---

Back home, the house is all ready for Erik and Clara, who are arriving in the evening. There's a casserole in the oven and peonies in the guest bedroom. When they hear a car pulling into the driveway, Malti hurries outside to unchain the gate, Benjamin behind her. Erik drives in and kills the engine. As he pushes the car door shut with one hand, he walks straight to Malti to pull his old friend into a hug.

'It's so good to see you,' Malti pats her friend's cheek, and then hugs Clara. But Benjamin hasn't said anything.

'Hello, Benjamin,' Clara says.

'Oh, hey,' he replies, but his voice sounds funny. The words are exhaled rather than spoken. He gives Clara a loose hug and shakes Erik's hand, the two men thumping each other on the back the way they usually do. Benjamin's eyes are fixed on the car, frowning. The car's red duco is smooth and waxed, loving care in its gleam. Its shape is sleek and streamlined—even Malti can recognise that.

'Is that yours?' Benjamin demands.

Erik grins. 'Brand new.'

'It's nice,' says Malti.

'Nice?' Benjamin repeats, looking at her. 'Malti, it's a Lamborghini.'

'I'll take you out for a spin, if you'd like?' Erik offers.

'A ride would be good,' Ben replies, raising his eyebrows. 'I can't imagine ever wanting to spend that much money on a car, to be honest, so it's probably the only time I'll get to drive in one.'

Clara purses her lips, but Erik just smiles. They walk to the house and, in the doorway, Benjamin pauses to look back at the car.

Malti uncorks a bottle of shiraz for the others and they all sit in the lounge room, catching up. Erik and Malti are mostly trading work stories—talking current cases. Clara works in finance and chimes in from time to time. Ben stares out the window.

An hour or so later, Maeve arrives with her partner, Robert, and greyhound.

'Sorry we're late—I'm drowning in a mountain of marking right now,' Maeve says, rubbing her temples and sinking onto a spare chair.

Between the empty wineglasses and the laughter, it feels like they might have wandered back in time to third-year uni, perched on mismatched moth-eaten furniture in one of the halls of residence.

When they move to the dinner table, Malti takes the casserole out of the oven and the guests make small noises of disappointment.

'I thought you'd make Indian!' Maeve exclaims.

'I did too,' Clara admits.

Malti tilts her head. 'I thought you'd prefer Western cuisine. Sorry! It'll be roti and fish curry next time.'

Dinner conversation is easy. They talk as a group for a while and then the discussion splits into smaller segments—Malti talks mostly to Clara and Maeve. But as Malti places a trifle on the table, there's a lull in chatter and Benjamin's voice rings through from his conversation with Erik.

'I like my job. Linguistics is very meaningful. We work with so many diverse communities, and preserving, recording and analysing the way people use language is hugely important. It's our primary means of communication—there's real value in understanding how and why it's operating at any given time.'

Erik nods. 'I know what you mean. Not all areas of law have the same overarching social and ethical implications, and I certainly struggle with some of the things I have to do in my job. But truth be told, I find my work meaningful too.'

Ben shakes his head. 'It's not the same,' he says flatly. 'I think it's naive to pretend corporate law isn't about profiteering. Anyone who spends their spare cash on sports cars is in it for the money, right?' His tone is jocular, though the words are combative.

'Ben!' Malti rebukes him.

'No, I'm just saying—there are more important things than making a lot of money.'

'Obviously,' Malti snaps.

Erik doesn't seem perturbed. But Maeve shifts in her seat and Robert checks his watch. Clara's mouth is tight. And Malti feels anger that is so white hot, she wonders that it does not blister her skin.

'So, yea-ah,' Benjamin says into the silence, and the sound is sarcastic and syncopated.

---

Malti misses teasing that doesn't have an edge—the kind that's merely playful. All through her first few winters in Melbourne, she had burrowed in shawls and blankets. Benjamin would laugh at her: mittens on indoors and a snarl of scarves around her neck, a loose-knit shawl around shoulders.

'I'm from the tropics,' she would defend herself.

'This is a desert island, you know,' he'd tell her in return.

She had a rickety radiator in her halls of residence room that smelled so musty she distrusted it and wouldn't keep it on for more than ninety minutes at a time—and certainly never when she slept. Hot-water bottles would suffice through the night. But Benjamin was there now to sleepover and keep her warm.

People always stared at them when they were together. *Don't make a spectacle of yourself,* her mother had warned Malti as a child. But this time it was everyone else who was making her into a spectacle. Eyes were seeking her out and fixating on her fingers entwined with Benjamin's—the mismatched skin tones. Only one person ever said anything aloud: *Check out black and white over there,* she overheard one man say to another in a restaurant. But other people conveyed this same sentiment well enough with their cocked heads and raised eyebrows. On that bright-lit stage, she simply clasped Benjamin's hand that much tighter and made her curtsy. Or, as Benjamin said, 'Fuck them!'

They didn't agree on everything. Malti would drink a glass or two of wine, but was otherwise what she called 'sensible' and Benjamin called 'unadventurous'. Benjamin was keen to dabble in all facets of university life. He and his roommate got hold of a small marijuana plant and dried its leaves in the toaster. Malti didn't go near his dorm for several weeks after this, furious with him and worried that he would get caught. Ben had found this all very funny.

'You're still complicit. You know all about it. You, a future member of the legal profession! If we got caught, would you defend us?' they had teased her one evening when she dropped by. Their eyes were red and their mouths in droopy smiles. There was music playing on the stereo.

'What is this?' She jerked her head with dislike.

'King Crimson, don't you know.'

Malti had left when they started to raid their stash of food.

Late the next day, Ben had appeared at her dorm room: clear-eyed, contrite and promising not to partake again. 'I never want to disappoint you again. You know how I feel about you.'

And yet the first time she said *I love you* in the flesh, he couldn't say it back exactly. They were floating on her bed, windows open and curtains billowing like sails. There was a cigarette in his hand, aimed carelessly in the general direction of the window. Her hair was tangled like kelp across the pillows and her nose twitched periodically as the smoke caught her nostrils.

'I love you,' she said. She had rehearsed this in her head so many times, leading up to it for weeks. They had started signing off 'love' in their letters and notes to each other weeks ago. The moment the words had slipped from her mouth, he had looked at her and kissed her lips. But his jester's smile had fallen away and they were bound in seriousness.

'Isle of view too,' he had replied quietly.

She could taste disappointment in her mouth like bile.

'That's not the same thing' she told him.

'The sound is precisely the same. It is a phonetically identical phrase.'

'It doesn't mean the same thing, Ben.'

'No,' he agreed. 'But I do feel the same. Why do I have to say it?'

Except they both understood the importance of words.

---

It was five years after this that they got married in Suva. When they announced their engagement, friends gave them strange and pointed looks.

'But you've always been contemptuous of the institution,' they reminded Malti.

Yes, that was true. Malti had sneered at weddings for years. *Poor bastards*, she'd joke, whenever she drove past a bridal party congregating on the steps of a church.

'It's for visa reasons,' Malti explained. 'It'll be much easier for me to stay here if we're married.' She felt squirmy, hypocritical, but visas were a reason everyone could understand. Her friends, unconvinced, showed mostly a combination of smugness and delight, which Malti found totally irksome. 'We knew you'd get there eventually!' Malti and Benjamin had been living together, but unwed, even though Benjamin's Catholic family had continually entreated and wheedled.

'Darling, wouldn't it be nice if the two of you made it official?' Ben's mother had suggested tentatively from time to time. Agnes Fortune might only attend church sporadically, but the thought of her eldest son living in sin sat uncomfortably on her conscience.

Malti had never told her parents that she was living with Benjamin, but they seemed highly relieved to hear that their daughter was to be married. 'Congratulations!' they cried. After telling them, Malti hung up the phone feeling a bit gloomy. Who knew everyone was still so conservative?

'Let us know when you're planning to come,' her father had urged. 'You will be married here, of course?'

'I assume you want to wear my wedding sari?' her mother had said.

'Umm,' said Malti to both of them.

'Change of plans,' Malti told Benjamin apologetically that evening. 'We can't just go to the registry after all.'

It was a small event—mostly family and a few dedicated friends (Erik and Maeve among them), who could afford the time and expense of flying to Fiji. They got married on Saturday evening and stayed for two days, before leaving on their honeymoon. Malti wore her long hair loose around her shoulders, with Farrah Fawcett ends flicking backwards. No circlet of flowers for her. Elderly female relatives and her mother's friends looked at one another meaningfully. Malti understood the disapproval and chose to ignore it. The red-and-gold sari pleased them, but she wasn't wearing it for their sake. The silk was as bright as the hanging on her wall, and when he saw it Benjamin's eyes lit up in recognition. When she'd dressed that morning, she had wound it around her body and imagined its unwinding later that night. He would unwrap her like a present, literally.

After the pared-back ceremony (the priest modified it to be forty-five minutes, at Malti's insistence), when they could whisper quietly to each other as the formalities took place, Benjamin traced his finger over the gold embroidery and edging which peeked out from beneath the red silk.

'So much nicer than a white dress,' he said.

They danced a self-conscious waltz. The sari gaped a little at her hip, exposing a flash of skin—and his bare hand closed the gap.

Her hand on his shoulder, his at her hip. They swayed together, and then the music changed key, sliding a few notes higher, and they changed direction, moving to the left now. Benjamin suddenly laughed aloud, the hand at her hip squeezing affectionately.

'You're trying to lead again.'

'Sorry,' she apologised, laughing as well.

Her mother and aunts had cooked the food, in huge vats, more than big enough to fit both Hansel and Gretel. Pumpkin, okra and green bananas all found their way into curries, and the women stirred them with ladles like oars. Food was always en masse, no allotted portions here.

When Benjamin took his first bite at their reception, his eyes became as round as coconuts.

'I see what you mean,' he said. 'Your cooking really is average in comparison to this.'

'Gee, thanks, Ben,' said Malti, as eavesdropping aunts smiled broadly.

He hadn't met her extended family before, only her parents. But now there was an endless procession of new faces and names his tongue was not nimble enough to pronounce.

'It's easy,' Malti told him. 'Call all the women "aunty" and the men "uncle". Problem solved.'

Agnes and Timothy Fortune booked flights to attend their son's tropical wedding without question. Ben's grandma came too, and though she had wanted him to end up with a good Catholic girl, she had kissed the Indian bride with genuine warmth. As for Malti's family, the strain of straight English was too much after a few days. With the ceremony over and Benjamin's relatives departed, Malti's family slid into familiar modes of expression. On the second morning, at the breakfast table, the women began to lapse into Tamil when they spoke; sentences began in English and then suddenly slid into something else, mouths shaping words differently and syllables suddenly mysterious. Malti looked at her new husband and the incomprehension suffusing his face: furrowed brow and eyes clouding over. Malti wouldn't dare rebuke her relatives—her mother and aunts, fierce matriarchs every single one of them—but translated in soft undertones for Benjamin.

'I'm sorry about this,' she whispered.

'Don't be,' he breathed back. 'This is fascinating. It's called code-switching and it's very common in multilingual communities. We model our language behaviour to reflect our identity. It's actually a fascinating research area, you know.'

---

Two days later, they flew in the little barrel of a light plane to Taveuni. It was Benjamin's present to her—their honeymoon, arranged and paid for by him. He told her weeks ago that he'd prepared a surprise, but announced it on their wedding night.

'Oh,' she'd said, taken aback. 'What a lovely thing for you to do.'

Down below, the glistening ocean spread wide and the greenery was lush on each island they flew over. Malti was reminded of just how different the ocean was here; this was not Melbourne's Port Phillip Bay. As the plane began its descent, Malti looked out the window with a weary sort of appreciation. She'd visited Taveuni three times growing up, but Benjamin was excited as only a tourist could be. Novelty made him lean forwards in his seat, craning to see through the window—and she enjoyed watching that. She didn't have the heart to tell him that she'd seen this landscape several times before. But, then, she had seen it in his eyes this entire time: Fiji was exotic to him. He was ready to be impressed—susceptible to the charm of strange new customs, harmonised a cappella singing and waters which could not be described as anything other than turquoise.

By the time they were sitting in the resort shuttle, Benjamin's guidebook was already open in his lap.

'They call it the garden island,' he told her. 'It's supposed to be absolutely beautiful.'

'Yeah.'

'*The third largest island* . . .' he was reading snippets aloud. '*Tropical marine climate* . . . Ah, this is interesting. Did you know about the International Date Line?'

'Of course I know,' she snapped. 'It's my country.'

He looked up, a streak of hurt in his eyes.

'I'm not lecturing you,' he said. But he put the book away after that.

The resort was on the very edge of the water; a storm could wash those pretty thatched bungalows right into the sea. They walked over vividly green grass to reception and checked in with a friendly woman who said *bula* and wore seashells around her neck. Ben had booked the type of honeymoon suite they had only ever seen in magazines, and the woman smiled at them when she handed over their keys.

'The Fijians are so warm and welcoming,' Ben remarked to Malti.

In the room, Benjamin threw himself onto the cream-covered bed, arms and legs akimbo, like a child might, and Malti paused in the doorway, just watching him. And smiling.

Then he was up and pulling swimming trunks over his long legs.

'Well?' he asked over his shoulder. 'What are you waiting for?'

They spotted the rungs of a metal ladder four paces from the door, descending straight over the rocky incline into the ocean.

Malti waited on the rocks as Benjamin went first down the ladder. The black lycra of her one-piece was warming, even in the brief minutes that she'd been outside, just as her hair was already becoming hot and heavy, sucking in the sunlight and trapping it there.

Benjamin sighed as he sank into the water up to his neck. Malti followed him in, feeling the water wind around her as sinuously as a cat. As Benjamin fished for adjectives to describe the sensation, Malti twirled slowly in the water, using her legs to propel herself around. They affixed their snorkelling masks and flippers—should have done it on dry land—spitting in the goggles and washing the saliva away with distaste. But when they pressed the plastic and rubber to their faces, it was worth it. The coral they could suddenly see was bright and multihued, an aquatic version of flowers—blues, pinks, oranges and reds. Small fish threaded through hardness and softness in watery acrobatics all their own. Benjamin and Malti, dark shadows overhead, scared them out of hiding, and then followed those little fish away from shore and out towards deeper waters.

They were watching for sea kraits as they swam, their eyes darting sideways behind their snorkels. They never saw those long forms, but they had been warned about poisonous fangs and dead fishermen. The kraits' bodies were covered in black and white bands (Malti and Benjamin had seen photographs), and as they swam they took comfort in the vivid colour underneath and the blue above—no monochrome to be seen. (*Dadakulaci.* Benjamin had been repeating it to himself since he'd read the word in his guide-book. It had a much more interesting sound to it than *krait.* He liked these Fijian words, with their mysteriously appearing nasal consonants. He made a note of it in a little notebook and would spirit it back home to his PhD supervisor, one more linguistic souvenir from the honeymoon.) But the sea kraits were really the only things to watch out for; the encircling reef kept the waters safe. It was more dangerous to be in Australia, really, where every goddamn thing could kill you if it wanted.

They had been holding hands, but broke apart to follow their own pathways of coral. They were not really so very far from the shore. Malti's face was pressed horizontal to the water, but she looked up when she heard her new husband speak. He was emerging from a dive, exhaling the water out his snorkel spout as he reached the water's surface. Playing at being a whale.

'Jeez,' he said, as he removed his mask and shook out those droplets of water that had somehow managed to penetrate the seal. 'Jeez,' he said again. 'You sold this place short.'

He turned in the water, looking outwards to sea and then back to the shore—the greenery, the palm trees—and finally at Malti.

'Yes,' she admitted. 'Perhaps I did.'

Back on shore, already engulfed in humidity, he pulled her towards him and kissed her. She felt the coolness of his wet body and the warmth of the sky pressing down on her from above. They stood together, mouths locked. Their suits were still damp with the sea, but the salt on their bodies was sweat as well as sea water. And, with her face so close to his she noticed that the smell of sunshine was coming off his skin.

---

The International Date Line ran through Taveuni, and Benjamin's guidebook directed them to it. It wasn't much to look at—a gimmicky sign with a hole in the middle that needed a good coat of paint—but they took the obligatory photographs. They had to wait their turn, for there were a couple of other tourists there already, with one foot in today, one foot in yesterday. Or one foot in today, one foot in tomorrow. Malti had never been able to work out which it was. Intellectual time travelling. When they were finally alone, Benjamin wedged his body in the gap in the sign. She snapped a picture.

'Have you ever wanted to go back in time?' he asked, moving from one side to the other.

Malti laughed. 'Or see the future?' She moved to the other side.

If Malti gave Benjamin half a chance, he would describe the linguistic patterns he had heard around the island—and try to repeat all the different sounds aloud. The islands, melting pots of languages, were a linguist's wet dream (Benjamin's words). His textbooks were being brought to life. The alphabet did not align to the Fijian language the way English-speaking Benjamin would have expected. He was thrilled at this practical demonstration of half-forgotten learnings from his undergrad days. Taveuni was particularly special because rather than using the *k* consonant, they used a glottal stop—and Benjamin found this interesting for reasons Malti could not begin to fathom. There were little linguistic surprises and Janus-faced consonants which were not what they seemed: a written *c* sounded like *th* in conversation: *Timoce* was really *Timothy*. And that was just the start; *d* had a secret *n* sound before it when it was spoken (*Oondre Oondre* she thought, before pushing the thought away)—'Except when it appears as the first letter of the word,' Benjamin explained, wagging one finger like the professor he hoped one day to be. Only they were lying in bed and he wasn't wearing underpants. She kissed him to shut him up, which seemed to work. Ah, she thought, I must remember this trick.

—

At the back of the resort, the property became less shiny, less well maintained. The Real Thing, not for tourists' eyes. The huts where the hotel staff lived were located there and the grass, which was not mowed regularly, grew wayward and rough. But one of their walks had carried them this way. At the edge was a small patch of sugar cane, shivering in the wind. A man mending a window at a hut nearby was dismayed when he saw Malti and Benjamin.

'Please, there's really nothing to see out this way,' he said, trying to usher them back to the manicured grass.

But Malti's eyes were on the sugar cane; those tall stalks were the reason she had been born in Fiji rather than India. 'Could we maybe buy a tiny piece?' she asked.

'You know it?' the man asked in some surprise.

'I do,' she replied, and he smiled at her knowingly.

He clipped a piece for her and halved it so Benjamin could also try it, waving away her proffered coins. They walked back to the resort, onto the grass which was perfectly maintained.

'We used to do this as children,' she told Benjamin, handing him one of the stalks.

He handled it gingerly, unused to it. Then he ran his hands along its creases, as though it was a flute he could play.

'Do what?'

'Eat it.'

Sitting on one of the wooden chairs outside their bedroom, she showed him how to peel back the brown outer casing in long fibrous strips—he used a knife, she pulled it away with her teeth—and then they sat chewing the sugar cane in the sun. Juice filled their mouths and they spat the husky fibres on the ground when all the moisture was gone. Nice, isn't it? she wanted to ask. But Benjamin's expression remained carefully blank, and so she already had her answer. He chewed through his piece and then shook his head as he spat the last dried-out fibres to the ground.

'I feel like some Texan hick with chewing tobacco.'

Malti shrugged, a little disappointed.

---

On the plane home, he plaited their fingers together.

'This is just the beginning, you know.'

They were flying back to Melbourne, back to familiar territory, and he was not looking through the window anymore. Instead, he was looking at his new wife. 'Just the beginning,' he said again, for she had not replied.

Light was falling through the oval window across his left forearm, streaking it in gold.

'Just the beginning,' she confirmed.

And he kissed her.

---

Now, six years later, on an inauspicious Sunday in early May 1987—a couple of days after the Lamborghini has gone from the driveway leaving the house once again their own—Malti stands with her hands on her hips and Benjamin's arms are crossed against his chest. Angry words have been bottled up since the dinner on Friday night. Too many things that couldn't be said with friends staying in the downstairs room.

'How could you be so rude to Erik?'

'Oh, come off it,' Benjamin says, scrunching his face.

'You were so obnoxious to them.'

'Why? Because I pointed out the frivolousness of his lifestyle?'

'It was more than that—you were really hostile.'

'Surely you lawyer types can handle a bit of repartee.'

This isn't a misunderstanding, but a refusal to understand.

But it isn't just this weekend. The ghosts of generations of women stand behind her; she can feel them, wives standing in the kitchen or the living room, peering out the window or listening for the sound of a booted foot on the front doorstep. How on earth did she join these ranks? That's an issue to fester in her own mind, but for now she addresses her questions to Benjamin. She watches her husband with her head tilted sideways in confusion.

'What has happened to you?'

It's the question she has wanted to ask for the last three months. No—much longer than that. The words come out explosively and Benjamin rises to meet her. He is looking at her from across the room, arms crossed and eyes narrowed.

'Nothing's happened to me! What the hell happened to *you*? Where's the girl I married? Who is this person who's obsessed by houses and only talks about her cases?'

Malti stares at him, shocked. 'You wanted to move too—we were always working towards a house of our own. And I thought you liked hearing about my work.'

'It's all you talk about.'

'What would you prefer we spoke about—linguistics? Relationships are give and take, Ben.'

'I wonder if you've got anything left to give me anymore.'

'I don't understand what that even means.'

'That's the problem—you don't understand me, do you?'

Perhaps this is not a world of words, but a web of words. Words which have become trapping, ravenous, consuming—with a hunger of their own. Where did we go so wrong? she asks silently. But both her questions, the silent and the spoken, go unanswered.

As she looks at Benjamin's face—splotched and red with anger—she starts to wonder if maybe he has a point. Has he changed? Or has she changed? Maybe that's the problem. Sometimes she thinks that she has grown and Benjamin has stayed the same: the same laugh, smile and sense of joie de vivre. The same charming boy she took to a party eleven years ago.

She can feel her lips curving downwards and her chin dimpling—unstoppable and unbidden. Benjamin sees the signs too and it seems to increase his anger. He turns on his heel and walks out of the room, footsteps sharp and staccato. When he gets to their bedroom he slams the door so hard that the sound reverberates through the house.

Malti cries—not in sadness, but hot tears of frustration. She sinks onto the sofa and lets the memories of the past months linger in her mind. Maybe some things can't be repaired by a pregnancy and a new house. *Too far gone* is an expression she has always heard people use and wondered at it. *Gone where?* she always wanted to ask. But now she thinks she can answer, at least for herself and Benjamin: gone in different directions.

She feels her stomach flutter as their baby stretches inside her. She rests her hand lightly on the gentle dome on her stomach, rubs in a circle. To comfort the baby, of course.

When she goes upstairs, Benjamin is in their bed, turned away from her.

She kills the lights.

# chapter eight

SHE IS SITTING in her chambers a week later when the phone rings, and a truly uneasy feeling bubbles to life. It's immediate, visceral—triggered by the phone before she has even picked up the receiver. If the feeling had a colour it would be mustard yellow. The colour of warning. Rather than letting the call go to the machine the way she usually does, she answers it.

'Malti speaking.'

'Have you heard?' Benjamin's voice is urgent.

'Heard what?' She doesn't even know what he's talking about, but his tone has already seeded fear within her. The weeds of fear flower quicker than any other emotion. Malti knows it can grow, unwatered and unasked for, in almost any place. And it spreads. How quickly it spreads.

'There's been a coup.'

'What?!'

She doesn't need to ask which country he's talking about.

'It's all over the news. A group of armed men hijacked the government—the prime minister and cabinet have been taken away. There's no word yet on what's happened to them or if they are still alive. There are reports of violence on the streets—Indians being beaten, attacked by gangs . . .'

'I need to call my parents.' The mustard unease is rising within her, bilious and nauseating.

'Call them now,' Benjamin urges. 'Why don't you come home? We can call them from here.' He sounds just as worried as she is, and she feels a sudden flash of solidarity. Maybe she shouldn't be surprised—after all, it's where they got married. It's a part of him now too.

'Good idea,' she says.

She isn't in court today, so can simply lock the door of her room and walk away. She only has to wait ten minutes for a train and sits on the stained fabric seat, counting down the stops and clenching her fingers around her handbag.

Arriving at the house, Malti walks straight to the telephone from the front door and dials her parents' number, but she can't get a connection. The lines are tied up and all she can do is try and try again, listening to the monotone bleep that indicates a lack of success. Benjamin stands behind her as she leans over the kitchen bench, cord stretched to its fullest extent and receiver pressed to her ear, and she feels his hands settle on her shoulders. He makes her a mug of tea and coaxes her to sit in a chair. All the while, the radio newscaster repeats the word 'violence'. Benjamin eventually switches off the radio and closes the newspaper.

Friends call her throughout the day and she answers on the first ring, hoping to hear her father's voice. But it's only ever an Australian accent on the other end—Erik and Maeve first, but also friends, colleagues and acquaintances. They all offer the same words of concern and sympathy.

'Malti, I'm so sorry to hear the news. Is your family okay?'

'I don't know!' is the only thing she can say, before Benjamin gently takes the receiver from her and speaks the words of gratitude for both of them that Malti cannot summon. If she wasn't so panicked for her family, she'd be touched by the outpouring of concern, but right now all she wants is to hear her parents' voices. Again and again, Malti dials the number.

Almost twenty-four hours has passed when the phone call finally connects. Malti hears her father's voice and thinks she might faint from relief.

'We're all okay,' says her father. His voice, usually so melodic, is drained and flat.

'Mum? Aunty Rosie and Uncle Jack? Uncle Govind? And Mirdula? Bhaarati, Carmen and Dipika?'

'All fine,' he confirms. 'Just shaken.'

'Can I speak to Mum?'

'Not right now; she's lying down.'

'What's happening?'

'It isn't good,' her father says. The family might be safe, but others have not been so lucky. Nobody has died, but Indian homes and businesses have been burned to the ground or looted, hospital beds are filling up with people who've been assaulted—and the jewel of the Pacific has been smashed to pieces.

'I don't believe it,' she says once again to her father.

And yet she can see it, can sense the ticking of the time bomb: so unbelievable and yet believable. The mutual bitterness and the insurmountable differences. Hatred runs just as deep as fear and, at the end of the day, she wonders if they might not ultimately be the same thing.

Her father promises to call back when he can and they hang up.

Benjamin is watching from the kitchen doorway, questions on his face.

'Ah, Ben,' she says.

He doesn't say anything, but comes over and wraps his arms around her from behind.

'It's your homeland,' he says.

'My homeland, perhaps,' she concedes. 'But this is my home.'

'Is our family safe?'

*Our family*. The wording does not go unnoticed by Malti.

'Yes, I think so.'

She looks up into Ben's face and sees relief relaxing its lines—almost as much relief as she feels. They're his in-laws, after all.

'The hall where we got married was burned down,' she says.

She closes her eyes against nausea, a spiralling orange-peel shape descending from her throat into her belly.

—

Later that night, as she lies in bed, unable to sleep, she thinks of Udre Udre and cannibalism. And of how her birthplace has just eaten itself alive. Perhaps it's human nature to be ravening—to consume and destroy.

It wasn't long after their wedding that Malti had applied for Australian citizenship, filling out the form carefully in block letters. It felt like a strangely mundane way to begin such a significant process. Acceptance came relatively swiftly, and the ceremony was held thirteen months later. Benjamin's parents came, sitting with their son as Malti recited the citizenship pledge on the small wooden stage. They were excited for her. Perhaps more excited than she was. It was like an echo of her graduation, but it felt somehow strange to celebrate citizenship as an achievement. At the end of the ceremony, after the anthem had been sung and all the speeches delivered, she had made her way back to Benjamin, weaving through the swirl of the crowd—trios and quartets of people being congratulated. Benjamin's arms came around her and his parents had a bouquet of roses for her, which she held to her nose in gratitude. And so she had become Australian—a new piece of identity to claim, as she left another piece behind. She didn't really feel any more Australian. The label of citizenship was an important bureaucratic word, with no particular meaning at all. Words for documentation. As Benjamin drove them home, she watched the Melbourne scenes through her car window and did not feel any greater sense of belonging.

Malti's great-grandmother had been approached in the street of her Tamil Nadu village and persuaded to sign a contract she had not been able to read, which had seen her transported across the ocean to a colonised land. She'd been set to work for a pittance as an indentured labourer in the harshness of sugar cane plantations for white overseers and had never returned to her homeland. She was part of a generation of displaced Indians, just as much victims of the colonial project as the native Fijians, who had to suffer their country being colonised and their land used for farms. Malti is the third generation born in Fiji, but she is not Fijian. Her ancestors are from India, but she has never been to that country and the culture she knows is its own tropical variation of Indian traditions. She is connected to all three places—India, Fiji and Australia—and yet belongs truly to none of them. And the country she has settled in, Australia, has its own colonial past—she lives on land that belongs to the Indigenous people.

With her home country imploding, she calls her parents more often than usual. From a dutiful fortnightly check-in, she likes to hear their voices every second day now. At first reports of the coup flood the newspapers, but soon enough the stories creep off the front page and into the back pages. There are new problems and dramas, and the world doesn't slow down for one little island. But bits and pieces still reach Malti.

The exiled leader turned away from everywhere but New Zealand, and the beginning of an exodus.

'A flight of earls,' Ben comments.

Ten days after the coup, her father tells her that Jimmy Patel, with whom she went to high school, was beaten by a mob.

'Is he okay?' she asks in alarm.

'A broken arm and nose, I believe. But he's okay.'

'Awful,' she mutters. No other words come—not Benjamin's, not her own.

'It's the tip of the iceberg,' her father says sadly. 'This place doesn't feel safe anymore.'

---

But something else is not right. And this time it isn't Benjamin. Or Fiji.

May is almost at its close—the temperatures are starting to drop into single digits at night and the branches of the trees are spindly. One Wednesday morning, Malti sits at her desk at work fighting nausea. It takes her aback, as she hasn't been plagued by morning sickness much. Lunch was an egg salad sandwich from the deli: multigrain and wilted lettuce—apparently a bad choice. She doesn't have any appearances or appointments in the afternoon, so she takes the train home. The walk from the station is unpleasant and the nausea is getting worse. As soon as she's through the door, she sinks onto the sofa with a groan. Her lower back hurts too.

She turns on the television and tries to distract herself with a soap opera, but she is unable to focus. She wonders vaguely if she should put a video on instead—Benjamin had taped *Twelve Angry Men* off the television a few months ago—but the nausea makes her toes clench and turns her fingers into fists.

She braces two hands flat on the coffee table, struggling to push herself to her feet, and heads to the bathroom instead. But on her knees in front of the toilet, she can't seem to bring the sandwich up. She knows she'll feel better if she can get the damn thing out of her system, but her body will not cooperate. She strains and retches, but nothing will come.

Giving up, she decides to empty her bladder instead. And when she pulls her underwear down, there they are: enormous patches of blood, clotted and spherical, on the pale fabric. The redness coats her thighs too, a torrential stickiness she hasn't seen for many months now, dripping downwards until the toilet bowl is stained scarlet.

She brings her hands instinctively and protectively to her stomach. One thought forms in her mind: hospital. She is not sure if she is whimpering or moaning, but is dimly aware of small sounds escaping her mouth—not pained, but panicked. Half-running to the living room, underwear still around her knees, she claws the telephone receiver from its base.

There's no answer at Benjamin's office, but Maeve answers on the third ring.

'Jesus, what's the matter?'

'Maeve, I need help.'

'I'm on my way.'

# chapter nine

THE TRIAGE NURSE in the emergency room is kind, in a pragmatic sort of way.

'The doctor will come and see you as soon as possible,' she says and arranges for Malti to be taken to a cubicle.

It isn't much, but at least curtains can be drawn across the sides and there's a bed to lie on. Maeve sits next to her, squeezing her hand, though they do not speak.

The doctor is a young woman with tired eyes and a stethoscope looped around her neck. She asks questions and jots down notes on a clipboard.

'I've got you booked in for an ultrasound as soon as possible,' she says. 'And we're calling your obstetrician.'

It's only a twenty minute wait before an orderly appears with a wheelchair. Malti clambers into the seat to be wheeled away.

'See you soon,' Maeve says. 'I'll find a payphone in the meantime.'

The radiographer is waiting at the end of the windowless corridor. The process is familiar from her check-ups—the squirting jelly and tapered wand. Except this time her hands are clenched into fists on the pilled white sheet that covers the examination table and there is no excitement, just desperate prayers to every deity she can think of. The radiographer moves the sensor over Malti's abdomen. The woman does not comment on what she sees and her face is carefully neutral. Malti cannot see the screen the radiographer is watching, but she can tell from the woman's face—the reluctance to meet Malti's eyes, her hesitation—that the news isn't good.

'The doctor will come and speak with you again,' she murmurs and then falls quiet. The silence in the room is sepulchral.

---

Benjamin arrives at the hospital forty minutes later. Maeve is getting a cup of coffee and Malti is in the cubicle, staring at the ceiling. Benjamin is a whirlwind, running through the curtains. He is panting and has obviously sprinted from wherever he parked. When he sees Malti alert and sitting upright in the hospital bed, he clutches his chest.

'Thank fucking Christ,' he gasps.

There is relief on his face and it breaks her heart that this surprises her. He strides over to her and grips her shoulder. Tight. He is searching her face, looking for an answer.

'Have we lost the baby?' he asks quietly.

The baby. Nameless, sexless, but still their child—always their child, no matter what.

She shakes her head. 'I don't know,' she says. 'I think so.'

He sinks down onto the bed beside her and pulls her in towards his chest. 'Come here,' he whispers. 'It's okay.'

She feels the soft cotton against her cheek and the soft plastic buttons. She cries quiet and ugly, screwing up her face now that she can hide it against his shirt. Above her head, Benjamin's jaw clenches and works, then he cries too.

—

Their obstetrician arrives half an hour later.

'I'm so sorry,' he says. His voice is low and sympathetic as he confirms what Malti already knows. She will never get to hold her child.

'What happened?' Ben asks.

The doctor has no answer.

'This isn't uncommon,' he says. 'It usually means that something isn't right with the foetus.'

But they all know this already and thinking about it in these terms doesn't help.

'I know it's extremely hard,' the obstetrician says when nobody speaks, 'and I know you don't want to hear this right now, but it is probably for the best. There will be another baby.'

Malti can't even imagine that.

The doctor asks for privacy to examine her, and Benjamin and Maeve shuffle out. Maeve squeezes her shoulder as she passes. The doctor arranges a sheet over Malti's knees and puts on gloves. She feels him touching her.

'You're still bleeding a lot,' he says, pulling the sheet back down to cover her and frowning. He is saying something else. She watches his lips move through his moustache, but the words seem so far away. And strange. *D&C. Put you under. Ten minutes.* She hears snatches but can't entirely make sense of it. The doctor calls the others back in and repeats his words; Maeve and Benjamin seem to be following much better. Malti watches their heads bob as they nod.

'Malti, honey, they need to do a quick operation,' says Ben.

'We'll be waiting right here,' Maeve promises.

---

There's a small team of medical staff standing around when they wheel her bed into the operating theatre—the obstetrician, anaesthetist, a couple of medical students and a nurse.

'This should be quick and easy.' The anaesthetist smiles at her—she can see his eyes crinkle above the mask. 'See you soon,' he says.

The room dissolves.

---

She dreams that she is back in Rakiraki. The light is extremely dim, but too sepia for twilight. She's not in a car this time, but on foot. Barefoot. Her soles are pricked by the gravel and the humidity is like a pillow over her mouth. The air is pressing in on her like a hungry animal. But is it just the air? Over there—what's that? A shadowed figure is emerging from the trees. He pauses, just in front of the tree line. She feels rather than sees that she is being watched and, although she cannot see the face, she knows instinctively who it is. This is his gravesite, this is his territory. The ground and the air belong to him—she is a trespasser in this place. And what would Udre Udre do to a trespasser?

It's quick—a flash—and the figure is suddenly standing a metre away from her. He is still shadowed and Malti feels the familiar blossom of fear. Has he come for her? Is this her time? Maybe somewhere far away she lies bleeding out on an operating table. Will she now feel the sharp piercing of incisors sinking into her skin? But the figure moves no closer to her.

The dim light changes and, kaleidoscopic, his face comes into view. Lines arch out from the temples and across the forehead, and grey is peppered through his curly hair. His eyes are brown like hers and he watches her dispassionately. There is no antipathy there. Looking into the aged face, it strikes her that he is not actually a myth or a spirit, but a man—someone who lived and loved, laughed and wept, with fears of his own. The creeping uneasiness that has always lingered, the shadowed figure always at the periphery of her vision is suddenly dispelled as she looks into a face which is entirely human. What if the problem wasn't him, but her all along? What if she has been afraid of the wrong thing?

And now that she has stared at bloodied underwear with terror that cannot be put into words—has felt genuine fear for the tiny being within her body—what hold can phantoms have on her anymore?

Rakiraki fades out, not in darkness, but into prisms of light that refract and realign. She surfaces or maybe sinks into calmer sleep.

---

She rises to consciousness in a series of images. Fluorescent lights overhead, dull beeping from the corridor outside and Benjamin sitting next to her in a plastic chair. He is thumbing through a magazine, but pushes it aside when she stirs.

'Hey, angel.' He leans closer to her. 'How are you feeling? Are you okay?' He backtracks immediately. 'Sorry,' he mutters. 'Of course you're not okay. I meant—physically, are you in pain?'

She wants to answer yes, because there is pain constricting her chest like a vice, but that's not what he is asking.

'They gave me some painkillers.'

It's a dull ache, no worse than the womb-centred pain she sometimes gets during a period.

'I'll be okay. We'll be okay.' She is in fact asking a question.

She feels Benjamin's breath on the crown of her head.

'We will,' he affirms.

---

Malti is released from hospital that evening, though the staff insist on wheeling her to the car in a wheelchair. The sky is dark now and the lights are on in the hospital car park. She stares out the window as they drive. Benjamin does not talk either. When they arrive home, she goes straight upstairs to bed, hoping to sleep without dreams.

—

Malti takes three weeks off work and lies around the house, listless.

People call and she speaks to them as briefly as possible, hanging up quickly. She marvels that she is forming words and talking, when her insides have suddenly disappeared. Her breaths keep coming steadily and her heart beats as ever. How is this possible? She is now just an empty shell.

Maeve and Erik ring every day, and Maeve stops by after work. A few cards arrive from people at the office—one is even accompanied by some peonies: *We heard you have been unwell and send our best wishes for a speedy recovery. Ernst and Ilona Krause.*

Malti tries to get on with things—tries to make a list of things she needs to do: grocery shopping, pay the electricity bill, call her parents—but finds she can't be bothered. Benjamin is picking up a lot of the slack. He makes her his kumara soup for dinner and buys a crusty baguette to go with it. He has fallen back on old favourites. They sit at the table, skimming thick hunks of the bread across their bowls.

'Thanks, Ben,' she says, touched even through the torpor.

He seems relieved to see her smile.

When they finish dinner, it's Benjamin who clears the plates away and fills the sink with hot soapy water. Fifteen minutes later he returns with two mugs of English breakfast. She squeezes his hand in acknowledgement and he covers it with his own.

Benjamin is making excuses to stay home a lot at the moment. He goes to work as usual, but he arrives back in the late afternoon—the chaotic period at work seems to have passed. There are no late hours or business trips scheduled. Malti has a hunch that he has pulled away from some of his project commitments to spend more time with her. He seems less distracted. Increasingly, she can see glimmers of the Benjamin from two years ago. And she wonders if she, too, is softening—becoming more like the woman he married.

'You're different,' she says to him again one evening. 'You've changed.' This time it is a compliment.

Benjamin's eyes flicker before his mouth twists into something like a smile and he shrugs.

'I've remembered what's important,' he says quietly. But he looks somehow sad and Malti wishes she hadn't said anything at all—sometimes silence is the better option.

---

Even when she goes back to work after the three weeks, their rekindled closeness remains. They start to touch each other when they walk past again, and one evening when she gets home from work Benjamin meets her at the door and pulls her straight upstairs to bed. No baby now for him to be afraid of hurting. He takes the time to kiss her—her mouth, her shoulder blades, her ankle bone—and she lets him. Over the years their lovemaking has become quick and lazy, but tonight she remembers their beginnings. Afterwards, they lie in the sheets together and talk about small, familiar things.

Of course, Malti hasn't yet recovered. Will she ever?

Every day the grief catches in her throat and chest. Sometimes she finds her mind drifting out of focus during the day as she works on a brief or attends a hearing. The strength of will required to refocus is enormous. Once, on a lunch break, a pregnant woman walks into the deli where Malti is buying a pasta salad. Her belly curves and her smile is wide; she rests her hands on her stomach.

'Just over halfway there,' she says to the cashier, laughing, and Malti feels a frisson of grief. That would've been her too. She walks out without the salad and cries in her chambers, before taking the rest of the day off and going home.

There are some baby clothes in their bedroom closet—yellow and cream, carefully gender neutral. Malti hates seeing them there. She wonders if she should give them away and can't help recalling the shortest of stories, often (and apocryphally) attributed to Hemingway—*For sale: baby clothes, never worn.* When she brings it up with Benjamin, he gives her a strange look.

'We'll need them.'

He is planning to recycle the teddy bear he bought for the next pregnancy. Malti finds this a bit squirmy but doesn't say anything. She simply moves the baby clothes, still with their price tags in place, further into the depths of the closet.

She'll be glad when 24 September, the due date that was to be, has passed. It is pencilled into the calendar hanging on the fridge; she had scribbled it there the day they moved into the new house. Everything has been a countdown until that day and it is looming in front of her.

Benjamin isn't as mesmerised by that date as she is; his eyes don't seem to drift to it on the calendar the way hers do. His sadness is more contained. More abstract and less embodied, perhaps. He does not have to feel the emptiness and stillness in his belly like Malti. He is already thinking about the future.

One night as they sit together in silence on the sofa, he strokes her wrist.

'What do you think of Ellery for a girl?' he asks. 'Derived from "cheerful" in Latin.'

'Mmm.' Malti makes a noise against Benjamin's shoulder. 'Maybe. Cheerfulness is probably one of the best things we could give her.'

---

And a couple of months later, Malti takes a pregnancy test. She reads the instructions on the box and holds the stick with hands that tremble. She is unsurprised by the result—she has known before the stick confirms it. There is an ugly bud of fear within her that wasn't quite so prominent last time, but she also feels thrilled at the prospect of telling Ben.

And feels the sudden conviction that they will be okay.

# part 2

# 2000

# chapter ten

THEIR BAGS ARE packed and waiting by the door. Ellery stands beside them. Her shoelaces are already fastened in double knots and her hands cannot lie still in her lap. They writhe like caterpillars that will never become butterflies. She presses her forehead against the cool glass of the front room window and keeps her eyes fixed on Beach Road. She can see the street through the wide grille of the front gate and, even through the walls of the house, the sibilance of cars rushing past is clearly audible. They flash past the house in dots of colour, but no blue four-wheel drive is among them. None of these cars is the right one. And the right one is more than an hour late.

Verona couldn't care less about the time—she never seems to notice. Even now, she'll be on her tummy in front of the television: chin propped on wrists, bare feet sticking up in the air. Ellery can hear the *Rugrats* theme song repeating itself every half-hour as one episode moves into the next. Debris from yesterday lies around the house: new toys in the bedroom, the bin full of candy cane wrapping paper, and the fridge brimming with leftovers in Tupperware containers, including the forbidden brandy custard that every year Mum refuses to let them try.

Verona makes the most of her holidays. The day after school finished for the year, she painted her nails bright orange and now, between midday cartoons and nail polish, she is perfectly content. She does not ever seem to doubt that their father will arrive to pick them up as planned.

But Ellery is a full year older than her sister. Verona is only ten, whereas Ellery is already eleven. She'll be in high school next year.

'You're very grown up, aren't you?' adults tend to comment when she says this, as if she can't hear the laughter shadowing their voices. But eleven *is* grown up. And now, as she presses her face to the glass pane, she feels the heavy weight of her own maturity like a mantle around her shoulders. Verona may sit and blithely watch TV, expecting Dad any minute, but Ellery knows so much better. Seventy minutes have dripped by since he promised to be here. In that time, the sun has moved right to its zenith in the sky and baked the earth to its usual December heat.

Their mother has an important case to work on this week—the last week of 1999—but has taken this afternoon off to wait until Dad collects them. She'll take her own holiday next week, heading back to the country of her birth, but she has been working overtime in the lead-up. She'll no doubt go back to her chambers later today and, like Ellery, Mum's eyes swivel between her watch and the endless stream of cars on the street outside. Mum hasn't said anything, but she's blinking the way she does when she's angry: too many blinks, with the eyelid shuttering down too strongly. She blinks like that whenever John Howard makes an appearance on TV. Mum is sitting at the kitchen table with a mess of papers in front of her, but her eyes are magnetised to the watch on her wrist or the digital clock on the microwave. Still, when Ellery comes to the kitchen to fill a glass of water, her mother smiles reassuringly.

'Don't worry, he'll be here.'

Ellery shrugs and walks back to the window. The sun continues to move steadily across the sky and the wind starts to pick up.

Another forty minutes later and she sees it—the squat blue car turning into their driveway.

'He's here!' yells Ellery, and she can hear the answering flurry of movement in the other room. Although she can't see it, Ellery knows that Verona would have leaped up instantly, the television forgotten. There's the sound of Mum's chair scraping the floor.

Peering out the window, Ellery sees her father, long-legged and lean, climbing out of the car. Somehow, he is always taller and more vibrant than she remembers him to be. More real, rather than the voice on the phone that she's used to. She watches as he pulls the gate open, tethering the end with a frayed bit of rope, before driving forwards to park in the cobbled entrance of the front yard. He's deft with the gates—there's a trick to making the hinge cooperate, but he seems to remember it. Ellery has to remind herself that he once lived here. The tiny part of her that had been imagining a horrific car crash somewhere—a circle of ambulances and the blue bonnet engulfed in orange flame—is relieved. But the feeling is closely followed by a slump: so then he was just late. Again.

Verona, now wearing Converse, rushes into the room and peers out the window too.

'Dad!' the younger girl shrieks, excited now. 'Dad!'

In an instant, she's out through the door and into the front garden.

Their father half-crouches and spreads his arms wide.

'Where are my girls?' His voice is warm and eager.

In a wild tangle of hair, Verona throws herself at him and he hugs her tightly.

'Hello, Monkey.' He kisses her. 'Merry Christmas for yesterday—I've got your present in the car. Where's your sister?'

At this, Ellery gets slowly to her feet. The screen door whines as she goes through it and she pauses just past the bristly welcome mat. From ten metres away, she looks at her father, and in that second she splits into two: there's an overwhelming urge to copy Verona—to race to him for a bear hug and let the excitement of seeing him consume her. But there's also something sharp and spindly in her throat, something with jagged edges, which holds her in place as she swallows against it. She doesn't move.

'Hi, Dad.'

'Well? What about a hug for your old man?' He grins. 'Come on!'

He keeps one arm around Verona's shoulders and holds his other arm out to embrace Ellery. She can feel her stiffness as she walks over. She stands rigid as he hugs her and doesn't kiss his cheek.

'You're late,' Ellery tells him.

Looking over her head, he raises his eyebrows at their mother, who has poked her head around the doorway.

'Late, am I?' he repeats loudly, pointedly. 'I wonder where you got that from.'

'Well, don't look at me. And she's not wrong,' says Mum. 'You did promise to be here almost two hours ago.'

'Yeah, yeah, yeah.' He says it liltingly and melodically, like a song fragment.

Ellery has learned by now that they're not really angry with each other—that fire burned itself out long ago. But they tend to do this banter thing when they see each other. Mum comes out of the house now, slipping on a tattered pair of thongs to traverse the pathway into the garden. It looks bizarre with her formal court attire up above—the fitted skirt and the chiffon blouse—but even so she is still graceful when she moves.

'How are you, Ben?' Mum asks. They're right next to each other now. She kisses his cheek and he gives her a loose hug.

'Ah, can't complain, Malti. How's life treating you?'

'Very well, thank you. Merry Christmas for yesterday. What did you end up doing?'

'Same to you. I just hung out with some friends. Saw your name in the paper when you won that last case—good for you.'

'It's always gratifying.' Mum nods. 'And you're on holiday now, of course?'

'Yes, I've got a bit over a month of leave and the students won't be back on campus until March.'

'Academia has its benefits.'

'Few and far between. And you—are you excited to be going home?'

'I don't know that I'd call it home,' Mum says.

'Have you even been back since the wedding?'

'Twice. The last time was five years ago, I think, when you took the girls for Easter.'

'Oh, yeah. Guess I lost track of time. Well, give my best wishes to your folks.' This time when he looks at her, his head is tilted to the side and his eyes are soft and crinkled. 'I'll always have fond memories of that place.'

'Homemade curries and endless relatives?'

'Yes. And beautiful snorkelling, white sand, Fijian singing. You in a sari.'

'Ah,' says Mum. 'I have fond memories of those bits too.'

'Really?' Dad says. 'I didn't think you even saw them.'

'Something can be many things at once,' Mum replies.

There's a pause. They're smooth and polite with one another, full of pleasantries.

'You're a stunner as always,' Dad tells Mum appreciatively, like he always does, but she doesn't give her usual laugh.

'Why don't you two go collect your things?' she says to the girls.

Verona is immediately off to her room. She isn't a sporty girl, but she'll certainly run when Dad comes over. Her short curls bounce around her head as she darts back into the house to collect her bag and Ellery follows, much more slowly, all the while straining her ears to hear what the adults are saying.

'This holiday is gonna be great,' Verona announces to Ellery as they run upstairs to do a final check and for Verona to grab her new Tamagotchi. The Christmas tree, resplendent with tinsel, sits in the living room, already shedding pine needles. It'll be browning by the time they're back.

It takes them three minutes to collect all their things, and when they return Mum is speaking to their father in a low voice. Her hands are on her hips and Dad is half turned away from her. The girls pause in the doorway.

'All talk and no follow-through. No sincerity. You told them you'd be here at eleven and you just leave them waiting.'

'Oh, they don't care. They're fine.'

'No, they're not! It's two hours later. I don't understand—do you need a new wristwatch?'

'For God's sake, the clock shouldn't dictate life.'

'You're a budgerigar!' Mum hisses at him, shaking her head. But, at this, Dad laughs with sudden delight. He laughs easily and throws his head right back. No polite chuckling, just true joy.

'Budgerigar?' he repeats. 'I love that word. Most people don't realise that it has Indigenous origins—the etymology goes back to the Gamilaraay language, you know . . .'

Mum opens her mouth in a sharp shape, but quickly closes it again when she sees her daughters have returned. Both adults stop talking and smile in a determined kind of way; they never let the girls witness the behind-the-scenes arguments. United front and mutual respect always. Ellery sighs to herself. Verona might be young enough to fall for it, but do they really think Ellery is so easily fooled?

'Well, girls,' Dad says. 'Ready to go?'

Mum kisses her daughters goodbye. There's a hurriedness in her manner now. She has got to get back to work—she, too, will now be running late.

'Have a lovely time, my darlings,' she says brightly, as she packs their bags into the boot.

'Bye, Mum,' Verona replies indifferently; she is already getting into the back seat and telling Dad about school. They rotate the seating: Ellery gets the front seat on the way up and Verona takes the journey home. There's no seniority here.

'Bye, Mum.' Ellery dawdles. She gives her mother another hug and takes her time opening the passenger door. 'Have a great time on your holiday.'

'Thank you, sweetheart, I will. Look out for your sister while I'm gone. You two need to take care of each other.'

'Yes, Mum.'

'And remember that I'm at the other end of a phone. Call anytime.'

Ellery looks back at the house with its brick walls, wooden balconies and decks that Mum had painted mint green many years ago. The flowerbeds burst with colour—citrus trees and azaleas, splashes of yellow and pink side by side. She misses this place when she's away.

'Hurry up, kiddo, let's hit the road,' Dad calls from the driver's seat, one arm negligently on the wheel, the other propped against the window.

Ellery takes her place in the passenger seat. Her own reflection gazes solemnly back from the window's slight tint. The car reverses onto Beach Road and, turning around, Ellery watches Mum pull the gate shut behind them.

---

It's hard to stay angry with Dad. Even when he's serious, there's some remnant of laughter in his eyes and mouth. Boyish, people call him, one of those slippery words which is only half a compliment—or perhaps not even that. 'Lightness of spirit' is the phrase Mum uses to describe him, and Ellery thinks that it's the right choice. There's something bright and bubbling within him. Something deeper and more important than charm or levity. The Golden Boy, Granny Agnes likes to call him—even now when they visit her, she'll still ruffle her son's hair.

But Ellery isn't in the mood for Dad today. She is determined to remain cool. One hundred and twenty minutes late! The worry she'd felt is slowly fading, but leaving sharp and brittle things in its wake: hurt and anger. She isn't being unreasonable—this has happened before. And it's months since they've seen Dad, anyway. He hasn't set foot in Melbourne for twelve weeks at least—not since the September holidays. Ellery folds her arms and watches the streets skitter past the left hand side of the car. The heat is picking up and Dad has switched the AC on high. Verona chats from the back seat, always talkative around Dad. Verona usually veers between unguarded conversation and sudden moods that wash over her. It isn't uncommon for Verona to fall suddenly silent; she will get hooked by some thought in her own mind and her conversation will trail off as she follows it. *Girl with the curl,* their mother says as she tugs one of Verona's swirled brown locks affectionately, and Ellery thinks it's kind of a pity that her sister matches the nursery rhyme quite so neatly. Ellery is only half-listening, but Dad is attentive—murmuring soft sounds and asking questions. Beyond the window, the beach disappears and Brighton's wide, tree-lined streets are far behind them.

When Verona's chatter fades to a lull, Dad glances at his eldest child.

'And how's my Elly?'

She doesn't say anything and Dad's voice gets gentler. 'Ferret?'

She's Ferret and Verona is Monkey. Neither of them has any idea where he got the names from.

'I'm fine.'

Dad sighs. 'Well, come on. Out with it. What's the matter?'

'Nothing.'

'Clearly there's something bothering you or you wouldn't be staring out the window sulking.' There's a slight flavour of impatience in his voice now, as he likes to get things out in the open. He isn't passive aggressive and doesn't hold grudges, but he's quick to grow irritable or even angry. He tends to flare up—sudden and heated, like a match. Verona is like that too.

Ellery watches the nature strip slide past, not green but yellow. And soon brown.

'Why were you so late?' she asks after a while.

'Look, I had things to do, alright?' The last word is emphasised slightly, warning her off. In the back, Verona shifts on her seat. Dad's driving gets jerkier when he's annoyed, with sudden bursts of acceleration that brush against the edges of the speed limit.

'Two hours,' Ellery points out.

'I said I'm sorry. The trip from the airport took twice as long as I expected.'

'Actually, you didn't say you're sorry! And you've made the drive plenty of times before—how could it possibly take you by surprise? If you'd wanted to be on time, then I'm sure you could've been.'

'We're on our way, aren't we?'

'That's not the point.'

'Yes, it is. You need to live in the moment a bit more. There's no need to be in a strop around me coming a little late.'

'I'm not in a strop,' Ellery retorts.

'Oh really? Looks like a strop to me.' There's a hint of playfulness entering his voice now. The heat has seeped out as though it were never there. He glances over his shoulder to the back seat. 'What do you think, Verona? Is it a strop?'

'Yep!' Verona agrees, starting to grin. Traitor. Typical that she'd side with Dad.

'I'm not in a strop,' Ellery insists again.

'Ooh, sounding even stroppier.' And now he's smiling widely. He winks at Verona in the rear-view mirror and she laughs. And he laughs. Until finally, grudgingly, Ellery can't help herself: she laughs too.

What is it with laughter? It's a very different car ride after that. Cross words might never have been exchanged. Verona is humming under her breath and Dad is making easy conversation.

'She's quite a woman, your mum,' he says, shaking his head. 'Budgerigar,' he repeats fondly and laughs, as though it had all been a joke.

'What happened? How come you got divorced?' Ellery can't help asking.

'You know the story.' Dad is airy, unconcerned.

'Kind of.'

'Sometimes people just don't fit together. She's quite a woman, your mum,' he repeats.

She opens her mouth to ask, but Dad pre-empts her. 'Too many questions, Ferret.' He smiles. And, just like that, the opportunity is lost. Levity must continue to reign.

But Mum never says much about it either. Ellery had asked her a few months ago as they stood at the sink one evening, Mum scrubbing the dinner plates and Ellery using the tea towel to dry them. Verona was supposed to be putting them away, but she had disappeared into the front room after dinner. They're not allowed to watch television in the evening, but there are plenty of books to choose from and Mum always approves of them reading.

'Why did you get divorced?'

Mum had sighed and squeezed the sponge, soapy water trailing over her hands like foamy gloves.

'People change, Ellery.'

When nothing else came, Ellery prodded again.

'But he had an affair?'

'Yes,' Mum said shortly. 'A woman he worked with. Amanda.'

'How could he have done that?'

Mum shrugged. 'He wasn't very happy. Relationships are complex.'

Mum had turned the tap on to wash the suds from the sink and the rush of water had carried away any further possibility for conversation. Ellery hadn't asked any more questions, she'd stood wiping the rivulets of clean water from the dishes and, beside her with the tap roaring, Mum had looked lost in thought too.

---

Dad drives them all the way to Ferntree Gully. *First star to the right and straight on till morning.* Car travel is one of Ellery's favourite things. She has noticed that people are more likely to talk in that enclosed space. The womb-like bubble seems to draw forth things they wouldn't usually share, creating some sort of transient honesty. Car trips with Dad aren't quite like that, though. There's always singing involved when he's at the wheel. He puts on CDs and hums a harmony, encouraging the girls to join in, or he simply sings from his memory. His voice is strong and he can make the melody wheel right around the car. He likes to introduce the girls to old tunes which are new to them: Phil Ochs is the favourite—'Men Behind the Guns' and 'The Highwayman' always get a run-through—but he also teaches them songs by Leonard Cohen, Neil Young, Judy Collins and Nick Drake. Both girls can carry a tune, so they don't mind this little ritual of his. They sing along behind him.

The mountains are up ahead, getting closer. Verona winds the window down and it is not just fresh air that seeps into the car through that sliver: it is anticipation. Cramped suburbia is now mostly behind them; they are on its outskirts, where the houses are a bit sparser and the yards are bigger. It's just them and Dad, and even Ellery feels the wild thrill of that. Dad isn't like any other adult she's ever met; adventure is perpetually lighting up his eyes. He's Peter Pan and they are his duo of lost girls.

# chapter eleven

THE HOUSE AHEAD of them is made for adults. There is a formal dining room and cream-coloured furniture. There is also a wine cellar under the staircase, bottles displaying labels whose significance she cannot fathom. Grange . . . like Hermione Granger? But Dad brings Neverland with him wherever he goes. The house is set on a hill with a view out over the nearby mountains and the vast sloping yard has many corners in which to play—there have been countless games of hide-and-seek over the years. *Come out, come out, wherever you are!*

This isn't actually Dad's house—it belongs to his parents—but neither Ellery nor Verona make the distinction. The house is simply theirs. Agnes and Timothy vacate to their beach house and Dad stays in their place when he visits Melbourne on school holidays.

Dad unlocks the door, and they carry their things into the hallway. Then it's straight to the kitchen to rustle up sandwiches—corned beef on Wonder White.

'Are we going to Susan's tomorrow?' Ellery asks as she adds mustard to her bread. Susan lives in Flemington and makes incredible lasagne. After dinner she serves tiramisu with cloud-like sponge and layers of mascarpone (she omits the marsala when she's cooking for the girls). Both girls enjoy visiting. When Dad takes them along, they watch movies together on Susan's charcoal L-shaped sofa. They like her even more than her tiramisu. She has a warm smile and her widow's peak gives her face the shape of a heart. She seems to genuinely enjoy spending time with her boyfriend's daughters, doesn't see them as rivals or nuisances. She doesn't fight them for his attention. And she gives great hugs: the tight, snuggly kind.

'Susan, Susan,' Dad repeats absently in a singsong voice. 'Susan and I aren't seeing each other anymore, Ferret.'

'What?' This is news to Ellery. 'Why?'

Dad shrugs. 'She's a bit cross with me and wants to cool things off.'

'Oh, but Susan's the best!' Verona chimes in, stabbing a fork into the pickle jar to add to her sandwich. 'I liked her even more than Janet or Shannon.'

'Or Lorraine or Rose,' Ellery agrees.

They had both adored Martina, a woman Dad had been with for a whole year when the girls were much smaller. But she was only a dim silhouette in their memories now.

'Yes, thank you both for that recital.'

'Why is Susan angry with you?' Ellery demands.

'Mind your own business, kiddo.'

Ellery wants to ask more, but Dad's voice promises only evasiveness. Having narrowly skirted a fight today, she doesn't want to push her luck.

'Right,' she settles for saying.

'I've got my two best girls with me—who else do I need? Just Elly and V.'

Ellery smiles, but feels a sinking sadness that Susan is to join the ghostly ranks of all Dad's other girlfriends. The carousel spins endlessly around, but the women never reappear. Always a new face with whom the girls have to start afresh, all the while knowing some giant hourglass, visible only to Dad, is already measuring the span of their relationship with the latest woman: one day she will disappear and they don't get a say in that. In recent years, Ellery has been tempted not to bother making an effort when Dad introduces them to a new girlfriend, but his women are usually so likeable she can't help it. Saying a gloomy farewell to Susan in her mind, she closes the lid of the mustard and takes a seat at the dining table.

The heat is thick and porous now and Dad has flicked on the overhead fan.

'How about we do Christmas presents?' he suggests. 'And then we could go for a swim.'

---

Even after an afternoon spent splashing around in the local outdoor pool, Ellery lies awake staring at the ceiling. She never sleeps well in this house. There's a new Nintendo 64 console and a couple of video games for the girls to share. She misses her own bedroom, and the dark mountains in the distance do not comfort her the way the lapping waves of the bay do. She's a water baby at heart—picked it up from Mum—and cannot be away from sandy shores for long. She stares into the darkness, wide-eyed, feeling tension she can't place or name threaded through her shoulders and behind her forehead.

Of course, in the brightness of daylight it's easy to appreciate being here. When Ellery goes downstairs the next morning, sunshine is already streaming into the breakfast room. She can see the mountains through the window and hear the cacophony of butcherbirds and magpies from the trees overhead. It's all green and gold out there today.

Dad is sitting at the table, drinking black coffee and reading the newspaper, with the broadsheet covering most of the table. He's scanning the letters to the editor, shaking his head.

'What a little berk!' he is muttering when Ellery walks in, taking umbrage with a letter writer from Prahran. Dad is usually distracted over breakfast and needs some caffeine through his veins in order to revive. He likes to sit and read the paper undisturbed; the only sounds in the room are his sighs and asides as he flips through the pages: 'Stupid fucking Ruddock.'

But after a couple of coffees, he will become chatty. He tells the girls stories from *Lord of the Rings*. He knows the book inside out and has been taking them through a slow serialisation. Each time they stay with him, he takes them a little further through—to Tom Bombadil's house, through the mines of Moria and the gardens of Ithilien. Ellery and Verona are still and silent, the images unfurling like movies in their minds.

Verona isn't usually an early bird, but she is always up before Ellery at Dad's place. She's lying on her tummy on the floor—the usual position—reading as well.

'There's my Elly!' Dad exclaims when he glances up and sees Ellery standing in the doorway. 'Sit, sit.'

'What's around for breakfast?'

Dad shrugs. 'Not exactly sure,' he says vaguely, eyes still on the back page. When Ellery checks the fridge, it's almost empty—just milk in the door and a withered zucchini in the crisper.

'Not much in the fridge,' she observes aloud.

'There's toast, plus peanut butter, Vegemite and jam in the cupboard. I've got cereal too, I think. There's always muesli. Er, do you eat muesli? And your sister had Coco Pops. Right?' He glances over at Verona.

'Coco Pops,' Verona confirms from the floor.

'Well, help yourself,' he says to Ellery, so she puts some muesli in a bowl and adds milk, bringing it back to the table.

By the time she sits down, Dad has finished with his paper and is swirling his coffee around in his cup to catch the dregs.

'So, I've been thinking up some fun things for us to do,' he announces.

'Like what?' Verona chimes in, looking up from her book.

'We could go to the St Kilda markets today,' he suggests.

'St Kilda,' Verona repeats, uncertain of where that is.

'St Kilda is ages away! That's right near home,' Ellery says, incredulous.

'So what? We're not in any rush. There's also the aquarium,' Dad offers. 'We could wander around there for a while and see the sea life.'

'Yeah, that would be fun,' Ellery admits.

'See the sea life.' Verona laughs. 'Or we could go to the zoo?' she adds.

'Absolutely!' Dad enthuses. 'And how about climbing trees in the park?'

'Yes! And go back to the pool!' shrieks Verona. 'And get ice cream again!'

'Or rollerblading,' Ellery hears herself say in the same rapid, high-pitched voice as her sister. 'There was a disco rink you took us to around here once. That was so much fun.'

'Right.' Dad nods his head solemnly. 'We're off on an adventure.'

---

It's always like this at Dad's. They work their way down the list over the next week—a new thing each day. Always something different, all kinds of summer activities. When they go to the pool, Dad doesn't sit watching from a sun lounger but is splashing around in the water as well. Or he's wearing too-tight rollerblades, circling around the rink right alongside them. He buys ice cream for all three of them from a Mr Whippy van, with its sinister music-box soundtrack. Mum would never let them near soft serve—something about bacteria—but those things don't matter to Dad. The girls are more adventurous with flavours than Dad, choosing raspberry or hokey-pokey or chocolate chunk. Dad doesn't even get the grown-up flavours, like pistachio; he only ever orders vanilla, which the girls agree is a total waste of a perfectly good ice-cream choice. It's the boring flavour and doesn't suit him at all.

They don't have set bedtimes but can go upstairs to their rooms when they choose. Dad half-heartedly reminds them to have showers, but never checks to see if they've cleaned their teeth or tidied their rooms. In fact, when he goes down to the service station to buy cigarettes in the evenings he'll usually bring both girls a chocolate bar or a rainbow jelly snake to eat in bed. Verona loves it. Ellery can see her little sister relaxing and unfolding, becoming more expansive. Away from their mother's rules, in Dad's chaotic playground, Verona sparks and sparkles. She likes the bedtime jelly snakes and the brightness of Dad with his solar smiles and easy jokes.

But Ellery thinks about home a lot. The Beach Road house lies empty—not even Mum is there. The gates are locked tight and the potted orchids have been dropped off at Maeve's for safekeeping. Mum has flown across the Pacific to the islands where she grew up.

'What will you do while we're away with Dad?' Ellery had asked a few months back as she helped Mum slice okra for dinner. *Bhindi*, Mum calls it.

Mum had smiled. 'Oh, I'm sure I'll think of something or other.'

'Like what?' asked Ellery dubiously.

It's all too easy to forget that Mum has a life beyond her daughters and does not exist in servitude to motherhood.

'I might go visit my parents,' Mum had said as Ellery stared at her. The okra had fallen onto the cutting board in wagon-wheel shapes, spilling seeds. She never says 'your grandparents'. For some reason, that label is reserved for Benjamin's parents.

'They should come here,' Ellery says. It's been several years since they last came to Melbourne.

'They're getting older and it's harder for them to travel.'

Ellery remembers the last time very clearly. Mum had picked them up from the airport and driven them home, where the girls were waiting.

'Touch their feet,' Mum had whispered, nudging the girls. 'Both hands.'

'Huh?' Verona had looked at their mother. 'Yuck.'

Ellery had moved forwards. Feeling upright and stiff, she had bobbed down and touched toes through thick socks. Both grandparents had smiled. She had asked about it later, when Mum came upstairs that night to tuck them in.

'It's a sign of respect,' Mum explained.

'It's kind of weird,' Ellery said.

'Says who?' Mum replied. 'What makes it weird?'

Ellery had no answer to that.

'It's different,' Mum corrected.

For the two weeks Mum's parents had stayed, fragrant steam had billowed constantly from the kitchen and new dishes had appeared on the table each night. The girls, only used to mild chilli, had panted and run for glasses of milk to soothe swollen tongues.

'Your girls can't tolerate their chilli,' their grandmother had commented, frowning. 'And you need to update your spices.'

The next day, she went to the Indian shop and returned home with fresh garam masala and cardamom pods. Even now, the turmeric jar is written in the unique slanting lettering used by Mum's mother. There had been new words at home too—incomprehensible to Ellery and Verona. Her grandparents spoke a strange hybrid language, with every fifth word in English, ensconced in rolling sounds that seemed to bleed one into another.

'I'll give you the numbers you'll be able to reach me on,' Malti had assured them. 'I'll be in contact the whole time, just at the end of the phone.'

It was very rare for Mum to go away without them. A holiday by herself? How strange. How would she possibly have any fun without them?

Even Verona was paying attention. 'What are you going to do there?' the younger girl had asked, wide-eyed.

Mum had given them an A4 sheet of her itinerary to take to Dad's: Suva, Nadi, Lautoka and then the Blue Lagoon. Both the girls looked up at their mother. Blue Lagoon? That sounded rather intriguing. Like something out of a storybook. They have never paid much attention to where Mum grew up, but some things just sound good—like when Verona had thought that the Princess of Wales was the Princess of Whales. Ellery is starting to think that the world needs blue lagoons and cetacean royalty.

Mum had smiled at the wonderment she must have seen in their eyes.

'It's the route of a small cruise line,' she explained. 'I'll take you one day if you'd like.'

Verona had merely shrugged, but Ellery had been curious.

'Would we like it?'

'Yes, I think so. I think you'd find it pretty.'

Mum doesn't say much about her home country. Both girls are always surprised when they remember that she wasn't born in Melbourne. It was only when they studied immigration one term that Ellery had realised.

'You're an immigrant!' she had exclaimed to Mum.

'Yes,' Malti agreed. 'A large part of your heritage lies elsewhere.'

It's strange knowing Mum is not in the country; Ellery feels the prickle of missing her.

---

Over the next few days, Ellery also finds herself missing Susan. Dad didn't plan quite so many activities when Susan was around, but there was a home-cooked meal on the table by seven o'clock every night and bedtimes were always observed. Ellery likes the half-hour she spends reading before lights out, but she's always too tired to read when she's staying with Dad. And she misses Susan's place in Flemington, where the carpets were vacuumed every Saturday morning and aromatherapy candles burned in the bathrooms: French vanilla! Pomegranate and lime! Teak and lingonberry! Dad is fun, but Susan was caring. In the evenings, they would watch old movies together and Dad would wrap his arms around Susan's shoulders. *African Queen* on the screen, Ellery in the beanbag and Verona on the floor. It was all very nuclear.

'Are you going to call Susan?' she asks one night when they're making Milo before bed.

'No, Ferret.'

'You're not going to try to talk to her?'

'That relationship is over.'

'But you sound sad!'

'Of course I'm a bit sad, but there are plenty more fish in the sea.'

Ellery stares at him. 'People aren't fish,' she says indignantly.

He laughs. 'I don't know about that, kiddo. Talk to me again when you're older. Lots of shrimps and sharks and barracudas out there.'

'But—'

'Come on now, Elly. Drop it.' The warning note has crept into his voice. 'No, I didn't want the relationship with Susan to end, but sometimes in life you have to deal with things you don't like. I didn't want my marriage to your mother to end either, but you take it in your stride and you move on. Susan and I are over, and I don't want to keep talking about this. Is that clear?'

It's a stern-voiced and crease-browed fatherly edict.

'Yes,' Ellery mutters. She wants to argue with him, but doesn't have the nerve to pursue it. She will not mention Susan again. The name slides into the background, beside Janet, Shannon, Lorraine, Rose, Martina and Marianne.

---

New Year's Eve is a surprisingly low-key affair at Dad's. This New Year's Eve is the calendar error that's making everyone crazy.

'From 1999 to 2000 is just the turn of the century, it's not actually the new millennium,' Verona likes to point out. She's good with numbers in a way Ellery will never be.

At this, Dad ruffles her hair. 'Never let accuracy get in the way of a good time, kiddo,' he advises.

The abbreviation Y2K is making the rounds on television and being used in advertising slogans. Every city is trying to outdo itself and all others with fireworks, parties and grandeur. People are having fun guessing what Sydney might come up with and making bold, biased claims that Melbourne's celebrations will be better. This year Mum will get the New Year before them. Samoa and Tonga come first, but New Zealand and Fiji are next after that.

Dad, Verona and Ellery are going to stay home with pizza and watch the fireworks on television. The girls like Hawaiian and they pick off strips of plastic ham as they watch the fanfare.

'What if the television explodes?' Ellery asks nervously.

'Won't happen.' Verona is dismissive.

Dad drinks beer and periodically goes outside to smoke cigarettes. Smoke furls back into the house from the door left partially open.

At midnight, there are images from all around the world being shown, and Dad pours sparkling apple juice into the long glass flutes, and they pretend it's champagne. They clink and make a toast to the year 2000.

---

Over the next week, Dad stays up in front of the television when the girls go to bed, watching movies end on end. *Dune*, *Stargate*, *Alien*. He mostly likes science fiction; galaxies and nebulas fill the screen as he sips pinot noir and puffs on cigarettes. One night, Ellery dreams of empty chairs and flat lemonade, waking up with a fuzzy mouth that feels like cat hair. She crawls out of bed in the dark room and makes her way downstairs into the nimbus of light coming from the living room. Dad is on the sofa, partway through a movie. The microwave clock reads 12.45 am. He turns around when he hears Ellery's slippers on the black tiles, angling one arm along the edge of the sofa, the same way he does when he reverses the car.

'Ferret!' he exclaims, pausing the video. 'What are you doing up?'

'Needed a drink,' Ellery mumbles as she fills a glass of water.

'Bad dream?' Dad asks.

'Not exactly.' Ellery yawns, eyes still two-thirds closed. She drains the glass and turns to head back upstairs.

'Where are you going?' he asks, surprised. 'Why don't you finish watching the movie with me? This is a very interesting one—very thought-provoking.'

He brandishes the blockish case and she sees *Silence of the Lambs* written on the front. She's never heard of that one.

'It sounds really boring.'

'Oh, don't be too sure of that. Come on, pull up a pew!'

Ellery stares at him. 'Dad, it's late.'

He waves this away. 'You're on holidays, aren't you? You can sleep in tomorrow.'

Anthony Hopkins's face stares out at her from the screen. 'No, it looks weird.' She frowns. 'I'm going to go back to bed.'

'Fine, fine, have it your way,' Dad replies, sounding disappointed. He turns his back to her and picks up his wineglass. He hits play on the remote control and the VCR whirs to life again.

# chapter twelve

DAD IS RESTLESS. His leg jiggles and he drums his fingers on the table when he sits. Ellery doesn't bring up Susan again, but her absence seeps through the house. Dad is different without Susan around. It isn't just the meals; his face is less relaxed and his eyes are often unfocused when the girls talk. On Wednesday of their second week, he takes them to the park to climb trees and throw a frisbee around. Tall trees that Ellery cannot name strain towards the sky. She and Verona have often nestled in their low branches, searching for the perfect foothold to get just a bit higher, and they both have their own small museums of scars on each knee from tumbles: red raw sores which have faded with time to white lines and patches, each one the memory of a mishap.

'It would be more fun to be the frisbee and get to fly through the air,' Verona remarks, neatly catching the fluoro disc as they stand in the paddock together.

They switch to shuttlecock after that. Dad plays the first few rounds with them and then unfolds a banana lounge to adjudicate from the sidelines. They eat cheese and tomato sandwiches in the park for lunch, but the icy poles Dad bought have melted to orange puddles.

'How about we stop for ice cream on the way home?' Dad suggests as an alternative when they're packing up an hour later. But as the car sits stopped at a set of traffic lights on their way back to Ferntree Gully, his eyes snag on a pub where people are milling onto the nature strip, men holding glasses of amber liquid and women in sundresses. 'You know what, how about we stop for a quick drink? I reckon they'll have ice cream.'

Even before the girls nod politely, Dad is already turning into the car park. When they're seated inside at a high table in a dim room, the waitress shakes her head.

'Sorry, no ice cream. We could do you vanilla slice, though? It's the house specialty.'

'Now that sounds pretty damn good.' Dad smiles. 'Three, please.'

Dad also orders a glass of red wine for himself and red lemonade for the girls—Barmaid's Blush, he calls it, which makes the waitress laugh. Ellery doesn't know why; it wasn't particularly funny. The waitress has written the order on a notepad, but pauses at the table, fingers trailing on the watermarked wood.

'Your daughters, obviously,' she says, glancing at Ellery.

The shape of Ellery's eyes is straight from Dad—a hand-me-down from Granny Agnes—and her hair is a much lighter shade of brown. 'My, you look like your dad!' people have always said to Ellery, which makes both her and Verona scowl. Ellery from offence: *Do I look like a man?* And Verona from resentment: with lush dark curls and eyes like blackberries, she looks much more like their mother. Both girls felt they got the worse end of the deal and would prefer to look like the other parent.

'Peas in a pod,' agrees Dad in what Ellery thinks of as his Ironic Voice.

This makes the waitress laugh again, and she smiles back at Dad over her shoulder as she heads to the bar.

Women always tend to smile at Dad when they walk past the table. Waitresses often linger and touch him on the shoulder when they take his order. He seems to like it; he finds excuses to strike up conversations with them.

Ellery has noticed that hours in a pub seem to pass very easily for adults. Thirty minutes later, Verona is yawning while Ellery is tearing her paper napkin. But Dad is sipping his merlot and reading the wine list again. He is chatting to them, but his eyes are roaming the room.

Two hours later and they're still sitting at the small, high table. The waitress took pity on them and brought over some crayons and the butcher's paper they use to cover the tables in the bistro area. Verona is drawing a praying mantis and Ellery is inventing a signature. Some woman called Anna has joined them at Dad's invitation and is deep in conversation with him. Her right knee is hooked over the left and her hands are gesticulating, swimming through the air like pink fish. She looks about the same age as

Mum and is speaking with such animation that her entire face is illuminated. Dad is leaning forwards slightly across the table, which makes his hair fall across his forehead.

When the waitress returns and asks if they need anything, Dad sends her away. He has switched to beer now and Anna is halfway through a glass of something clear, but which is not water. People have started making their way in for dinner—the early bird crowd. The girls catch the smell of fish and chips from the kitchen: Ellery's face swivels towards the clear pane, where they can see the chefs hurrying around, and Verona copies the move. Dad looks up.

'You girls hungry?'

'Yeah!' Verona exclaims.

'How about we get some chow here? Feel like fish and chips?'

'Yeah!' That's Verona again. Dinner sorted and on its way, she turns back to her picture, now drawing what looks like a tree with strawberries on it.

Dad turns back to Anna. 'Care to join us for dinner?'

She smiles at Dad. 'I'd love to. I'm just going to run to the bathroom.' She gestures to her drink, almost empty. 'Would you order me another?'

'Coming right up.' When she has left the table, Dad turns back to his daughters. 'How are my girls doing?'

'Good,' says Verona, still drawing. 'Pretty hungry, though. Can we get the fish and chips now?'

'I'll order them as soon as the waitress comes over, sweets. Are you hungry too, Elly?'

Ellery has crossed her arms. 'No, I'm bored. We've been here all afternoon . . . I thought we were just coming in for ice cream?'

'It's been a lovely afternoon!' Dad exclaims, wide-eyed. 'Us all sitting together. You two drawing and me getting to know Anna.'

'It's been so boring.'

Dad sighs. 'A bit of spontaneity isn't always a bad thing. Just go with it.'

'Anna's the only thing you're interested in here,' Ellery accuses. 'You haven't said a word to us—you're just talking to her.'

'That isn't true.'

'Yes it is.'

'I'm spending time with you guys too.'

'No you're not. You're not like any of my friends' fathers. Can't we just go home?'

There's a long pause and Ellery can feel her middle sentence hanging in the air, poisoning it. It's too late to take it back. But if she could open her mouth and swallow it, she would.

'Is that really what you'd like to do?' Dad asks. His voice is uninflected and Ellery can't tell if he's angry, sad or just disappointed.

'Yes!'

'How about you, V?'

'No, I want fish and chips.'

Anna is returning, wending her way through the clump of people clustered around bar tables.

'There's no food in the house, Ellery, and it would be rude to scarper when I've already invited Anna for dinner. But I'll tell you what—we'll order and eat quickly, then go home. Deal?'

'Fine.'

Anna takes her seat and smiles at Dad, flicking her longish hair over one shoulder. 'So, what did I miss?'

Dad is true to his word. He catches the waitress's eye immediately and orders their food. He resumes his conversation with Anna, but now tries to draw the girls in. Verona is embellishing her drawing and only responds sporadically, whereas Ellery feels the beginnings of something twisting inside her stomach. Maybe she's being unreasonable. She tries to join in the conversation, but there isn't really much for her to say.

Anna's forehead is slightly wrinkled as she watches Dad—he's more distant now, and their conversation has fallen into awkward stops and starts. Ellery notices the woman surreptitiously check her watch. As soon as Anna's fork has come to rest on the plate, Dad tilts his head towards her, apologetic.

'I have to get the girls home.' He pauses, teetering on the verge of something, but in the end simply gives her a smile. 'It was lovely to meet you.'

'Oh. Yeah, you too. Well, bye, girls.'

Dad pays for dinner and bundles them out the door, with Anna watching them leave—brow still crinkled like crepe paper. The hurt look in her eyes makes Ellery squirm.

Dad doesn't speak as they get into the car, but his face is starched, teeth mashed together. He twists the key in the ignition in a way that makes Ellery's arm scurry to the armrest. He reverses out of the car park and flicks on the radio. No songs to sing this time. The streets are narrow, made for slowness and caution, not for these rough turns he's making.

'Dad?' Ellery says into the prickly silence. 'You're being weird.'

'Honestly, I'm just a bit disappointed, Ellery.'

'What? In me?'

He doesn't respond to this directly. 'You made me feel really awful back there. I don't always get it right, but I love you girls very much. And being a good father means a lot to me.'

Her throwaway comment before dinner comes floating dimly back to her, but Dad's foot is on the accelerator, and he takes the next turn at speed. Ellery is gripping the passenger handle now. This is the fight that has been simmering for days. As the streetlights flash overhead, Ellery suddenly realises that it had never been diffused, simply delayed. The inevitable cannot be avoided—this was crashing down on them all along.

'Don't,' she snaps, but he ignores her. 'Listen to me! If you're going to drive like that, let me out of the car right now.'

No response. They both know what an empty threat it is. Dad's foot just presses down harder and the car screams in acceleration.

Ellery is afraid. Even Verona looks uneasy; Ellery turns around and sees her sister's small face echoing her own.

You never know what you're going to get with Dad. Peter Pan and his Lost Girls.

When Dad pulls into the garage, Ellery is out of the car before he has even stopped the engine. She stands at the front door, arms folded. Verona follows at her heels, which is unusual—she usually waits for Dad. The sisters look at one another as he comes to unlock the door. He lets the girls walk inside first. He doesn't quite slam the door behind him, but there's enough force there to make it thud. The cowbell slung around the doorknob clangs against the dark wood.

'Get to bed, girls,' he says and then walks into the lounge room. He grabs a beer from the fridge, then settles onto the sofa and turns on the television.

It's almost 8 pm and Verona pads obediently upstairs to her room to read. Ellery, however, pauses, half hidden in the shadows of the room. Veiled by the canned music of the television advertisements, she tiptoes to the itinerary on the fridge and scribbles the telephone number for Mum's parents' house in Suva on her hand.

The house stretches across several floors. The garage opens onto the lounge room and kitchen; upstairs are the bedrooms; and on the lowest floor is a formal sitting area that has never once been used, alongside a poky study with Granny Agnes and Papa Timothy's endless books. And a telephone.

Ellery heads to the study now and dials the number on the back of her hand. She has never dialled this number before by herself—Mum usually makes the calls and they get on the phone after her to say a quick hello to their grandparents. The girls do this a bit awkwardly, passing the phone to each other like a hot potato. Ellery wonders vaguely whether there is a time difference as she listens to the dial tone.

In her mind she mentally rehearses a hello to her grandparents. *Hello Paati, hello, Thatha. May I please speak with Mum?* But there's no need; it's Mum herself who answers.

'Ellery!' she exclaims, her voice concerned. 'Is everything okay? Goodness, why are you calling so late?'

'I want to go home.'

It feels good to say out loud. As she says the words, she flashes on another beloved children's book—not J.M. Barrie this time, but Frank L. Baum. *There's no place like home.* The words had been a mantra in her head the whole drive home to Ferntree Gully as Dad sped around the corners.

'Why? What's happened?' Mum asks.

'I don't like being here with Dad.'

'Why not?'

'He got really cross with me today.'

'How come?'

Mum always constructs a gentle cross-examination with them. Ellery mumbles the story. The bar, the boredom and, finally, the car ride home.

'So, can I go home?' Ellery asks. 'We could get Megan to babysit.' Megan is studying commerce at university and sometimes comes to look after them if Mum is at a work function. 'Or we could stay with Maeve?'

But there's a long pause on the other end.

'Have you spoken to your father about this?' Mum asks.

'No. He wouldn't listen to me—he never does. He wouldn't even pay attention in the car when I told him to slow down.'

'Give it a try,' Mum encourages her. 'Go back upstairs and tell him that you didn't like the way he handled the afternoon—tell him how it made you feel. He loves you, Ellery, he'll listen.'

Now it's Ellery's turn to be silent.

'Can't I just go home?'

Mum sighs. 'Ellery, you'll have to sort this out with your father. This is your time with him, and if you're having problems, you two need to discuss it. There's nobody to take care of you, anyway—Megan will be busy with her family and Maeve is in Hawaii.'

Ellery stands in the darkened study and looks out onto the street. She can see the pinpricks of windows in the valley below and her own face reflected in the glass from the light of the reading lamp, hand clenched around the receiver.

'When are you coming home?'

'In a week, darling.'

Ellery presses her forehead against the cool glass of the window. 'How's it going over there?'

'It's fine. Being back reminds me of why I left. When you haven't always belonged, it's easy to forget that Melbourne is home. How's Verona?'

'Oh, she's fine,' says Ellery tartly, and Mum actually laughs.

'Okay,' says Mum. 'Why don't you put your father on the phone.'

It's more awkward than Ellery had expected to climb back upstairs. Verona must be in her bedroom and Dad is reclined on the couch watching some kind of cop show on TV. There's a beer bottle on a coaster beside him and one bare foot rests on the knee of the other.

'Um, Dad?'

'Yeah?' He speaks without turning around.

'Can you come downstairs? Mum's on the phone.'

'Your mother?' Now he turns around, his voice low and worried. 'Why did she call so late? Is everything okay? Has something happened?'

'She didn't—I called her.'

Three long seconds go by.

'And aren't you supposed to be in bed?' Dad asks. His voice is neutral; his crossness in the car has scattered away.

'Well, yes, but if I want to talk to Mum you can't stop me.' Ellery is defensive, but Dad holds up his hands, fingers spread.

'I'm not having a go at you.'

He mutes the television and picks up the phone's second receiver, which is on the wall a few metres away.

'Hi, Malti,' he says, then he murmurs to Ellery, 'Will you go downstairs and hang up?'

She nods and heads back to the study, glad to leave the room.

'Oh, for goodness sake,' she hears Dad exclaim to something her mother says.

Downstairs, Ellery picks up the receiver to return it to its cradle, and as she does she can hear her parents' voices. The temptation is too irresistible and, careful not to breathe audibly into the mouthpiece, she lifts the phone to her ear.

'. . . I'm sure it would if you talked to her,' Mum is saying. 'She's just looking for a bit of your time and attention.'

'Exactly. She wants my attention focused entirely on her, but Verona's here too and I've got other things in my life. Tonight was a prime example—I talk to somebody else for half an hour and she flies off the handle.'

Half an hour? The clock had swivelled around at least twice as they sat in that bar tonight.

'She's only eleven,' Mum reminds him. 'She's a child.'

A child?

'An immature eleven.'

'Oh, come on, Benjamin. She's not a demanding kid. The girls don't see you much. You relocated to Brisbane almost a decade ago.' Mum never reprimands him in front of the girls, but here in the privacy of a phone call, her voice is acid.

'Eight years,' Dad interjects hotly.

'Same difference. I mean, what did you expect? When was the last time you even came to visit? Would it really kill you to give them your undivided attention while they're with you?'

Dad's voice is spiky. 'Do you have any idea how much pressure the university puts on us to publish? Academia is incredibly demanding.'

Quietly, quietly, Ellery replaces the phone and stares at the receiver. She sits on the floor of the office, hugging her knees.

Fifteen minutes later, Dad's voice calls her name from upstairs and she follows it up. The phone has been replaced on its holder: no Mum.

'I've spoken to your mother,' Dad tells her. 'If you want to go home, I'll drop you back in the morning. I'll find someone to come and stay with you for the next week.'

'Really?' Ellery blinks at him.

'Yes.' He sighs and rubs his hands roughly through the sides of his hair. His eyes are smaller than usual and tired. 'But I hope you don't. I'd really like you to stay.'

Ellery half-expects him to offer an apology, but it never comes. The incision of hurt from the conversation she wasn't meant to hear is there—she feels it jaggedly somewhere beneath her ribs. So why do these words make everything okay? They shouldn't—they won't—but somehow they do.

---

Later that night, Ellery lies awake. She's thinking about the stories Mum told them when they were little: sharks, octopuses and princesses turned into flowers. But there were also stories of gods with elephant heads, goddesses in lotus flowers and women swallowed by the ground. So many stories. Despite the heat, Ellery shivers and pulls the covers up higher over her body and tucks her limbs further in towards the centre of the bed, as though any limb outside the safe square of the mattress might fall prey to a *vetala* in the dark. Dad has always been the best raconteur—he knows how to hush his voice just right and how long to make each pause—but Mum's stories are better. She has always known the tales to get the heart racing with delicious terror or excitement—the kind that made Ellery forget that fiction is fiction. And yet, in that moment when the mind is captured and the whole body is consumed by the story, there's really no such thing as fiction at all.

She thinks of Dad downstairs, watching TV with his disappearing eyes, and of the arguments always at parboil in this house. The unanswered questions and evasions. Her parents' voices in her head. *An immature eleven. Just a child.*

Their mother is always there, consummately dependable. She packs the sandwiches and Just Juice into the lunchboxes every day and can be found waiting for the girls outside the school gates in the old Fiat each afternoon. Mum checks that they do their homework and reminds them to clean their teeth before bed. Her love is expected and freely given. And taken for granted. When their mother says *I love you*, the girls nod absently: they already know this. Dad is the wild card.

Like Verona, Ellery too has always counted down to Dad's visits. Privately, though—she does not mark the calendar hanging in her room, but she counts down nonetheless. But lying here now she wishes she was home. And although she's no longer thinking of leaving, the countdown has reversed. In the dark, she ticks off the days that have passed on her fingertips and whispers an invocation for time to hurry up.

# chapter thirteen

MUM IS PLAYING the soundtrack from *Bleu* when they arrive home. Its orchestral notes seethe behind the screen door, grand and gloomy. Neither of the girls sees eye to eye with Mum when it comes to music, so she must take advantage of their absence to play her own CDs.

Dad has pulled the car into the driveway through the iron gates and now unloads the girls' suitcases from the boot. Verona darts into the house to switch off the music and Ellery stands staring at Dad.

'Shall I bring these into the house for you?' he asks.

'I can do it.' She shrugs and takes the handle of her case. 'Well, thanks for having us.' Mum believes in manners and politeness, and has drilled boilerplate phrases into her daughters: *May I please be excused from the table? Ellery speaking, may I help you? May I know who's calling?*

'Ah, you're very welcome, Ferret. Nothing makes me happier than having my girls for the holidays,' Dad tells her with sunny sincerity. Except Dad's words don't always match up to his actions. The affirmations and promises uttered so earnestly all too easily fall away. They get carried away on the air as they leave his mouth. *Cheating at solitaire*, says Mum. *Being a flake*, says Ellery.

She can feel the bright chaos of the past few weeks like a sugar high lingering in her body. Exhilaration and fatigue. Ellery shifts her weight from one foot to the other, unsure of what to say to this person who is both parent and unknown quantity. From inside the house, the music suddenly stops—Verona must've reached the CD player.

Dad looks over. 'Where's your mother?'

'I don't know. Do you want to talk to her?'

'I'd like to see her if she's around.' He runs a hand through his thick blond hair to tousle it. He's always like this when Mum's around—flirtatious and eager. He seems to forget that they're divorced. He gives boyish grins and she gives cool smiles, as they perform two halves of one whole. Only maybe they're not even really performing anymore. Ellery doesn't think Mum's distant smile is a pretence. Nor Dad's eagerness.

Right on cue, the screen door quivers. Verona is back and, behind her, their mother. Mum is a warm cardigan. A mug of Milo. Hot buttered toast.

All Ellery knows is that she's getting a big hug and Mum is whispering, 'Hello, sweetheart,' against her hair, smoothing it back from her forehead to give her a kiss. 'Hello, Benjamin.'

'Looking good, Malti,' Dad says, half-reclining against the car.

'As always, apparently.' Mum raises her eyebrows.

Ellery wonders when they started talking like this, in subtext and one-liners.

'How was the trip?' Dad asks Mum.

'It's been a long time.' This, she seems to think, is answer enough.

'And how was Appaji?' Dad has always copied the words Mum uses for her parents. It sounds weird coming out of his mouth. He doesn't put the accent in the same places that Mum does.

'Getting older, but fine, I think. His knees are playing up . . .'

As their parents chat, Ellery is standing next to Mum and Verona is beside Dad. The fragmented family, facing each other like they're all about to square-dance.

But now Dad is looking at the road and the sky.

'Best be off,' he says. The first person falls easily out of his sentences.

'No!' The wail is Verona's. She hugs Dad around the middle, as though he is a tree trunk. 'Can't you stay a little longer? Can't you have dinner with us?' She looks towards Mum, but it's Dad who replies.

'Sorry, V. Not today. I've got a flight to catch tonight for a conference this week.' He pats her arm. 'But I'll see you again soon.'

Verona neither replies nor releases him. Even though she's still clutching him, Dad holds out his arms to Ellery. 'What about a hug for your old man?'

This is, of course, his eternal greeting and goodbye. He's smiling widely and his eyes are lit up as only Dad's eyes can be. Nobody else's eyes ever look as bright and alive as his.

And despite the ups and downs of the past weeks, Ellery doesn't hesitate. She rushes forwards.

---

It's a slow rehab being back home after a few weeks with Dad. Mum has rules and edicts that must be followed. Bedtime is sacrosanct, every meal is served with leafy greens, dishes are never left in the sink, and no rainbow jelly snakes slither to them as they read in their rooms at night. Ellery lies in her white metal bed with roses painted on the frame. After the hyperventilation of Dad, this is like taking slow deep breaths.

Mum, fresh off the plane from tropical sunshine, is tanned. Her arms are brown and she smiles often. But after a few nights of working late, the smiles become briefer and more close-lipped—as though she hasn't had a holiday at all. Ellery and Verona sleep in, but Mum gets up early to do yoga on the balcony each day. Ellery and Verona watch dubiously from the sidelines: adult life seems to be terribly skewed towards work. Grown-ups all have frown lines etched between their eyebrows and worry lines carved into their foreheads, yet somehow their smile lines are never as pronounced. Except on Dad.

They spend the last two weeks of the holiday at home while Mum goes in to work. Mum has decided that they don't need Megan the babysitter anymore through the day, but when she's out and they're home alone, she calls them every lunchtime from work to check on them. *I'll let the phone ring three times, hang up, and then call you again, okay? Under no other circumstances should you answer the phone.* On the weekend there are books and stationery to buy for school. They have migrated from Dad's hedonistic anarchy to Mum's benign dictatorship.

Ellery is going into year seven at a co-educational private school around the corner—the first year of high school and the year most of her friends will become teenagers. Ellery is slightly young for her year (Verona is too), and won't turn thirteen until the next year, but she will be twelve soon enough. This must be the moment of true transition between childhood and growing up—the point of demarcation. One night, she runs this theory by Mum, who cannot suppress a bubbling laugh.

'Oh, sweetheart, you're a treasure.'

Ellery's close friends are all staying on at the same school for year seven. They have their routine, cross-legged in summer learning French braids from Gabby or playing Uno. It's warm and familiar, a small patch of belonging. School work comes easily to Ellery too—the report cards she brings home at the end of each term are approving.

Verona is brilliant at maths, but has never really been able to negotiate the fog of English. She could participate more in class, the teachers write in their reports. On the other hand, she often reads in the library at lunchtime. Ellery sees her through the glass double doors as she walks with her friends to the front lawn. Verona's head will be bent over a book, legs swinging, but her lips curve upwards and her eyes are bright. She gets on fine with others in her year level, but seems to prefer her own company. Ellery watches her from afar with a mix of consternation and envy, for Verona has something Ellery does not: she doesn't care what people think.

---

The Monday that school starts is hot and dry, with dusty winds from the north. The return to school is always marked by sweat and sweltering heat. Mum drops the girls off at the school gates then drives to the station. For the first time, Verona and Ellery turn in different directions—Verona threading downwards to the junior school and Ellery turning left up the brick pathway that takes her to the year seven halls. They belong to different worlds now.

'Have a good first day, V,' she calls to her sister, who does not turn around.

Heading to the new corridors, Ellery walks the way she has seen their mother do: shoulders back and chin parallel to the ground. The other four girls in her group are already standing on the verandah outside the new classrooms.

'We waited for you,' they tell her as she approaches them. 'Are you ready for this?'

'Of course I am,' Ellery replies, surprised to hear that a slight quaver has crept into her voice. 'Let's do this.'

They push open the classroom doors, where new faces and old faces are already colliding into a blur. Ellery knows that she is in a class with Sylvia and Meg, while Liv and Gabby are in a different class together. It'll be the first time since year one that she and

Gabby haven't had classes together. They've been friends a long time. Ellery doesn't much like hierarchies, but she and Gabby own two parts of a Best Friends bracelet. The quintet has already sworn to keep hanging out together at lunch. *Nothing has to change just because we aren't in the same classes anymore*, they had promised each other when the class lists were released at the end of last term. Sitting in their new chairs, they are given timetables with strange subjects: science, history and geography. Ellery has spent an afternoon carefully covering all her books with contact paper, but the subjects are opaque. The history textbook has pictures of archaeological dig sites, while the science one has a diagram of a Bunsen burner. Which subject will be her favourite? She can vaguely perceive that this choice will somehow matter going forwards.

When lunchtime comes around, she is exhausted by newness, nervousness and excitement. It's a relief to sink onto the grass and eat her cheese sandwich. Liv and Gabby are slightly late coming to lunch and, when they arrive at their usual spot on the lawn, there is another girl trailing behind them. She's carrying a tennis racquet and her hair is up in a short ponytail.

'This is Sophie,' Gabby says. 'She's new. Liv and I said she could have lunch with us today.'

Ellery, Meg and Sylvia look at each other and then say what is expected of them.

'Of course! Come join us!'

They all shift backwards on the grass to widen the circle, as Sophie nods her thanks and takes a seat on the grass.

---

When Mum picks them up after school, she immediately probes for stories.

'How was the first day?'

Verona shrugs. 'Not much different. My form teacher seems nicer than Mr McMillan last year.'

'That's great, V. How about you, Elly?'

'Good, I think,' she says, wondering whether or not this is true.

---

Ellery is curious about Fiji, a mystery to her and yet also somehow part of who she is, something that sets her apart and marks her as different from Gabby, Liv, Sylvia and Meg, with their blue eyes and blonde hair. (Liv's hair is actually brown, but she is porcelain pale, just like the others.)

'What was it like going back?' she asks Mum on Friday afternoon, when the first week of year seven is officially over. Mum is making a curry for dinner and Ellery stands beside her, helping her peel the pumpkin and fetching the mustard seeds from the cupboard.

'It was fine,' Mum replies.

'Different from the last time you were there?'

Mum considers this. 'Yes.'

'More tourists?'

'It wasn't that.'

'So what then?'

'Well, it's more that the country itself has changed. There weren't bars on windows when I was growing up, for example.'

Ellery has never seen bars on windows. She tries to visualise it, but all she can think of is prisons.

'I've only been back three times since 1987, you know,' Mum adds.

'Why? What happened in 1987?'

'A lot of things, Ellery.'

Ellery turns her attention back to the pumpkin and reflects.

---

Every so often the phone rings and Dad's cheery voice floats down the line. He promises to call weekly, but the phone usually rings at two- or three-week intervals. He does make a point of calling after their first week back at school.

Verona speaks to him first, chatting away about clarinet lessons. She only reluctantly hands the receiver over to Ellery. 'He wants to talk to you.'

Dad's warm voice somehow dissolves the distance between Melbourne and Brisbane. 'How has school been? Any new friends? How's year seven?'

'First week was okay. We're starting a bunch of new subjects and reading a good book in English. There's a new girl, Sophie, who's hanging out with us.'

Dad asks more questions, wanting to know about her teachers, and Ellery hears herself chatting away much the same as Verona. She tells him about Mrs Morgan, the art teacher who wears tights with crazy patterns, and about swimming lessons, and Dad laughs in all the right places. Then he draws a breath and she knows what's coming.

'Alright, kiddo. I've got to run now.'

Quickly, she asks a question of her own—the one that's always on her mind.

'When are you coming down to see us?' Ellery asks.

'Soon, Ferret. Very soon.' The words are so airy that they might just blow away.

'Brisbane isn't far!'

'Work is terribly busy, Elly. I often need to go to Sydney at the last minute, or Adelaide. I don't want to make a commitment to the two of you unless I know I can keep it.'

It's such a sweet-sounding excuse. She thinks about pressing him—the words are on her tongue—but an incredible weariness suddenly comes over her and she closes her mouth again, letting the words just slide down her oesophagus.

Ellery is trying to be understanding, but why won't he make firm plans? Beneath her blossoming frustration is something darker and more insidious. It keeps her up at night from time to time, weird questions haunting her mind. Somewhere along the way, she has begun to ask why, and the problem is she has no answer to this. The only logical reasons she can come up with are not appealing. The one thing she hasn't factored in before is herself: what if the reason is actually her? She finds herself thinking back to their last visit and replaying her words and actions in her mind. She knows she offended him that afternoon in the bar and when she asked to go home. Were those things bad enough to make him avoid visiting? Or maybe it's something else. Maybe it's because she didn't stay and watch the movie that night. Or maybe she didn't sound grateful enough when he took them to the swimming pool. Or did she ask about Susan too often? At night, Ellery makes these lists in her head, and in the morning shakes them off as ridiculous—feeling the heat of anger towards him flare again in her stomach. She feels cool, cross and in control. Through the day this is the shield that protects her, but where does it melt away to at night? Why does it always disappear and leave her defenceless?

Ellery knows that Mum has private theories of her own. Mum often talks to her friends at night, especially Uncle Erik. After the girls have gone to bed, Mum will recline on her bed with a mug of Genmaicha beside her and the phone cord twisted around her fingers. Ellery doesn't set out to snoop deliberately, but if she gets up to go to the toilet at night, sometimes a few words of the conversation will float down the hall. It's mostly about Mum's cases, news about relatives or general chitchat about books and movies. But tonight the word 'Benjamin' catches Ellery's attention. She looks at the nimbus of orange light arcing out from Mum's half-open door. She silently pads a bit closer to hear the conversation.

'. . . drugs and alcohol, no doubt,' Mum is saying. She is keeping her voice soft and low, but obviously doesn't expect to be overheard. It's 1 am and the girls should be fast sleep—she must be talking to one of her friends from the States. They call each other at strange times, somehow able to do the mysterious time-zone maths that Ellery has always found confusing.

'Well, I don't know,' Mum continues. 'I'm not married to him anymore, am I? . . . Yes, but he wouldn't tell me, would he? . . . Oh, nothing like that I'm sure . . . Yes, I heard . . .'

Ellery can't hear what whoever is on the other end is saying, but Mum's side of the conversation is punctuated by long gaps and she is obviously responding to questions. 'He wasn't like that when I was married to him, was he? I'm sure he wasn't . . . Yes, seeing someone new, no doubt; he doesn't wait around.'

Is this why he won't plan ahead to come and see them? A new girlfriend?

'Oh, Hattie, I've called so many times. I've told him the girls miss him and need to hear from him, but I don't know, it's like I'm beating my head against the wall . . .'

This is news to Ellery. Mum never comments on or critiques Dad's absences. Ellery has heard enough. She creeps away from the sliver of doorway, careful that her feet don't make those telltale sliding sounds on the carpet. Back in her bed, she mulls over what she has heard and the note of anxiety and confusion in Mum's voice. Maybe she expected him to be a different kind of father too.

---

The Easter holidays are spent at home. They toast hot cross buns under the grill, slathering them with extra butter, and watch movies on the sofa. On Easter Sunday, Mum hides Easter eggs around the house and in the garden. The girls go out in the morning, feeling the bracing April air, eyes peeled for the glint of colourful foil among the kumquat trees and hydrangeas. The flowerbeds are lush and it's nice, peeking under the leaves in search of eggs.

This is the kind of thing Dad would usually do for them, but he is not coming to visit these holidays. Ellery brings it up with Verona as they scramble around the rosebushes.

'You must be missing Dad,' Ellery says.

'Of course,' Verona replies. She is only chatty with Dad—she doesn't talk much to Ellery or Mum.

'It doesn't bother you that he hasn't visited us these holidays?'

Verona shrugs. 'He'd be here if he could,' she says. 'If he isn't here, he has a good reason, and he calls us. Besides, I just save up my stories to tell him next time.' She frowns and tilts her head to one side. 'I don't understand why you give him such a hard time.'

'I just wish we saw him more.'

But Verona shakes her head. 'No, you want him to be someone else.' And then she dives into a rosebush, emerging with a tiny rainbow bunny in her hand.

The game is over all too quickly. Mum doesn't have the same knack for hiding places as Dad—she thinks like an adult, along logical lines. Dad is the one who will keep them guessing, stowing the chocolates in zany nooks and crannies. They combine the spoils and then divvy them up evenly on Mum's orders.

In the end, Ellery doesn't mind that they've spent the holidays at home. She sees her friends every few days, mostly at Liv's place because she has a pool table, but the group comes to the Beach Road house for Ellery's twelfth birthday sleepover. It's just the original five and Ellery feels a relief that she cannot pinpoint or describe. The familiarity of the laughter and easy banter makes her hands clench involuntarily in her lap, as though it's something they are desperate to hold on to.

---

And then it is term two. Year seven turns out to be not so very different to any other year—just with more homework and new subjects. Ellery is swimming, not sinking, in the crowd, with new friends and old friends. People say hello to her when she walks past them in the corridor and she is invited to go to movies on the weekends. The bells still chime at the same time, the teachers have the same deep shadows beneath their eyes. Yet they get to traverse different parts of the school now—twice a week they head downstairs to the laboratories on the bottom floor of the main building. The rooms are cold and, even though the summer has not quite finished, the girls all pull on their woollen jumpers as they study diagrams of the greenhouse effect and learn what photosynthesis means. The beakers and Bunsen burners sit on the high shelves, where the year nine and ten students can reach far more easily. Ellery prefers history, which takes place in their sunny homeroom. Mrs Harris, the subject teacher, has red hair and big square glasses. She gets excited when she talks about ancient civilisations and waves her hands around in the air. Everyone has to study two languages, so Ellery chooses French and Indonesian. She memorises long lists of vocabulary and how to conjugate basic verbs.

'Your understanding of grammatical terms is good,' the French teacher comments one day, eyebrows arched.

'My father is a linguist and Mum's a lawyer,' Ellery explains, and the teacher laughs.

'Oh, there's no hope for you—you'll be a word nerd, just like me.'

Ellery smiles but inside she cringes a bit. Nerd? No, thank you.

The girls tease her about it at lunch that day. The lunchtime circle has expanded to include a few new students, including Sophie, who joins them every day now.

'Elly the nerd.' Liv grins.

'You might be a nerd, but we still love you,' Gabby says.

But Sophie is frowning at Ellery's lunchbox. 'What is that? A pancake?'

'No,' Ellery explains, 'it's a roti.'

'What?'

'Haven't you eaten Indian takeaway?' Ellery asks incredulously. 'It's like a kind of bread that you can roll up. My mum makes them for me and my sister instead of sandwiches sometimes. She puts scrambled eggs in the middle.'

'They're nice,' Gabby pipes up. 'I've had them at Elly's house.'

Sophie doesn't say anything but continues to stare, frowning slightly, at the roti.

'Do you want to try some?' Ellery offers, after a long pause in which no-one says anything.

'No, thanks,' Sophie replies, dropping her gaze as she bites into her BLT.

---

The weekends are busy too, with soccer practice on Saturday morning and tennis matches in the afternoon. By Saturday night, Ellery is flushed and tired, sweaty tendrils of hair plastered to her face, knees and shins often bruised from falling over—despite her shinguards. In the evening, Ellery and Verona will usually sit and watch a movie together. Mum always used to join them on the sofa, but lately she has been going out a bit more, leaving them with Megan if she's planning to be home late. She wears long dresses, heels and dark lipstick, and her shoulders are always square and back, head held high. Ellery watches her mother and wonders if she will ever be half as elegant.

'Who is she meeting, do you think?' Ellery asks Verona one evening, as Megan makes popcorn in the microwave.

Verona shrugs, uninterested, but Ellery is deeply curious.

---

The air has become sharp and cold, starting to nip at exposed hands and faces. Somehow, suddenly, summer is a distant memory—Ellery can't imagine craving ice cream or wanting to go swimming. Old people always talk about how quickly time moves—*Oh my goodness, time is flying*, they always say, shaking their greying heads. But Ellery can kind of see what they mean. Each year, time seems to pass just a little quicker. Is this something that happens automatically as you get older? How do you make it slow down and stop? She doesn't want to be an old person like that, sad and mourning lost time.

# chapter fourteen

IT'S A SATURDAY morning in May, halfway through term two, when Ellery comes downstairs to find their mother looking very serious. She is reading the newspaper with a frown on her face and her left toe tapping the floor with agitation.

'What's wrong?' Ellery asks. The frown is contagious and springs from her mother's face onto her own.

Mum's eyes do not leave the broadsheet.

'There's been another coup in Fiji.'

'A coup?' Ellery tries the word in her mouth. It sounds familiar. She feels as though she has heard this word before. But what does it mean?

'A coup d'etat,' Mum elaborates. 'It's when the elected government is overthrown by its citizens or the military.'

'Why?'

Mum is turning the pages of the paper with a feverish rapidity.

'Because some people aren't happy with the way things are going.'

Ellery mulls this over. 'But doesn't somebody get elected because most people like their ideas and voted for them?'

At this, Mum smiles broadly—she likes it when her children show lawyerly instincts. She lets go of the paper and throws her hands in the air. Mum always uses her hands when she speaks. If she had to sit on her hands, she wouldn't be able to say anything at all, Dad sometimes jokes.

'Precisely!' Mum cries. 'That's the premise of democracy. The elected representatives have a mandate to govern because the majority of people in a country have voted in their favour.' The smile falls away. 'But of course, it doesn't always happen like that. And sometimes small groups have enough power or determination to disrupt the whole system.'

'So when did this coup happen?' Ellery asks.

'Yesterday. And so history repeats itself. Déjà vu.' Mum shakes her head.

'You mean this has happened before?'

'Oh, yes. In 1987 the elected government was overthrown in a military coup.'

'That's awful,' says Ellery, uncertain but taking her cue from the look on Mum's face.

'It was terrible—a miscarriage of justice and a scary time for everyone.'

'Why has it happened again, then?'

Mum shakes her head. 'I don't have an answer for you. It's a country with a lot of tension and a clash of cultures—an indigenous population who were dispossessed and another population who were displaced into the country as glorified slaves. Both victims in different ways.'

'Victims of what?'

'Race, colonialism, the Empire.'

'I still don't understand,' Ellery admits.

'Neither do I,' Mum says. 'If you figure it out, let me know.' She lets out a laugh.

Can a laugh be an expression of sadness? That's what Mum's sounds like to Ellery right now. Mum folds the paper into quarters and leaves it on the table.

She walks to the phone in the kitchen and dials one of the numbers on the cardboard list of contacts mounted on the wall. She stands with her arms folded as she waits, the phone wedged between her ear and her shoulder.

'Ama! Is everything alright?' Mum asks after several long beats. Her voice is higher than usual and more hurried. 'Is everyone okay? You're safe?' There's the indistinct buzz of a reply at the other end.

Safe? Ellery is surprised. What could possibly happen? But there's tension in Mum's shoulders. The next few sentences are spoken in Tamil. Ellery listens hard, trying to understand, but she never learned enough. She only knows *thank you*, so at least she can be polite in her ignorance.

'Well that's a relief,' Mum is saying, sliding fluidly back into English. 'No violence? Please keep in touch and let me know that everyone is fine.'

She hangs up the phone and turns to Ellery, who has picked up the discarded paper and is skimming the headline: IT'S A TAKEOVER, BY GEORGE. Mum's shoulders have dropped about two inches—back down from around her ears. 'Your grandparents are safe and well,' Mum says reassuringly, and Ellery senses that she ought to have been more worried. But Mum's hand shakes slightly as she holds it to her forehead. 'Maybe I'm getting used to this.'

Mum's parents are the only family members still in Fiji. There are far more of Mum's relatives in Australia, New Zealand and Canada now. Family members have suddenly appeared in Sydney and Adelaide. Ellery won't learn the word 'diaspora' until her first year of university; 'exodus' she learns earlier. At least those who have come to Australia from Fiji can go on and get jobs, work in their chosen industries easily enough—they are the lucky ones. In the coming years, Ellery will meet Afghani cardiothoracic surgeons working as scrub nurses and cab drivers from Maputo with PhDs in economics. But for now it's all a bit hazy in her mind. Moving from one place to another does not seem like a big deal. It's a seamless transition in her mind, an easy geographical transplant.

Why don't her grandparents just come here anyway? she wonders. If this has happened before, why would anyone want to live there? When she says this aloud, it's greeted with a frown.

'Fiji is their home,' Mum reminds her.

'You didn't like it there,' Ellery points out.

'Yes, but that was me. It certainly isn't true for everyone. My family has lived there for a hundred years. My parents were born there, my grandparents were born there—even my great-grandparents. It's their home,' she repeats.

The girls have always seen Fiji through Mum's eyes. Some of the kids at school have been there on holidays and Ellery hears them refer to it authoritatively as paradise. There's a particular way they speak about it, with a sudden dreamy look in their eyes. Ellery can almost see the turquoise water reflected back to her from their blue irises. *There's nowhere like it*, they tell her and Ellery, thinking of Mum's stories of being suffocated by its smallness, has always been puzzled. Which account is true? And if she is half Mum and half Dad, how much of this unknown country is part of her?

'Will you take me? I want to see it. I think I need to know.'

Mum's eyebrows raise. 'Yes, sweetheart. Of course. If things settle down and it's safe, of course I will.'

---

Later that afternoon, there's even a call from Dad.

'I heard the news. Things aren't good in your mum's home country. Thank God she wasn't there when it happened,' he says to Ellery, who answers the phone. 'Can you put her on?'

'You don't want to talk to me or Verona?'

'Well, of course I do, Elly. I just want a quick chat with your mother first.'

Ellery fetches Mum from the balcony, where she's watching the ocean and drinking tea.

Her parents' conversation isn't a 'quick chat'; it actually goes for forty minutes. Dad obviously knows what questions to ask better than Ellery does. Tired of waiting for her turn, Ellery drifts upstairs to where Verona is watching a cartoon. But an hour later, when she wanders downstairs, the receiver is back in its cradle. The surprise knifes through her and Ellery stops to stare at the phone.

'He had to go, darling,' Mum tells her gently from the kitchen table. 'He got called in to work. But he'll try and call back later. He's coming down to Melbourne for the June holidays and he's invited you and Verona to stay with him.'

'Called in to work? It's a Saturday—I didn't think there were classes today.'

'It'll be to do with his research,' Mum says soothingly. 'It's only a few weeks and then you'll get a chunk of time with him.'

'We haven't even seen him since the summer holidays.'

Mum sighs. 'I know.' But she doesn't repeat any of the things Ellery overheard her say to the friend on the phone. Party unity always.

Ellery bites her lip as a new thought erupts in her mind. 'What if I don't want to go?'

Mum doesn't take this seriously. 'Of course you do.'

But the prospect of more Peter Pan escapades leaves her feeling cold. And the fights from last time stand sharply in her mind.

Verona pinballs around the house in excitement when Mum tells her the holiday plans, but for her part, Ellery thinks she'd rather just stay home. And Dad's place isn't home.

---

The subjects at school are getting more interesting. Mrs Harris announces that their main project for term two will be an investigation essay into an ancient culture of their choice. Most people are gravitating towards Greece and Egypt, but Ellery has something different in mind. That evening she goes into Mum's study and takes down one of the heavy coffee table books. It lives so high on the shelf that she has to stand on Mum's swivelling office chair to reach it, and when she has it in her hands, she finds a faint sheen of dust across the dark green cover. *Indian Culture and Mythology*. She carries the book to the kitchen table and opens it. It's laid out encyclopaedia style, with blocks of text accompanied by illustrations and photographs—dusty streets, women in silk, spices and lentils piled high, stone ruins and a sea of cars. Ellery pauses when she sees an etching of a small boy with a wide grin on a page dedicated to mythological creatures. There is something familiar about that smile and she bends lower to read the caption. *Kuttichathan, the little imp.* The book describes a trickster spirit who appears in the guise of a twelve-year-old boy, always mirthful and playing pranks. Kuttichathan is amused by stubbed toes, burned dinners and plans gone awry. He'll cause chaos just for fun and laugh from the sidelines. Although he is not malicious, mischief lights up behind his eyes and everything is a game. Ellery is vividly reminded of someone else she knows—not quite a prankster or a trickster, but a boy eternal. Except that Dad's games come in the form of words.

When Mum comes past to flick on the kettle, she peers over Ellery's shoulder.

'What are you doing reading that one, darling?'

'History project. I'm going to write about India.'

'I see.' Mum is looking at her, head tilted and face impassive. Then she smiles. 'I think that's an excellent idea.'

'Do you know anything about Kuttichathan?' she asks Mum, her tongue sounding out the word awkwardly.

Mum looks thoughtful. 'If I recall correctly, there's a movie about it. *My Dear Kuttichathan*. I think it's a Kerala story, though. It's not one of the tales my family told.'

---

In history class the next day, the others are bored and grumbling.

'What's the point of learning about the past anyway?' Sylvia says to Meg in an undertone.

'You have to understand the past to understand the present,' says Mrs Harris from behind, making them all jump, guilty and surprised. 'If we don't know where we come from, how can we know who we are?'

The girls nod politely.

'Check behind you before you speak,' Meg hisses to Sylvia.

But Ellery is thinking about those words and wondering if they're true.

She brings it up on the car ride home and Mum nods.

'I think that's very perceptive,' she says. 'I would agree with Mrs Harris.'

'Well, I don't,' Verona pipes up from the back seat. 'I think it's stupid to get hung up on stuff that's in the past. Why should it matter anymore?' Verona's head is turned, looking out the window.

Ellery keeps thinking about this as she sits at the dining table working on the project later that night. It's due next week, on the last day of term. It has been interesting reading about India, looking at the pictures. Yet she has also been thinking about Fiji and the headlines in the newspapers.

'How's the project going?' Mum says, standing at her shoulder.

'Good,' Ellery says. 'It's weird, though. Are we really Indian?'

'We're Fiji-Indian. But yes, we're Indian.'

'So where do we belong?'

'Everywhere and nowhere. Belonging is what you make it and where you feel at home. At the end of the day, whatever else you are, you're also Australian.'

But Ellery thinks inexplicably of Sophie's face, the cold eyes and slight frown.

'I have to keep working, Mum,' she says and bends over the page.

She also adds a small section on mythology to her assignment and writes about Kuttichathan. She double-checks the encyclopaedia and comes across a small paragraph she had only skimmed before on the Kuttichathan page: if you do penance, you can control Kuttichathan, and so he tries to prevent this. Although she cannot quite place why this is important, she writes it down anyway. Ellery reads over what she has written, trying to see it from Mrs Harris's perspective.

When she writes the final sentence later than night, she doesn't just write her first name and surname—for the first time in her life, she adds her middle name to the document. Ellery Vinita Fortune. Vinita: Tamil for knowledge. Vinita: the unspoken word in the centre of her name.

# chapter fifteen

WHEN DAD PULLS through the front gates to pick them up for the midyear holidays, Ellery does not feel the usual butterflies of excitement. Her stomach is calm and her mind is thinking ahead to the week. As expected, Verona scampers out the front door to meet Dad at the car, towing her bag behind her. Back in the house, Ellery checks the clock on the microwave. Only twenty minutes late this time—for Dad, that's early. But surely he doesn't turn up late when he's giving a lecture? Isn't punctuality really just a matter of priorities? Keen to avoid a fight (and a speeding car ride), she keeps this particular observation to herself.

Mum is already at work, so Ellery locks the front door with the keys they hide in the aloe vera pot and then takes her place in the passenger seat.

'How are you both?' Dad shouts as he starts the car. 'It's good to see my girls.'

Looking at Dad, Ellery wonders why she has never noticed how impish that smile is. Not Peter Pan after all, perhaps, but Kuttichathan.

'I missed you,' Verona tells him, and he looks at her in the rear-view mirror.

'Me too, Monkey, me too.'

Ellery looks out the window. She has thought about things she wants to say to him many times, rehearsed these in her head. *Six months, Dad. It's been six months since we've seen you.* But now the words have all blown away like the dead autumn leaves no longer on the ground.

Dad chats away, telling them he's making spicy kumara soup for dinner. It's the only thing he can really cook. Neither of the girls loves it—Verona doesn't like spice and Ellery finds soup unsatisfying, but they both murmur appropriately appreciative things. Dad sings his songs and Verona joins in as the mountains draw closer and closer, and the house soon enough comes into view. But still those butterflies have not revived. Ellery glances up at the big house crouching on the hill and waits for the familiar giddy feeling. Where has it gone?

After pulling into the garage, Dad helps them carry their cases into their bedrooms and makes them lunch.

'I stocked up the fridge and everything,' he says proudly. 'See?'

Sure enough, the shelves are full. He takes the corned beef out of the fridge and lays slices of bread on their plates like blank canvases.

'I've got so many exciting things planned for us,' he chirps. It could be last December. 'We'll do winter things this time. I was thinking we could go to the big ice rink they've set up in the city! Doesn't that sound like fun? You two are such champions on rollerblades, I'm sure you'll take to it like ducks to water. We'll go to Luna Park too. And there are a ton of great flicks on. We could even take a drive up to the snow next weekend. You've never been to Buller, have you? I'd love to teach you kids to ski. I'm not actually a bad skier, you know.'

Dad's recital continues, with Verona nodding her head vigorously at each of his proposals. She and Dad are sliding right back into the usual groove. But Ellery feels like she's watching him through a fog—his mouth is moving but his words are lost in vapour. Back to jelly snakes and chaos.

Mum's a whiz with a vegetable peeler, but Dad takes a while to scrape away the roughened skins of the kumara for his soup. The orange flesh has chisel marks when he's done. He ties one of Granny Agnes's frilly aprons around his waist and stands over the pot, humming and stirring. Verona turns the television on and lies in the family room on her tummy. Ellery remains in the kitchen with Dad, watching him. Maybe he'll talk to her properly now Verona is elsewhere. Maybe he has a good reason for not being around the past few months, and he has just been waiting for the right time to discuss it. Maybe he's secretly an international spy. Maybe he was on assignment to Cuba this whole time and didn't have much access to phones.

Well, if he is a spy, Dad is guarding his secret well.

'This,' he tells Ellery over his shoulder when he reaches for the cumin, 'is going to be delicious.'

'Isn't soup usually served as an appetiser?' she says coldly, but he doesn't seem to notice.

———

Later that evening, Dad stacks the unwashed soup bowls in the sink then takes the girls to the video store to rent movies.

'It's twelve for twelve dollars; we can each choose four. Think you girls can get through eight movies in a week?' They each have a VCR in their room at the Ferntree Gully house. Dad pads around, choosing his own films from the science fiction section. He likes to chat with the woman behind the counter, who smiles and tosses her hair when he walks past her.

'Did you hear that they're making a movie of *Lord of the Rings*?' she asks him as she checks out their movies. 'Didn't you say that's your favourite book?'

'Yeah, good memory! I hadn't heard there's a movie coming,' Dad says.

He buys Ellery and Verona jelly snakes to celebrate.

That night, Verona eats the long rainbow coil of her jelly snake in bed as they re-watch movies from last year, but Ellery leaves her snake next to her bed uneaten and, in the morning, throws it out.

For once, there doesn't seem to be a new girlfriend on the scene. No new names edge into the conversation and there are no mysterious outings or long whispered phone calls. Ellery thinks rather wistfully of Susan, but does not mention her name to Dad.

———

On Wednesday, Dad makes good on his plan to take them to Luna Park. Ellery and Verona are keen to get going early, but Dad lingers over the paper. It's early afternoon by the time they leave, dressed in jumpers and scarves—the late afternoon sun is no help at all; its white gold rays contain no real warmth. The drive takes a good hour and parking takes half as long again. Ellery gazes out the window as they circle the St Kilda streets looking for a park.

'There's one!' the girls cry from time to time, leaning forwards eagerly—only to slump back when the space turns out to be occupied by a small car, hidden by a patch of shade. Eventually they spot a mother wrestling her toddler into a car seat and wait for her to pull out. But she also needs to fold up the pram and stow a bag of what Ellery suspects is dirty nappies in the boot.

By the time they have parked and walk towards the Luna Park entrance—a gigantic painted face, with a leering smile for a gate—they are buffeted by hordes of people coming in the other direction, fairy floss in their hands or newly won teddy bears under their arms.

'Maybe there was an event on,' Dad says. 'Come on.' He leads the girls under the toothed maw and up to the ticket counter, where no-one is now queued. 'Er, some day passes, please,' he says to the cashier. 'Two children and one adult.'

Three children, really, Ellery thinks. Dad has taken out a fifty expectantly but the woman is apologetic.

'Sorry, sir, we're not selling passes anymore. Most of the rides are closing soon—we're actually closing a bit early tonight for a private function. You can buy single ride tickets, if you would like? The Ferris wheel should be open for a while longer.'

The three of them turn and watch its slow-wheeling process, with couples on dates holding hands as they spin around.

'Boring,' Verona pronounces.

'Ah, sorry, kids . . .'

'We should've left earlier,' Ellery says. 'We told you.'

Verona glances a bit wistfully at the ghost train and Ellery eyes the rollercoaster, but these lie dormant and unmanned.

'Sorry, girls,' Dad says again, sheepishly. 'Why don't we have a late afternoon tea in Acland Street instead?'

They eat cakes from one of the ubiquitous pastry shops there—cream buns and vanilla slices. The window displays are terribly impressive—maraschino cherries, glazed peaches and sugared violets galore—but taste like bicarb of soda. Ellery scrunches up her face and pushes the half-eaten pastry away and Verona soon follows suit.

No matter.

Two days later they go to the movies instead. Except when they get to the cinema all the immediate screenings for *Center Stage* are full, and there are lots of adolescent girls stocking up on licorice bullets and Cokes before the session begins. The carpet has crumbs and all kinds of grit over it from so many patrons; only its multicolour pattern saves it from looking outright dirty.

'You should have booked,' the woman at the ticket booth rebukes them gently as she taps away on her computer. 'We recommend coming fifteen minutes early at peak times. The next available session doesn't start for another four hours; I can book you in and you could come back then?'

'We live forty-five minutes away,' Dad says. 'There's no point driving home and then all the way back, and I think that's a bit too long to wait around the shopping centre.'

The woman points to a screen above her head. 'There are a few other films showing. Would you like to see something else?'

They all stare up at the screen. *Gladiator* is showing, and Dad looks at the girls hopefully.

'I wouldn't mind seeing that one again,' he says.

Verona looks dubious but says nothing. It is Ellery who puts her foot down; she will not be dragged into another violent movie.

'No,' she snaps. 'I definitely don't want to see it. It's rated for fifteen and over, anyway.'

'I could book you in for *Center Stage* tomorrow,' the cashier offers, clearly trying to defuse the tension.

Ellery folds her arms across her chest. 'Let's just go home.'

Dad buys them some popcorn to share on the drive back and, that night, it's a movie on the sofa instead.

---

Verona and Dad laugh at the organisational mishaps, but Ellery feels her face stiffen with irritation. Their plans are always shattered, thwarted and withered. It's almost better when they stay in the house, where they end up watching eight movies in three days. Dad takes them to the video store every few days and they come back with armfuls of films.

Dad is his cheery self. He doesn't bring work home the way Mum does—doesn't spend hours in the office—but reclines on the sofa reading novels. He doesn't like being interrupted in the middle of a page, but at the end of a chapter, when he takes his pack of cigarettes outside, he likes to chat.

'Get a job at a university, girls,' he tells them. 'Short semesters.'

Verona often follows him outside and sits on the steps as he smokes. Ellery overhears them talking about his research and the intricacies of language change—anything to do with words and he's off.

'We've also borrowed French words for things that make us uncomfortable, like *toilet* and *brassiere*. It's like a euphemism, a way of purifying difficult or embarrassing concepts. And these borrowed words have eventually taken over . . .' Ellery hears him say as she passes the open door, inhaling the plume of smoke that billows into the house. Granny Agnes and Papa Timothy will not be impressed.

'So,' Verona says slowly. 'You're saying everything is better in French?'

It's six months later and yet everything is just the same. Dad and Verona have simply picked everything back up like they're knitting a scarf; the needles click in the air and the wool is twined together into the same long pattern. But not for Ellery. She carries the absence and inconsistency with her, knotted in her stomach. Each day she waits for Dad to bring it up, but he never does. Maybe he's waiting for me to do it, she thinks. Is the ball in my court?

She watches him closely for the next few days, waiting for an opening. On Wednesday, he puts a Neil Diamond CD on as he washes potatoes for dinner. There are three crumbed fish fillets in the oven. With no girlfriend to cook and a limited repertoire, it's mostly things out of packets, or else soup or pasta.

Ellery stands in the kitchen, taking out the crockery to set the table. She takes a deep breath. 'Dad, do you think we should talk?'

'About anything you like, Elly! School, politics, the environment. I can tell you what it's like to smoke marijuana, if you'd like. Or the time your mother walked into an apple tree.'

'Um, no, thanks. I was thinking maybe something more personal?'

'I see.' Dad stops scrubbing the potato skin and looks awkward. 'Is this the sex talk?'

'No!'

Dad looks relieved. 'You should talk to your mother about those things.'

'I want to talk to you about the last six months. What happened?'

'Oh, sweets. I was just very busy.'

'Too busy to visit us even once?'

Dad is fussing around in the pantry for some cayenne pepper and takes his time answering.

'Well, I was in the Northern Territory doing some field work, and then when I got home I was very busy analysing the data.'

'But how long were you away for?'

'A month.'

'Only a month? We haven't seen you for six.'

'There's a lot of work involved in the research, Ferret. Actually, it's interesting stuff, as I've been telling your sister. So, I'm looking at gendered language change. I'll tell you a bit about it—I think you'll find it quite fascinating . . .'

---

On the last night of their stay, they order pizza and sit up at the table. There's a video ready to go and a tin of Milo for hot chocolate after dinner. The rain is slanting diagonally against the window.

'It's been lovely having you,' Dad says, helping himself to a slice of Verona's Hawaiian. He's on his third beer and the girls are drinking lemonade. Verona smiles, but Ellery keeps her face blank.

'Us too, Dad,' says Verona, with a half-glance at Ellery. 'We've had a great time. We always do.'

'Excellent!' Dad claps his hands together. He opens the pizza box again and wafts it towards the girls, flapping the lid like some giant winged bird.

'This is stupid.' It bursts out despite Ellery's best intentions. 'It hasn't been a fun holiday.'

'Hey! I've had fun,' Verona retorts.

'That's because you're a puppy dog.'

'Don't you talk to your sister like that,' Dad says sharply.

'But it's true!'

'If you've got a problem, you talk about it with me.'

'I've tried to talk to you and you won't let me.'

Dad shakes his head. 'You're living in the past, Ellery. You're just like your mother. Can't you see that it doesn't matter what came before? All we have is the moment. Rather than enjoying being together, you've spent the whole time determined to be unhappy. If you'd actually let yourself go, maybe you would've created memories this holiday rather than just grievances.'

'That's really unfair,' Ellery whispers and is astonished to feel a rising watery heat behind her eyes. 'Maybe you're just a bad father.'

The grin has slid right off his face and his eyes do not twinkle.

'There's no winning with you, is there?' he says.

The rain lashes the window and the chill is now coming off the glass. Verona takes another slice of pizza and nibbles at the end. Dad and Ellery stare at each other across the table, but neither says anything. Dad, the linguist, is out of words. And Ellery is out of both forgiveness and apologies. This is a stalemate.

Dinner wraps up pretty quickly after that.

'Go to bed, girls,' Dad tells them. 'You can watch the movie together in one of your rooms if you'd like. I'm heading upstairs myself. I'll see you in the morning.' The sound of his bedroom door closing echoes through the house.

Verona ejects the tape from the player and takes it upstairs, but Ellery doesn't follow immediately. Instead, she goes down to the study and sits among the bookshelves. It reminds her of home. She thinks back to the night in the summer holidays when she listened in to the conversation she was never meant to hear. To her parents she is just a child and immature, except that this isn't how she thinks of herself and is not the way she thought others saw her. Now she's confused and truth implodes and undoes itself.

Everything has a use-by date if you don't take proper care of it.

When she goes upstairs, Verona is staring at the TV screen and doesn't look up at the sound of the door. Ellery watches her sister's profile for a minute; the ghostly blue rippling across her face is tidal as one scene changes to the next.

'V, I'm sorry.'

Verona doesn't reply.

'Really, V—I didn't mean what I said.'

'Yes you did,' Verona contradicts her, turning briefly away from the screen and back again as Ellery considers denying it.

'You think that the way you feel about Dad is the way I have to feel too.'

'It's not that,' Ellery says. 'I just don't understand how you can ignore the fact that this is only the second time we've seen him all year and sometimes it will be weeks between his phone calls.'

But Verona looks genuinely puzzled. 'He's here now, isn't he? What else matters?'

They sit together on the bed as the movie plays, but when the credits roll, Verona brings it up again.

'Why are you being so horrible to him?' she asks.

Ellery pretends to be concentrating on the names of the assistant costume designers and doesn't reply immediately. Her sister's face is angled towards her and waiting for an answer.

'Did you ever think of asking him why he's being so horrible to us?'

'He isn't, though. He takes us to do things—okay, so he isn't that organised—but he does care. He tries to make holidays as fun as possible for us.'

'Punctuated by long periods of neglect.'

'You just can't accept that he's different to Mum.'

Verona's face is hard and set; she meets Ellery's eyes squarely and Ellery is taken aback. Does her sister really believe that?

---

Dad drops them back home to Brighton late the next morning. There's a Stones CD playing, but the car ride is otherwise silent.

Dad's jaw is clenched tight. He's been like this since she got up. She can't ever remember a bad mood not blowing itself out by morning before, but there had been no pet names at the breakfast table or recitals of *Lord of the Rings*. Dad had just sipped his black coffee in silence. Verona, too, is taciturn. She and Dad sit in the front seats of the car, united in disapproval. Ellery, the pariah, sits in the back.

This time when they pull off Beach Road and drive through the gates of home, Dad doesn't ask to see Mum. He heaves their cases from the boot, all the while leaving the driver's side door open, ready to get back in. Verona gives him a hug, which he returns briefly, before getting in the car. Ellery watches from the door, arms folded, but Dad doesn't look at her again.

'Bye, girls,' he calls as Ellery stoops to fish the key from the flowerpot.

But when they open the door, Mum is coming towards them.

'I thought I heard my girls! Where's your father?' She opens the screen door and peers into the yard, but Dad is long gone. Mum looks at their faces, frowning. 'Another fight?' She addresses the question to both of them and Verona snorts.

'Ask Ellery.'

She picks up her case and the way she walks off into the house could only be described as a flounce.

'Again?' Mum asks Ellery, who covers her face.

'Oh, sweetheart.' Mum holds out her arms.

---

In the kitchen, Mum puts on the kettle and fusses with loose-leaf tea as Ellery sits at the table and recounts the fight.

Mum is always the peacemaker. 'You shouldn't have said that to him,' she says when Ellery has finished. 'Or to your sister.'

'But it's true!' Ellery protests.

'Perhaps,' says Mum. 'But it wasn't kind.'

'I know.' Ellery feels squirmy now.

'Did you apologise to Verona?'

'Yeah.'

'To your dad?'

'No.'

'I think you should talk to him.'

---

Later in the afternoon, guilt settling in her stomach, Ellery tries to call. Benjamin doesn't fly back to Brisbane until the next day, so she calls his parents' house. She holds her breath as she dials, but the phone rings out into silence. She tries twice more, but there is no answer. At the beep, she leaves a hasty message.

'Um, Dad. Hi. It's me. Ellery, I mean. I just wanted to say sorry. Call me when you get this.'

But he doesn't.

Ellery can't help thinking about Kuttichathan and penance. She has heard the word penance in passing during the fortnightly religious education classes they take at school—repentance for wrongdoing, confession and absolution—but does not fully understand what it means. Is it the same thing as apologising? No wonder Kuttichathan hates it; apologies feel awful.

---

A few days later, on her way to the bathroom at night, Ellery overhears snippets of conversation from Mum's room.

'Really, Benjamin!' Mum is saying, exasperated. 'You're the adult.'

Three days after that, there's a phone call from Dad for Ellery with a formal and carefully worded apology.

'I apologise if I hurt your feelings; that was not my intention. When I'm next in Melbourne, I think we should make a time to meet and talk this out.' His voice is all parental and authoritative.

'Why?' Said aloud, it sounds more petulant than she intended.

'We need to figure this out.'

'I don't think so.'

'We do,' Dad insists. 'You're my daughter and I love you.'

'But you're good with words, aren't you, Dad? You always say the right thing, but it's never reflected in your actions.'

There's a sharp exhalation at the other end. 'Get that from your mother, did you? That doesn't sound like you. The Ellery I know is a sweet girl, not this cranky creature you seem to have become.'

Ellery doesn't dignify that with an answer—she simply hangs up the phone.

# chapter sixteen

AS ELLERY WALKS through the school gates on the first day of term three, she is glad of the heavy tartan skirt and thick blazer. Beside her, Verona is even wearing a scarf. Ellery tugs the end of it. 'Have a good day, V.'

When Ellery reaches the homeroom, the two friends in her class are already waiting for roll call. Sylvia and Meg both jump up to give Ellery a hug. For a moment it feels like old times—except Gabby and Liv aren't here, and Sophie, with her barbed questions, will be there at lunch.

Sure enough, when the bell rings at noon, Sophie is following when Gabby joins them outside. The grass is damp from rain overnight so the girls decide to find a spare classroom to sit in—they're allowed inside on wet days.

'So how were your holidays?' Gabby asks, as she and Ellery sit down next to one another, and Ellery mutters the story.

'Wow, you actually said that to your father?' Gabby asks, wide-eyed. 'I would never!'

'Nor me,' says Liv.

Ellery puts her hands on her hips. 'We'd never let our friends treat us badly without speaking up. Why should we tolerate bad behaviour from family?'

'Because they're family,' Gabby says, frowning.

'Well, I'm not accepting it anymore.'

But she sees the others exchange glances when they think she isn't looking.

'What did you do, then?' Ellery asks Gabby.

'Ah, not much. I mostly stayed at home. My brother got a new PlayStation for his birthday so we used that quite a lot.'

'You came to Daylesford too,' Sophie chimes in.

'Yeah,' Gabby says, not looking at Ellery.

'How come you were in Daylesford?' Ellery asks, but it is Sophie who answers.

'My family have a house there. Gab, Liv, Meg and Sylvia all came down.'

The other girls are looking at their shoes and their cuticles. Ellery has swallowed something spiky that has lodged in her oesophagus, but she smiles. 'Oh, lovely.'

And then there's a silence. Sometimes silence is a cacophony.

'You were with your dad,' Liv says finally. 'We know you don't get to see him much; we didn't think you'd be able to come.'

Retorts flash through Ellery's mind, but her mouth stays closed.

---

In history class after lunch, Mrs Harris hands back their assignments from last term. She walks around the class to deliver them to each table, face down, as the class fills out a worksheet, most students chewing on the ends of their pencils or gazing out the window. When Ellery turns the paper over, there is her name—Ellery Vinita Fortune—and next to it, the grade, written in blue: A+. Despite the sour feeling that has stayed with her since lunch, Ellery feels the thrill of achievement. She sits up slightly straighter in her chair and Mrs Harris, returning to the front of the classroom, gives her a faint smile. This is becoming a familiar feeling—the same thing happened with the flower diagram project for Mr York. Familiar now, too, is the hunger for more. That smile on Mrs Harris's face or Mr York's approving nod—these are things worth working for.

---

Dad doesn't call again and nor does Ellery dial his number. Neither will make the first move.

Mum is Dad's greatest advocate. She supports Ellery's decisions, but tries gently to change her daughter's mind. Mum calls her own parents every fortnight, no matter where she is in the world or what she is doing, and this schism between parent and child is unfathomable to her.

'Why don't you just try talking to him?' she says again and again. 'He loves you; he wants to make it right.'

But he doesn't, Ellery thinks glumly. He's just good at grand gestures and elaborate words. She will not make the mistake again of confusing that for consistency or care.

Until it's six weeks later, over halfway through term three. This is by far the longest she has have ever gone without speaking to Dad. They crossed that invisible threshold some weeks ago. There's no blueprint for this now, just instincts and feelings. Not talking to Dad is painful and yet at the same time it's easier. Everything is out in the open now, and Ellery knows where she stands. No more waiting for phone calls or pretending it's okay when Dad drifts away for months at a time.

Dad still calls Verona every few weeks, but does not ask to speak to Ellery, which means she does not get a chance to refuse to come to the phone.

---

Winter is in full swing. The sea outside the house is iron grey every day and the dogs being walked on the fierce windy beach start to look reluctant to be there. Tennis lessons have shifted to the indoor courts and soccer practice is often cancelled due to thunderstorms. But Ellery doesn't mind playing in the rain. There's something satisfying about the long hot shower afterwards and watching the mud slide off her body.

One Sunday, Mum makes gulab jamun. It's a favourite dessert of both girls. Verona squeals when she comes to the kitchen for her Weet-Bix and sees Mum shaping the dough into small logs. She flies at Mum and hugs her around the middle.

'What's the occasion?' Ellery asks. Gulab jamun is usually reserved for birthdays.

'Uncle Erik's in town from Sydney,' Mum replies. 'He's coming to dinner tonight.'

Erik, family friend and adopted uncle.

'He should come more often,' Verona says, eyeing the gulab jamun.

Mum laughs. 'I agree.'

The girls stand in the kitchen watching the dough turn a sizzling golden brown as Mum drops them into hot oil. But Mum won't let them eat sweets until dessert. 'You'll ruin your appetite,' she says severely, and won't be persuaded by the girls' denials.

Dinner is therefore a slow event. Adults take so long to eat—sipping wine and constantly putting their cutlery down. They usually eat with their fingers if Mum has cooked curry and it feels a bit weird using the silverware.

'Curry!' Uncle Erik enthuses, inhaling deeply.

'I wouldn't dare make a casserole again,' Mum says.

Ellery and Verona are quick to help clear the dinner plates when Uncle Erik finally puts his knife and fork together. Mum goes into the kitchen and brings out the gulab jamun, served in silver bowls with a rosewater syrup.

'These look magnificent, Malti,' Erik says. 'I've missed them. They never taste the same in restaurants.'

'Not enough *elaichi*,' Mum says—cardamom—and her smile is smug.

The first bite is somehow even better than Ellery had remembered. She closes her eyes as she eats, letting the sweetness circle around her mouth. There is silence as they eat—this is the power of gulab jamun.

---

The next day at school, Ellery opens her lunchbox with excitement. And, sure enough, there it is: last night's leftover gulab jamun wrapped in aluminium. She resists eating it at recess, saving it for lunch. The girls take their seats on the grass and Ellery forces herself to chew her sandwich slowly, even though she wants to scoff it down. Then, at last, she can unwrap the foil and pluck out the sweet. She has just taken a bite, eyes closing involuntarily, when a sharp voice rings out.

'What is that?'

Ellery opens her eyes to find all the other girls looking from Sophie to her.

'It's called gulab jamun.'

'What?'

It's strange—Sophie isn't smiling, but there's an undertone of laughter in her voice.

'It's kind of like a doughnut,' Ellery explains, but the comparison feels uncomfortable.

'I don't like doughnuts much.' Sophie is dismissive.

'Nor me,' Liv agrees.

'It isn't exactly like a doughnut,' Ellery amends. 'It's got spices and stuff.'

'Like a curry?' Sophie makes a face. 'No, thanks.'

'These guys have had it before.' Ellery looks at Gabby, Liv, Meg and Sylvia. 'Mum makes it for my birthday every year.'

But the girls don't meet her eyes. At her birthday party in April, they had all gone back for seconds—even thirds. Why are they sitting there so silently now?

'I don't remember it,' Gabby says.

'Me either,' the other girls mutter, shaking their heads.

'Your food is so weird,' Sophie says. 'It doesn't look like a doughnut—it looks like a dog poo.'

At this, the other girls burst into laughter.

'Ellery is eating dog poo!' Sophie says again.

Ellery looks around the circle at the faces of her friends. Even Gabby is laughing.

Ellery looks away and, in her peripheral vision, can't help noticing that the circle they're sitting in looks more like a hexagon, with sharp points and edges.

---

One Tuesday, a large envelope arrives in the mail. Ellery's name is on the front and she recognises the handwriting. The postmark is from Brisbane. Mum hands it to her without comment.

It turns out to be a hand-drawn comic. It's on butcher's paper and done in blue biro, but Dad has ruled neat little boxes onto the page and drawn beautifully intricate pictures within them. The panels tell the story of a pirate captain with two daughters whom he loves. The captain sails the high seas with a parrot on his shoulder, but he is often away for long periods and cannot come home. Still, all the while he misses his girls terribly. Then, angry about his absences, one of the daughters stops talking to him. The captain is very sad and he doesn't know what to do—his parrot stops talking and his handlebar moustache begins to droop. He keeps sailing around the world and hopes that one day the daughter will let him back into her life. But no matter what he sees, he can never feel like himself without both his daughters in his life. Dad is good with a pen—Ellery can even see vestiges of her own face in the little cartoon boxes. She takes her time reading it, running her hand over the ink. It's easy to see how much time and thought has gone into these small drawings. She puts it carefully in the drawer of her bedside table.

Kuttichathan, the imp child, flashes into Ellery's mind. Like Mum, she believes that magic is real. There are too many inexplicable things in the world to believe otherwise.

'You're a little clone of your mother,' Dad likes to say sometimes, but it isn't really true.

What if the essence of penance is not about punishment, but about something else? Forgiveness. Accountability. What if the power that Kuttichathan fears is actually the power of forgiveness? Mum is big on forgiveness. *Forgiving isn't about them, it's about you*, she likes to say. *Forgiveness is liberation—it will set you free.*

For the first time in eight weeks, Ellery goes to the phone in the kitchen and dials Dad's number. She can't resist looking over her shoulder, not wanting to be interrupted by Mum or Verona. This is a private moment for her and Dad. The receiver is clenched to her ear as the phone trills its ring tone and she waits for him to pick up, wondering if he's even home. But after another few seconds, that familiar voice is on the other end.

'Hel-lo?' He always answers the phone like that, with a jaunty upwards inflection on the second syllable. The sound of his voice makes her close her eyes against the sudden press of tears. It's been too long since she has heard that voice.

'Hi, Dad.'

'Elly!'

'Yeah.'

'Ferret, it's so nice to hear your voice. How are you?'

'I'm fine. I just wanted to say thank you for the comic. I really liked it.'

'You're most welcome.'

'I didn't know you felt like that.'

'Like what?'

'That you miss us when you're not around.'

'Of course I do. I love you and your sister very much. It's been awful not talking to you.' But his tone is light and airy. 'I'm actually right in the middle of something, Ferret. Can I call you back?'

'Oh—okay. Yes, of course.'

'I'll call you tomorrow evening.'

Except that he doesn't. He calls five days later. Five whole days, in which every time the phone rings, she jumps to her feet and runs to it.

At 8.30 pm, Mum knocks on the door of Ellery's room to tell her that Dad's on the line.

'He said you called him,' Mum says, not managing to hide either her surprise or her smile.

'It was the drawing,' Ellery says, handing it to Mum to read. As Ellery races downstairs to take the call, she glances back to see Mum sink onto her bed, flipping through the comic.

'Hi,' she breathes into the receiver when she gets to the phone, slightly puffed from sprinting.

'How are you, Ferret?'

'I'm fine, Dad.' She considers bringing up the delay in returning her call and decides against it. At least they're talking now.

'Good, good. How's school? What's been happening?'

His questions catch her off guard and she answers them mechanically.

'School's good, I like my subjects.'

'What's your favourite? History was mine at school. Although, when I was a kid, we didn't have as much choice. We had to study English, maths, history, geography—'

Ellery cuts him off. 'Dad, aren't we going to talk?'

'Isn't that what we're doing?'

'You know what I mean. Talk about the past eight weeks.'

There's a pause on his end. 'What about them?'

'Why weren't you in touch?'

'Why weren't you in touch with me?' he counters.

'I've been really angry with you.'

'And I've been really hurt by your behaviour. What's the point in going over all of this? I love you, and you should know that. The comic I sent you said it all. What else can I say? Let's put this whole thing behind us and move on. We're talking now, aren't we? You should tell me more about school—how are you enjoying history?'

Ellery doesn't know what to say to that.

'I have to go, Dad,' she says and hangs up the phone, feeling winded, as though someone has sunk a fist right into her abdomen. She braces against the wall. She has never realised how physical emotions actually are until now, and it's a lesson she would have preferred not to learn.

Behind her, Verona says crossly, 'Did you speak to Dad without putting me on?'

---

'What's this?' Mum asks a few days later as she empties the waste-paper baskets in the girls' bedrooms.

Ellery glances at her mother and then back to the maths worksheet she is completing. 'Dad's comic.' Torn into five uneven, crumpled pieces.

'Oh, Ellery,' Mum says.

Ellery looks at her mother squarely, aiming for defiance rather than the creeping guilt she began to feel the moment the paper first gave way in her hands. The comic—the Trojan horse—the gift that wasn't really a gift, just another manipulation.

'It was mine to do what I wanted with.'

'Oh, Ellery,' Mum says again. 'Why would you do that? You might have wanted it one day.' Her voice is so full of disappointment that Ellery can't meet her eyes. She drops her gaze hurriedly.

Mum fishes the fragments out of the bin and, a few hours later, Ellery sees her straightening them under the heavy wooden fruit bowl, bananas, apples and pears adding their weight. Once straightened, Mum tries to fit them back together—sticky tape at the ready. But they've been torn too unevenly and will not be mended. Mum gives up and the remnants end up back in the trash: Dad's painstakingly drawn comic, carted off to be landfill somewhere.

Some things cannot be resurrected.

# chapter seventeen

BY TERM FOUR, they have the routine sorted. They're back at school after a lazy September holidays spent with Mum (Dad hadn't come down to Melbourne, even to see Verona). Year seven is three-quarters of the way through now. Ellery will soon be in her second year of high school, and Verona will be turning into the high school gates herself, starting year seven. The group has been re-established, with Sophie a part of the circle and ostensibly one of Ellery's friends. She has opened up now and jokes around with the others, but is never particularly responsive when Ellery tries to get to know her. The others seem different with Sophie around, too—they're cooler and more detached. They look to her when they make a joke, like they want to make her laugh. Ellery misses the easygoing afternoons on the grass and feeling Gabby's hands braiding her hair. Maybe things will be better when the weather heats up and they can sprawl on the grass once again, rather than sitting upright in a classroom at lunchtime. Yet, imperfect as it is, she has a group of friends. For Ellery, Sophie is the sharp note, but there's still a harmony.

When the bell chimes, summoning them back to class, the girls file out. Gabby is at the back and, following a sudden impulse, Ellery pulls her aside.

'Do you want to hang out this weekend, just you and me? I thought that maybe we could play tennis or something.'

Gabby smiles. 'Elly, I'd love to. I haven't seen much of you this year and I miss hanging out.'

With some people, you just have to ask.

---

Dad calls to speak with Verona from time to time, but he does not ask to talk to Ellery again. Ellery leaves the room whenever she sees his name flash up on caller ID.

In October, an envelope arrives for Mum. The letter inside is on school stationery. In formal wording, it announces that Ellery has won a state-wide essay-writing competition for her year level.

'Well done, darling—what a fantastic achievement.' Mum squeezes her tight and Ellery can hear the pride in her voice. 'This is a prestigious award.'

Ellery, skimming the letter, is perplexed. 'I never entered a competition.'

'Apparently Mrs Harris submitted your history essay.'

'The one on India from last term?'

'That's what it says here.'

Ellery can't help but feel that Kuttichathan is playing a prank on her. Could she really have won a contest? She fancies that the imp is hiding in a corner laughing at her and that, at any minute, she will wake up.

But when she gets to school the next day, Mrs Harris is all smiles and announces Ellery's achievement to the class, and there's a small poster on the noticeboard about her win.

Mum says Ellery can have a few friends over as a reward.

The girls from school come along, plus a few others from tennis and soccer. They play music in the living room and create dance routines. At Ellery's request, Mum makes gulab jamun. The girls look at each other a little hesitantly.

'It's my party and I demand everyone tries it,' Ellery says.

The friends from soccer and tennis go first. Then Gabby. Then Liv, Sylvia and Meg. And, finally, Sophie nibbles an end. Ellery, catching her eye, gives her a wink. At the end of the party, the tray of gulab jamun is completely gone.

And a present even comes from Dad in the mail—a pair of bell-bottomed striped pants which look like they've come straight out of 1977 and a red-and-white t-shirt with a squiggly outline of an upside-down pineapple across the chest. The outfit comes in billowing cream tissue paper, and it smells of new fabric and scented candles: white peony and Douglas fir. On top is a note:

Elly, your mum told me about your big win. Congratulations! These are some trendy threads to celebrate. I hope you like them. The saleswoman said they're all the rage for a girl your age—you'll be the coolest kid on the block. Love, Dad.

She holds the pants up straight and the long folded legs unfurl. Trendy? Threads? These are grown-ups' words—only ever used by imposters trying to be cool.

'Does he actually think I'd wear this? Would anyone wear this?'

Mum, standing at her shoulder, points to the label.

'It's a Chapel Street designer,' she says. 'He's making an effort.'

'Yes, but it just shows he doesn't know me at all. And buying me expensive clothes doesn't fix anything.'

'Maybe it's about the intention, not the result,' Mum says. 'He's left a receipt in here. You can exchange them if you don't like them.' Mum's voice is neutral—she always lets Ellery make her own decisions.

'Yeah, I'll do that.' Ellery takes the receipt and the clothes fall in a heap on the tissue. 'Two hundred and fifty dollars!'

---

Later that week, Mum drives her to Prahran to return the clothes. The brand has a few stores around the country and, in the middle of the shop, Ellery has a sudden image of her dad in the Brisbane outlet. She can picture him talking to the young saleslady, hideously out of his depth; she can see him determined to get it right, browsing through the racks and smiling when he finds the pineapple top he genuinely thinks she will enjoy. Ellery hesitates, hands in the fabric of a red skirt she likes much better.

Maybe she should keep the present after all? But then she thinks of their last phone call and she can feel her jaw clench. She swaps his choice for a red skirt she shoves in her wardrobe and forgets about. For the one and only time in her life, she doesn't acknowledge a gift with a thankyou note and takes a guilty kind of pleasure in the rudeness.

---

The teachers announce that the students will be sitting exams for the first time in their schooling and hand out notes on letterhead to take home to their parents. Exams! Even the words sounds scary, somehow, with the letter 'x' hunkered in the middle like that. Mum reads the letter with a half-smile.

'Your first exams, huh? That'll be a bit different for you.'

'What are they like?'

'Oh, they're alright. Law is full of exams. I always liked them much better than assignments actually. You just have to keep a cool head and the rest is easy—you'll be fine.'

At school the next day, her friends report similar reactions from their own parents—shrugs and smiles. They're all a bit irritated by this lack of fanfare from the adults.

'What would they know anyway?' Sylvia says. 'Year seven is hard.'

---

One lunchtime in November, Gabby asks Ellery to come away with her for the New Year. Gabby's family has recently purchased a boat which they're going to sail around the Whitsundays, and she is allowed to invite a friend to keep her company. *Weird Sundays*, Ellery thinks Gabby is saying at first.

'You're asking me to go where?'

'It'll be paradise—I've seen pictures—it's just so beautiful,' Gabby enthuses.

*Paradise*. How many times has she heard that word over the years? It's a tawdry greeting-card word.

'We'll spend the day reading magazines and playing board games as we sail. Then, when we moor somewhere for the evening, we'll swim off the back of the boat and go fishing.' Gabby's face is dreamy. 'It'll be so much fun—please come!'

---

'The Whitsundays is very beautiful,' Mum confirms when Ellery runs the idea past her that evening. 'But are you sure you want to be away for New Year's Eve?'

'Yes,' Ellery says.

Mum speaks with Gabby's parents on the phone a few days later. And just like that, it's all arranged. Mum books her a plane ticket to Proserpine and gives some money to Gabby's parents to pay for food during the ten-day trip. She'll leave on Boxing Day.

'You should probably mention this to your dad?' Mum suggests. 'He usually spends the holidays with you—he'll want to know there's been a change of plans.'

Change of heart, Ellery thinks but does not say aloud.

'I haven't spoken to him for months. He isn't expecting me to come and stay. Benjamin's hopeless.' She's been calling him this in her mind now for a long time, but hasn't had the nerve to say it in front of Mum.

Sure enough: 'Dad,' Mum reproves her.

But this time, Ellery shakes her head. 'No,' she insists. 'Benjamin.'

Mum doesn't argue.

---

All through early December, Ellery sees Mum glancing anxiously at her daughters, but they are both privately happy with the arrangements. Ellery can tell that Verona doesn't mind having Dad to herself, and Ellery is much happier to have plans with Gabby to look forward to. Everyone said year seven would bring change.

---

When exam week arrives, they walk into the classrooms to find the desks have been rearranged; they are evenly spaced, no longer in the usual haphazard shape around the classroom. They are told to take their seats and they watch in tense silence as the teacher hands out a sheet of questions and blank paper. They have had exam conditions explained to them and know that they are not to talk to each other or check their notes. Ellery has her eyes on the clock, and when she hears the word 'Begin' she hunches over the faintly lined page.

---

The group celebrates finishing year seven with a small party. The parents drop them off for tenpin bowling, where the shoes squeeze their toes and the pizza slices are as big as dinner plates. Gabby brings a small disposable camera, and she clicks away until the film is at an end. Together, they have done this. They have survived the year.

When it is time for their parents to pick them up, Gabby gives Ellery a hug. 'See you in a couple of weeks.'

One by one, the other girls are picked up and driven away, until it is just Sophie and Ellery, sitting on the kerb. They've never been alone together before. Neither girl speaks and the air is full of cactus shards. Sophie's arms are around her knees and she's scuffing her Converse against the ground.

'Have you enjoyed being at the school? Is it better than your old school?' Ellery asks eventually.

'Yeah, it's been good,' Sophie replies, not looking at her.

'Much on for Christmas?'

'Not really. Just family stuff.'

'Do you have a big family?'

'I guess.'

Ellery has seen Sophie laugh at Gabby's jokes and donate the Mars Bar in her lunchbox when Liv was having a bad day. She speaks her mind in class and is chosen early when they pick teams in PE. Everyone is pleased with this latest addition to their friendship circle, yet between Sophie and Ellery there is only silence, difference and the memory of stinging words. Looking across at Sophie, hugging her knees, Ellery does not know how—or whether—to span the distance. She knows too well that not all relationships can be redeemed. Before her, many options spread out.

*Sophie, are we okay? It's just that sometimes I get the feeling you have an issue with me.*

*Sophie, have I done something to offend you?*

*Sophie, would you like to come over sometime? I'd like to get to know you a bit better.*

But Ellery remains silent. She and Sophie sit in the quiet until Mum's old Fiat pulls into view.

'Have a good summer, Sophie.' Ellery smiles and walks over to the car, but Mum is reluctant to drive away.

'Would you like to come and sit in the car?' Mum calls out the window to Sophie. 'Or we can give you a lift home?'

'No, thanks,' Sophie replies, not looking at Mum.

'We're not leaving until her parents get here,' Mum tells Ellery as she winds up the window.

Ellery laughs. 'I knew you'd say that.'

---

In mid-December Ellery gets a two-line Christmas card from Benjamin, which she throws in her bedroom's wastepaper bin the day she receives it. Verona will be staying with him as usual. The day Ellery heads for Queensland will be the day Verona packs her bags and disappears to Ferntree Gully for New Year. It's always been their time with Dad, but they've only ever visited him in a pair and Ellery wonders what it will be like for her little sister this time. Ellery has felt the limits of Benjamin's patience, but Verona has not. She has always had Ellery as a buffer—never borne the brunt of Benjamin's irritation. Verona is happy to entertain herself; at home she plays her CDs in her room and reads her Brian Jacques books.

---

The boat is white against the blue of the sea and the skies. Blue and white: sailor colours. Gabby stands taller on the boat and strides around the deck with confidence. *Windhover*, it's called, but Gabby merely shrugs when Ellery asks what it means.

It's bigger than Ellery had anticipated; she had been picturing something like a dinghy. The girls have their own little bunks just below deck and Gabby's parents sleep in a cramped double bed in a separate cabin. There's a table they fold down from the wall for meals, and a small toilet. But the boat still feels rather like a campervan on the water. The fact that Gabby's parents now own a boat is a big deal to the others at the school and gives her family some kind of status that Ellery can't quite fathom. ('It's associated with luxury and affluence,' Mum had tried to explain.) She doesn't really get the appeal of the boat until they start moving. The churning waters pass beneath them and she feels the roughness of salt on her forehead and cheeks. In front of them is just ocean, blue waters and tangerine sky.

'Paradise,' Gabby repeats happily as they lean against the front rail on the first evening. When Ellery lies in bed that night, her skin smells of sunscreen and her hair tangles on the pillow. Life here is as Gabby described. Her parents steer the boat and the girls relax on deck, reading *Dolly* magazine and talking. The boat isn't going anywhere in particular—eventually they'll end up back at the marina—but they are always moving forwards, whatever that means.

Every day they swim, enfolded by warm water. With her long hair fanning behind her, Ellery fancies herself to be a mermaid. *The ocean will be like bathwater*, Mum had told her. This turns out to be hyperbole—it's still cool, as any ocean must be, but it's not the fanged iciness of Port Phillip Bay. Both girls wear bikinis but can't help tugging at the edges, painfully aware of how much skin is showing and of the newness of their adolescent bodies. Ellery catches Gabby appraising her out of the corner of her eye and knows she is secretly comparing their relative thinness to each other; Ellery has done the same thing herself. On passing boats, the older teenagers—more women than girls—wear their two-pieces with unconscious confidence. They cannonball fearlessly into the water and shriek as their boyfriends wrap tanned arms around them. Ellery and Gabby watch quietly from afar; as yet these teenage rituals remain mysteries to them, but curiosity is slowly giving way to wistfulness.

When they dock at the next set of islands, Ellery calls Mum for a chat.

'Are you missing your father?' Mum asks. 'You'd usually be with him at this time.'

'No!' Ellery says, scornful and defiant. But this is a lie. She thinks about him as often as she thinks of her mother.

On New Year's Eve, they have docked the boat at Airlie Beach. A table has been booked at one of the local restaurants and they'll be able to watch the fireworks on television. It's nice to spend a whole evening on land. Ellery has become so used to the swaying motion of the boat, it feels almost unnatural at first. She walks to the restaurant, bandy-legged. Both she and Gabby are wearing little flared miniskirts to look older than they are, but no-one is fooled.

Gabby's father gives his name to the hostess and she leads them to a table. Strangers smile as they pass. The bar is crowded and everyone seems to have a beer in hand, but the atmosphere is jolly rather than raucous. Yes, this is a good place to ring in a new year.

The adults order champagne. Entrées and mains come and go. Ellery orders barramundi and then regrets it, discovering that she doesn't actually like its muddy taste. Despite the cheerful atmosphere and Gabby's chatter, by the dessert course Ellery is feeling distracted and restless. The adults are already wine-soaked. There are empty bottles piling up on the table—more beer and wine than plates of food.

'Do you mind if I call home and say hello?' Ellery asks Gabby's mother.

'Of course not, doll. There's a payphone just outside if you want to use that. Do you need some money?'

'No, thanks.' Ellery pats her little purse. 'Mum gave me some before I left.'

Feeding money into the coin slot, Ellery dials her home number and Mum picks up on the other end.

'My goodness, darling, I wasn't expecting to hear from you tonight! Is everything okay?'

'Yeah. I just wanted to say Happy New Year.'

'How lovely! Aren't you a sweetheart? Thank you. Happy New Year to you too.'

Mum's at home with a group of friends, waiting to watch the fireworks over the city from their balcony. But there's still twenty minutes left until midnight. Mum starts to ask about Ellery's day and Airlie Beach, wanting to know details, but Ellery cuts her off.

'I have to go, Mum. I just wanted to say hi.'

'Of course, of course. Call again whenever you want to. Have a great evening, darling! I love you so much.'

But when Ellery hangs up, she simply stares at the phone on the hook. She's been out here for ten minutes now and knows she should go back inside. But she can't help herself. There is one other call to make, one other person she has been thinking about. She picks up the receiver again and dials the only other number she knows by heart. She waits, dry-mouthed, feeling weak-willed and hating herself.

The phone rings and rings and rings—she thinks it's going to ring out into nothingness—until it hits the recorded voicemail. The familiar voice of Granny Agnes: *You're reached Agnes and Timothy Fortune. We're not available to take your call. Please leave a message.*

But she doesn't. She can't. She waits another thirty seconds and calls again, but there is no answer. Benjamin and Verona mustn't be home.

She cannot, will not, leave a message. And in the distance, carried on the wind, she can hear Kuttichathan laughing.

# part 3

# 2006

# chapter eighteen

DAD'S FUNERAL IS being held on Friday. She has had six months to prepare and yet, when the time comes, Verona finds that she isn't prepared at all.

They lucked into the last available seats on a Thursday evening Qantas flight and the cabin is full of business people—men in check shirts and women in pencil skirts. Laptops are out on every tray table and there's a kind of weary urgency in the air; everyone is postponing the moment when they have to switch their phones to flight mode. Ellery is looking past Verona out to the tarmac as the plane hums its readiness for flight. Verona's hands clench and unclench in her lap. In her head she recites the statistics for death by air travel that she looked up last night. You are more likely to drown in a bathtub—three hundred and thirty-five deaths a year, she chants to herself, waiting to feel comforted. Numbers are usually soothing, but not today.

Having Ellery beside her isn't a great help. It's only now that they are alone that Verona realises just how long it has been since they last spent time together—and now they will have three entire days with only each other for company. She is prepared for either quarrels or awkward silences. Occasionally, Ellery invites Verona to join her group of girlfriends for a coffee and carrot cake at the Elm Tree cafe or agrees to drive Verona home from band practice. But Verona couldn't tell you what classes Ellery is taking at uni or how long she has been dating Josh. And Ellery doesn't know the names of Verona's friends.

They haven't had to worry about the service arrangements—Dad's widow, Gertrude, has taken care of everything. She placed the death notices in the papers and informed his friends and colleagues. She ordered the catering for the wake and gave the instructions to the funeral director. All the girls have to do is show up. Their mother offered to fly up with them, but she has not been invited to the funeral.

Gertrude had called Verona with the service details earlier in the week.

'You'll pass all this on to your sister, won't you? But Benjamin wouldn't have wanted your mother there. She was part of his past, so please make sure she doesn't come.'

'Now why would she assume that?' Ellery had asked indignantly when Verona had relayed the conversation.

Verona had shrugged. 'It's not like our parents had a good relationship.'

'Our parents always got on fine after the divorce,' Ellery retorted. 'I don't know who Gertrude thinks she is, making these assumptions.'

'She's his wife,' Verona replied. 'Gertrude's alright. You'd know that if you'd ever spent time with her.'

Neither of the girls think of Gertrude as their stepmother and no endearments pass her lips for them. It's the same with Conner, Mum's partner. The girls had slunk downstairs together to tell Mum that she wasn't welcome at the funeral. Mum had been sitting at the kitchen table drinking orange juice and making notes on a yellow notepad. Conner, behind her, stood with empty husks of half-oranges around him. He'd only recently bought the juicer and set it up in the corner of the kitchen, just as his sleek metallic bicycle had come to rest in the front halfway. His shirts hung on the washing line alongside the girls' clothes and there was now shaving cream written on the shopping list on the fridge—fragments of male domesticity that are jarring in their house of women. Conner had looked up as the girls entered the room.

'Fresh juice going, girls! Can I make you a glass before school, Verona?'

Conner was still eager to please and fighting to win them over with something between sweetness and desperation.

'No, thanks,' Ellery had said as Verona shook her head. By tacit agreement, Ellery was spokeswoman. Mum had listened to Gertrude's edict impassively, Conner's hands on her shoulders.

'Are you okay not being there?'

'Of course,' Mum said. 'My time with Benjamin was a lifetime ago—you girls were babies when we split. But it would've been nice to say goodbye.'

And so it's just the two girls, without Mum there to mediate. Verona glances sideways at her sister. Although Melbourne winter is in full swing, Ellery wears a buttery sundress in preparation for Brisbane warmth. Her hands are folded neatly in her lap and her face is turned towards the window. Verona watches her with disapproval; nobody would guess Ellery was on her way to their father's funeral. Verona's jeans and t-shirt are dark, with a black dress packed away in the carry-on suitcase.

This will be Verona's first funeral. She laid out three possible outfits on her bed last night—clothes tumbling out of her wardrobe, but nothing she wanted to wear. The black dress, with its hem that flaps stiffly around her knees and its neckline that clings to her clavicles, was her final muddled choice. It is sober and sombre: Dad would have loathed it. But she cannot bring herself to wear a colourful outfit in his memory—that's asking too much. The black symbolises her respect and her sadness.

Ellery's voice intrudes.

'It's surreal, isn't it? I can't actually imagine him dead. I keep trying to picture it and my mind just goes blank.'

'Mmm.' Verona has been thinking the same thing, but doesn't want to talk about it with Ellery.

'You know, I keep thinking that if they ever make *The Hobbit* into a movie, Benjamin won't be there to see it.'

'Mmm.'

'This must be particularly difficult for you. I mean, you two were quite close—much closer than he and I ever were.'

Quite close? That's typical of Ellery: superiority and obnoxious qualifiers.

'What would you know?' she snaps.

But Ellery just gives her trademark patronising smile. 'Was he really that close to either of us, V?'

'Don't call me that.'

Ellery spreads her fingers in surrender and they lapse into silence as the plane begins its grumbling ascent.

Once airborne, the flight attendants wheel trolleys down the aisle and hand out grey tea on grey trays. Where has all the colour gone? Verona keeps looking around at the other passengers. They tap on their laptop keyboards, turn the black-and-white pages of their newspapers or stare unseeingly into the middle distance. It's like the dry cabin air has sucked the expressions right off their faces. Do she and Ellery look like that too? Are their faces so smooth and composed?

The unwavering loudness of the engine is enough to give Verona a headache. She can feel Ellery looking at her from time to time. Blueness and sparkle slide beneath the belly of the plane, the outskirts of the city gradually coming into view ahead of them. Brisbane is Dad's territory and Verona will always associate the city with him. She knows Ellery feels the same; that's probably why her sister doesn't like the place. The plane shudders slightly and it seems as though the nose tilts downwards.

'Is that normal?' Verona asks, and hears her voice coming out higher than usual.

'It just means we've started the descent,' Ellery says reassuringly. 'It's so weird seeing you get apprehensive about something.'

Verona can't figure out whether or not this is a taunt. You are more likely to die from falling out of bed—four hundred and fifty deaths a year, she reminds herself as her fingers grip the armrests.

---

Sure enough, they do land safely and Verona, wheeling her case through the airport, feels a mixture of foolishness and relief. Usually Verona would take a bus to Gertrude's house in West End—she has the system sussed out by now and knows which fares to ask for as well as the location of the stops. But today she is heading to a new part of the city, and when Ellery suggests that they spring for a cab Verona nods her acquiescence. After two hours on an aeroplane, she feels choked by the thickness and heat of crowds. The leather silence of the taxi is perfect.

When they're on the kerb with their bags in New Farm, Verona looks up at the two-storey B&B.

'Cute, isn't it?' says Ellery.

It's a quaint old townhouse with lemon paint and stocks starting to bloom in the garden in country cottage glory. She knows that there will be poached eggs, buttermilk pancakes and some kind of boutique marmalade served for breakfast. Trust Ellery to choose somewhere like this—Verona would have picked somewhere sparse and economical in the inner city.

'Did you charge this to Mum's card?' Verona asks, and Ellery looks at her with wide eyes.

'Of course not! Mum arranged the accommodation. Do you really think I'd book us into somewhere so fancy?'

The landlady checks them in and gives them keys.

'Three nights?' she confirms as she scribbles in a leather-bound appointment book, her grey hair slanting forwards as she writes.

'That's right,' Ellery says.

'Just here for a holiday?'

'Family event,' Ellery replies, smooth and sweet, not looking at Verona.

'Oh, lovely!' the woman responds enthusiastically, no doubt imagining reunions and birthday cakes.

'Yes, lovely,' Verona repeats, and the sarcasm earns a sharp look from her sister.

---

Their room is light-filled with creamy wallpaper. Ellery commandeers the wardrobe and Verona chooses the bed closest to the window. Thank God they won't have to share a bed.

Once they've unpacked, there isn't much to do except wait until 11 am tomorrow.

'Fancy a walk?' Ellery asks.

Verona shakes her head and holds up one of the thick textbooks she has packed. There are three in her suitcase.

'Mind if I make a call?' Without waiting for an answer, Ellery takes her Nokia outside onto the small balcony. Calling Josh, Verona presumes.

Exams are inching closer, but when Ellery has passed through the double doors onto the balcony, Verona stares listlessly at the open page. Unable to help imitating their mother, Ellery started law school this year. Verona is intending to do the same course, which always raises eyebrows, as most of her subjects at school are science-based.

'Why would you want to follow in Mum's footsteps?' Ellery has asked several times. 'You've never been close to her.'

'Who says I'm taking after Mum?' Verona always replies.

'Who else?'

'It'd be nice to remind everyone that you're not the only one capable of getting top grades,' Verona says.

It isn't just Ellery. Everybody seems surprised by her desire to enter a profession of words.

'But you're such a numbers girl!'

Yes, a numbers person in a family of logophiles. Mum is always proud when Verona gets good grades in physics and chemistry. When Verona was offered a place in the maths extension program, Mum stuck the letter on the fridge with a border of yellow magnets. But is it her imagination that Mum smiles slightly brighter when Ellery wins an essay-writing competition or tops history?

Dad was more plain-spoken. 'Gotta get good at English, V. Language is what counts.'

But no matter how many hours she spends at her desk making notes on *Othello* or reading about the Russian Revolution, her grades remain capped at a B.

*Oxidation is loss reduction is gain*, is the dull chant in her mind as she stares at the front cover of the chemistry textbook, but she feels no desire to actually open it. Instead, she takes out the pieces of A4 paper on which she wrote the eulogy eight days ago. There are barely any crossings-out; she knows exactly what she wants to say and how she wants to remember her dad. It's written for him. Cross-legged on the floor, surrounded by her textbooks, she reads it through again, chewing her lip.

Ellery can't sit still when she's on the phone, but paces endlessly in giant, looping infinity circles. Verona can only hear one side of the conversation—and even that only faintly—but she can imagine Josh's deep voice asking questions on the other end. Ellery's voice always gets breathier and higher when she talks to him. It's weird. They've got their own little turtledove language—they murmur and coo to each other. It's nauseating. Verona's world is empty of boys. Or girls. Never had a boyfriend. No-one has ever even asked her out. But she is seventeen and feels the press of time with desperate acuteness. The fact that she hasn't had sex yet is horrifying. She feels her lack of experience like a sluggish casing and sometimes she wonders if she'll ever get to do it. What if I'm stuck a virgin forever? What if it doesn't happen at all? That's possible too, right? Ellery, on the other hand, has been on the pill for years—Josh is her second serious boyfriend. The little packet sits in their shared bathroom (Ellery uses it as a toothbrush holder so she doesn't forget to take it), mocking Verona.

After half an hour, Ellery wanders back into the room from the balcony. She's off the phone, but there's a little smile around her mouth and rhythm in her walk. She busies herself with teacups and puts the kettle on, hovering at Verona's shoulder as it boils.

'How's it going?' she asks, her voice as bright as her dress.

'Fine.'

'Are you studying?' Ellery eyes the textbooks with some surprise.

'Just pretending to. I haven't been very productive. How's Josh?'

'He's good. He said to say hi and hopes you're okay.'

'That's nice,' Verona says. 'A platitude for every occasion.'

Josh is by the book: he's the sort of person who never puts his elbows on the table and holds the door open for old people.

The kettle screeches and Ellery rushes towards it. Both girls like making tea—it's a ritual they picked up from their mother. At home they infuse tea-leaves in teapots, but here Dilmah teabags will have to do. All the same, Ellery steeps them carefully and adds the pale dash of milk. She has graduated to coffee since starting uni, while Verona still has to fight the urge to say 'expresso'. Ellery returns with two cups carefully balanced on saucers and hands one off to Verona, then sinks onto the couch, legs tucked neatly underneath her.

'Do you know what you're going to say tomorrow?' Ellery asks. Her head is tilted to the side slightly and her eyes on Verona's face are soft. Ellery's face does all the right things—something else learned from Mum—and people like to confide in her. When she tilts her head like that, the stories just spill out of them. No judgement ever flickers where it shouldn't and she seems to know exactly the right thing to say. Verona does not share these skills. Not suffering fools gladly is Mum's polite euphemism, but Verona has overheard earthier words being applied to her at school. She wonders why she doesn't care.

Verona circles her hands around the cup and takes a sip. 'Yes, I've got it all written down.'

'Are you nervous about it?'

Verona shrugs. 'Not much point being nervous.'

'But are you?'

'Not really. I'm just going to talk for Dad.'

'Well, you won't be short of things to say,' Ellery notes. 'Benjamin was nothing if not interesting.'

'Oh yes.' Verona can hear the warm flash of enthusiasm in her own voice. It's like the room has come alight; Dad's presence conjured by the mere utterance of his name and memories swirling. 'He knew so much! He did so much. Remember all those trips around Australia and to the outback? And the photographs he took? Remember the folklore he taught us when we were kids?' Verona asks with a half-smile.

'They're Mum's stories, not Dad's,' Ellery points out.

They had loved those stories when they were little. At first Mum had been reluctant to share the darker narratives—eerie folklore to rival the Grimm Brothers' darkest retelling of Cinderella. She recounted tales of heartbreak, lost love, decapitations, tired eyes and spilled tears—the shark locked in ferocious battle with the turtle in the ocean and Rama rescuing Sita from the demon king. Fijian stories and Indian stories, told in tandem. And the all-powerful trinity—gods counterbalanced with powerful goddesses: you can't create without wisdom, you can't preserve without wealth and you can't destroy without power. But Verona's favourite had been the ghost stories—tales of the *bhoot*, an Indian variant of departed spirits. The places where the dead are cremated and scattered are charged and electric—the air remembers the ashes of the dead, annihilated fragments of humanity, and this is the birthplace of the *bhoot*. A *bhoot* is unable to forget its life or relinquish the human world—it remembers too well what it is missing. Mum had always described them as menacing figures; rather than the West's kindly Casper the ghost, the *bhoot* was something darker and more urgent. However, Verona had preferred to imagine these spirits as simply unquiet and restless.

Mum had been astonished when she saw the girls' widening eyes and rapt attention, their tiny bodies leaning forwards for the next word. She recounted the tales slowly and steadily, her deep voice endlessly calm and uninflected. Dad had liked to tell them the same stories, but he told them differently, voice lowered to a stage whisper and hands stirring the air.

'You're just a frustrated actor,' Mum had said to him once as she watched from the doorway, torn between amusement and annoyance. These had been her stories first.

'Excuse me? I believe you're the lawyer. Your entire profession is built on theatrics.'

They had shut the door behind them and the girls' bedroom had been cast in darkness, but their parents could be heard laughing outside. Ellery is the one who has recounted this incident—Verona has no memory of their parents together. The girls had been small enough to share a bedroom then, twin beds, a dollhouse and a wicker basket filled with plush toys. Verona could picture her wide-eyed toddler self with the pixie haircut, sheets pulled up to her chin. Even after the divorce Dad had still told the girls the stories, but Mum had stopped. It was as though Dad had claimed them in the divorce. *Appropriation* is Ellery's new word for it. First year cultural studies has her all fired up.

'Words and stories can be stolen too, you know. In fact, they're one of the most valuable things that can be taken.'

But Verona isn't so sure. 'You're way overanalysing this,' she tells her sister.

She thinks that Dad just couldn't quite help himself when it came to words. Like any passionate collector, he'd scoop up the floating ones in a butterfly net and make a glittering collection of them. What was so wrong with that?

'He was a lot of fun,' Ellery says now, but the way she says it doesn't sound complimentary.

The two of them never discuss Dad—not since the estrangement between him and Ellery. Verona would fly up to Brisbane every six months to see him, while Ellery stayed in Melbourne with Mum.

'He's just so light-hearted,' Verona says, only realising after she has spoken that she has slipped into present tense again. 'So much fun to be around. But it's always been like I could tell him anything. He was just there with an open ear.'

'Not always there,' Ellery corrects gently. 'Remember when he went on that research trip for nine months and didn't even call once?'

'He was in a remote location,' Verona retorts. 'It was field work.'

'He could've got to a phone once or twice.'

Verona shrugs and she can feel her clavicles and shoulder blades moving under her skin, as sharp as her expression. Ellery, diplomatic, allows all the other examples that Verona can see queuing in her eyes to fall silent on her tongue. Verona's mouth is stoppered up tight and no words against Dad will make their way past.

'What happened in June?' she asks Ellery abruptly.

Ellery saw Dad once before he died. A thirty-minute meeting after six years of estrangement—Benjamin's request.

Ellery sighs. 'I gave him a chance, V. He wasn't interested.'

And with that, she picks up the outdated copy of *Vogue* from the coffee table and flips its glossy pages with her fingertips. They order in a pizza and spend most of the evening in silence, with Verona whispering the eulogy to herself over and over again.

# chapter nineteen

VERONA KNEW THAT Dad had been writing to Ellery all year. Weekly emails and more. It had started the month he was diagnosed. Ellery had logged into her inbox one morning and his name was there: a short message addressed to her and a word document attached to it: *To Ellery, I hope you read this. Luv, Ben.* What would it be? Ellery had admitted to being intensely curious and suddenly nervous when she opened the file—to find a short story about his first time on a surfboard. This was it? She read it and then clicked out without saving it.

She had sent a reply a few days later. The politeness Mum had inculcated into them as kids has its own code of conduct for adulthood. Ellery and Verona know that they are supposed to reply promptly to emails and take either wine, flowers or chocolates for the host when they visit someone else's house for dinner. Ellery had settled on a few short lines of her own: *Hi Benjamin, I was sorry to hear the news. Wishing you a speedy recovery. Take care, Ellery.* But Dad never replied to that.

The next week, the same thing. Dad had sent Ellery a one-line message in an email and a short story attached—this one about the Port Hedland mine he'd worked at for cash during the university breaks. *And you wouldn't believe how I sweated out iron ore for months—you should have seen my shirt collars!*

These weren't stories; they were memories. And Dad had sent them only to Ellery. When Verona had asked him about it, he'd been dismissive.

'You've heard these tales many times in the flesh; you don't need to read them.'

They had been put down on paper for his eldest daughter alone. But six years into an estrangement, Ellery had claimed they felt like a stranger's obscure remembrances—meaningless, miscellaneous tales she couldn't see the point in reading. The stories of surfing mishaps and open-cut mines, of linguists' hijinks and boyhood pranks, could not stir her. She always did Benjamin the courtesy of reading them—careless, dutiful skimming—but then left them in her email inbox without bothering to save them to her computer's hard drive. The stories were always prefaced with the same short message and the same sign-off: *luv, Ben.* Luv? The bastardised three-letter word that wasn't even a word, impoverished of its full meaning. One vowel missing and the other so jarringly incorrect. A linguist ought to have known better.

But one week in June, there was no story attached. The email was a simple request. *Would you come up to Brisbane and see me?* And so she had.

Although the meeting had only taken place last month, Dad's illness spread very quickly since then. Perhaps he had been waiting for Ellery to come—Verona has heard that people will sometimes hang onto life if there's unfinished business to resolve. Now he's gone and tomorrow is the last goodbye. Verona needs the day to be perfect.

---

But the funeral the next day is a botched affair.

When the girls walk in together, they immediately attract stares and whispers. Verona doesn't care, but Ellery scans the room and bites her lip. Today Ellery's walk is not its usual confident stride. She hovers near the doorway looking tentative, like she has wandered into the wrong room.

The curiosity does not abate but follows them around the room in sideways glances and muttered asides as they cross to the neat grid of chairs. Most people here know Verona, but Ellery with her long hair and dainty features is new to them. Prettiness always attracts attention. Age hasn't made the girls look any more like sisters—they share Malti's thin frame, but not much else. And in a room full of black, Ellery's fawn skirt and white blouse are garnering glances of their own.

It's a small crowd—maybe thirty people, no more than that—but rather than feeling close and intimate, Verona thinks it feels kind of sad. Dad came all the way to the end with only a handful gathered to drink a toast to his memory and send him off. Verona wonders whether not many people knew her father after all—or whether there were others who knew him and don't care that he has died. That's even harder to contemplate, and she stares around the room, troubled and dissatisfied.

The faces she sees are mostly Gertrude's friends and a few next-door neighbours. There are a couple of other family members here too. Dad's father died several years ago, but his mother, Granny Agnes, stands commandingly near the front of the room. Granny Agnes is a strong woman, but hard-hearted with no softness to spare; it has been rationed out over her life in small annual quotas. She nods stiffly at Verona, but ignores Ellery altogether. She has no sympathy to spare for her granddaughters when her own heart is breaking for the death of the first and best-loved son. The other guests at the funeral are avoiding Granny Agnes's eyes; nobody wants to see the pain pooling there. At the centre of the room, Gertrude is dressed all in black. Her eyes are very red and there's a balled-up handkerchief in her hands. Ellery is dry-eyed and Verona will not shed tears in public, but Gertrude weeps openly.

'So dramatic,' Ellery whispers to Verona.

'She misses Dad,' Verona admonishes her sister, and Ellery looks contrite.

'Sorry, V. You're right.'

Verona loops around the room—the small-talk circuit. As she moves through the crowd, people squeeze her arm or murmur their sympathies. She nods and lets the gentle platitudes wash over her. It means nothing to hear a stranger give her their condolences.

'Your sister's quite a striking girl,' one of Benjamin's neighbours comments to Verona. 'Don't know about the outfit, though.'

Verona's high-necked black dress gets approving glances.

When Verona returns to stand beside Ellery, she sees that a few of the guests have approached.

'What are you studying?' Mrs Liu is asking.

'Law,' Ellery replies sweetly, and their eyes widen. She seems to enjoy the fuss people make—her mouth quirks up in a self-satisfied way.

'You must be a smart cookie.'

Mum gets the same reaction from people. Verona has watched their eyes brush over her black hair and the skin of her face curiously. Mum's clothes always look elegant and those are real pearls around her throat. People's eyes flicker between those lustrous beads and her face, visibly uncertain. From time to time, shop assistants will talk slowly and loudly to her—hands raised and ready to mime any words she does not understand. They do not register her fluid speech and extensive vocabulary. Only when she works the word 'lawyer' into the conversation do they snap to attention: *Oh, you're a lawyer!* It is the shibboleth used to command respect. When she has uttered it, cheeks redden as her interlocutors realise their mistake and conversation speeds back up to normal pace.

The same thing is happening now to Ellery. Everyone seems to have a relative in the legal profession and the other guests start mentioning that their children and second cousins are also lawyers.

This is only interrupted by the funeral director appearing beside them in his black suit. He materialises all of a sudden, gesturing towards the curtains at the back of the room.

'Would you like to say a last farewell?' he asks.

'Yes,' says Verona. 'But I'd like to see him alone.'

They enter a little alcove behind long, still drapes, with Verona on her tiptoes, not quite sure who or what she thinks she might be disturbing. Until there he is, inside a tiny casket. She would never mistake him for sleeping. The skin has sunken onto his face like a waxwork figurine.

'I'll give you a moment,' the funeral director says and melts away from the room, head bowed. It must get so tiring, pretending to be sad every day, Verona thinks—to work in a place where a smile is disrespectful.

In all Dad's stories from childhood, there was a mysterious plant to be eaten or a kiss to be had. Death was always reversible, never permanent. As she peers into the coffin, she feels cheated by this finality. And she is not superstitious enough to kiss the waxwork cheek. Those stories, just metaphors after all.

'Hello, Dad,' she says when they are alone, but the words sound unnaturally loud in this tiny space and she cannot override the knowledge that he no longer hears her. The words she wants to say, the final goodbyes, go unsaid. Instead, she just stares at his face until the funeral director returns. It smells like two-dollar incense in here and she wants to sit down.

'Do you want more time?' the man asks as he pokes his head around the door, and Verona hears herself laughing.

The celebrant taps a small metal gong with a ceremonial mallet and Verona is transported back to year one and a glockenspiel class. She and Ellery sit down on the stained velour chairs with the rest of the small crowd. At Ellery's insistence, they're a few rows from the front. The celebrant speaks first, peering over her glasses at the crowd. For someone who clearly never met Dad, she does a decent job of the biography. She must've spoken at some length to Gertrude and Granny Agnes.

The first eulogy is delivered by Uncle Patrick. Their uncle is a journalist and isn't bad with words himself, but the speech is strangely clumsy, punctuated with comments and asides that make Verona's teeth clench.

'He was an armchair philosopher, of course,' Uncle Patrick says wryly. 'An inactive activist. Ben loved to watch a good cause from the sidelines but heaven forbid he got off his arse to actually do anything about it.'

A bubble of laughter breaks over the crowd, but Verona is annoyed. Is that really how her father should be remembered? Aren't eulogies supposed to glorify the departed? Shouldn't jokes be left for later years when the hurt has faded? Does the ache ever fade?

Ellery watches without expression. Even her hair lies straight and smooth and she sits upright in her chair.

Uncle Patrick does not mention either of the girls—after all, talking about Verona means that Ellery also has to be explained. Uncle Patrick doesn't mention their mother, either. In fact, he acts like Benjamin's first marriage never happened.

'Wine and women, that was my brother,' is Patrick's summary of Benjamin's life before his second marriage.

To her left, Verona sees that Ellery is starting to frown now too. Both girls have crossed their arms, their elbows spiking outwards in angry points. Ellery would be cross for their mother's sake and feels the unfairness of Uncle Patrick's erasure. And Verona is furious on Dad's behalf: Patrick's final tribute to his brother casts their father as some sort of drunken womaniser. But the rest of the crowd seems amused in a sad-eyed sort of way.

Next is Gertrude.

'My husband was an awesome dude. A top bloke,' she begins. Her voice is hoarse and she leans heavily against the podium as she speaks. Halfway through, she presses the back of her hand to her forehead and has to be comforted by her brother, who rushes forwards from the front row to put an arm around her. Her voice breaks on the final line of her speech. 'Sleep sweetly, my *anam cara*, until we meet again.'

Then the celebrant is calling Verona to the podium. Her speech is folded in her pocket like failed origami. She takes it out now and smooths its uneven creases. She has never had a knack for public speaking. Although she is not troubled by nerves, she cannot perform for an audience the way that good oratory requires. When she plays her clarinet in the school band, she keeps her eyes on the music and her body still, refusing to add any flourishes. And this is how she reads her speech. It isn't long, and Verona reads without raising her face to the audience—words she wrote while lying on her bedroom floor the night he died.

'Dad was the brightest light in the room,' she says. 'He had the broadest smile, the easiest laugh—and the biggest heart.'

Every word ignites with affection and anguish.

But when she starts to read Allen Ginsberg's 'Things I'll Not Do (Nostalgias)', she chokes up. She hates crying in public—would bite her tongue in half to prevent it if she could—but today she is helpless. The wet trails anoint her face, from eyelid to chin. Ginsberg lists activities only available to the living, and Dad's dead body behind the podium is its own ode to things not done: he never saw the aurora borealis shimmer above his head, never tasted *lángos* in Budapest, never felt the waters of Adels Grove swirling around his torso. The finality of death is utterly incomprehensible. Verona reads the final line—'Not myself except in an urn of ashes'—and stumbles away from the podium. As she moves through her row to take her seat beside Ellery once again, people she doesn't know squeeze her shoulders or pat her on the back. And Ellery reaches out and grips her hand.

'Oh, V,' she whispers.

Verona isn't listening as the celebrant returns to the dais one final time. She feels only the rise and fall of her chest, the pattering rhythm at the inside of her wrist. That's something. Even these hot, humiliating streaks of salt are badges of aliveness.

Benjamin's brothers come to lift the casket between them, awkward-footed and rubbing their eyes on their sleeves. The casket is moved to the long black hearse, which pulls onto the street, where passing drivers watch it with curiosity and distaste.

The service finishes without Phil Ochs being played, but those tracks are on rotation in Verona's mind anyway—and one in particular: 'No More Songs'.

---

He had called her in January, only a few short months ago. In the dry, asphyxiating heat, his name had flashed up on her mobile as she sat in her room.

'Took you long enough,' Verona scolded laughingly. 'You promised me a call two weeks ago and then just dropped off the face of the earth as always.'

'I've got some bad news, V.'

'What's going on?' Her mind had immediately rushed ahead to the next holidays, when she had planned to go to Brisbane. He'd been too busy for a visit over Christmas and New Year.

'You know how I've been a bit unwell lately? Feeling tired?'

'Yeah?'

'I went to the doctor today and he says it's a bit more serious than I expected. Well, he reckons I've got cancer.'

'What?' she had exclaimed, but this was just a word. Playacting. She had never expected that he would actually go anywhere at all. Parents don't leave. He'll be fine, she had thought to herself—had never canvassed any other possibility. The words had washed over her: bowel cancer, radiotherapy, oncologist. A whole new vocabulary she'd never wanted to learn.

---

The wake is at Gertrude's house. The West End terrace has never felt like home. Even though he lived there for four years, Verona has never really thought of it as Dad's place. It isn't just because Gertrude's name is on the deed; her presence is spread all through the house—her horse-riding paraphernalia hanging around the living room, her battered pack of tarot cards in the ceramic fruit bowl and the abundance of amethysts in the guest room. This is Gertrude's territory. Only the bookshelves dotted through the house sing Dad's name. They boast an extensive collection: linguistics textbooks, science fiction novels, naval history, political biographies, literary criticism and poetry. All forms of the written word have made their way onto Dad's shelves; glossy hardcovers and second-hand paperbacks alike have been welcomed to his flock. Mum is exactly the same. Literary promiscuity, she calls it.

Dad was pithier. 'I'm a proud book slut.'

Now, Verona stares at the bookshelves as people mill around her. Dad's books. Asimov to Žižek. She trails her fingers over their broken spines. Books should be battered from love and use, she thinks: they should show the fullness of their lives, just as people should exit the world with smile lines and laugh creases. Dad had both. The mask-like face in the open casket rises in her mind, so shrunken without breath to fill his chest and his cheeks. What was it that had left him, to make him so tiny in death? She doesn't really want to remember that face in the coffin, but it has stuck tight in her mind. She shakes her head, but the image remains.

The sisters still stand together. Today they lean in towards one another, and work together to give Granny Agnes a wide berth.

'They were terrible eulogies,' Ellery shakes her head. 'Except yours.'

'Totally reductionist,' Verona agrees. She has picked this word up from Ellery, who looks surprised and then smiles.

'Exactly.'

When Ellery moves to get a glass of wine from the long table along the wall she brings an apple juice back for Verona. Verona watches her juggling the wineglass in one hand and piling nibbles onto a plate with her spare hand. She can see that Ellery has collected enough brie, crackers and grapes for the two of them. In Ellery's absence, people keep trying to draw Verona into conversation. As soon as she drifts off into a reverie, someone will touch her arm to offer their condolences and comment on her eulogy. With Verona, they talk about the past—reminiscing about Dad from years gone by. The few people who approach Ellery talk about the present.

Ellery is walking back to Verona when a grey-haired woman steps into her path. Verona recognises her as one of Dad and Gertrude's neighbours. At first Ellery smiles and nods as the woman speaks, however her expression quickly becomes guarded—tight mouth and shuttered eyes.

'. . . and he loved you so much, sweetie,' Verona hears the woman say. 'You have no idea how much it pained him not to talk to you. Not to have both his girls in his life.'

Even from a few metres away, Verona sees Ellery struggling to maintain politeness—her smile stiffening and then falling away. 'I'd prefer not to discuss this with you.'

The woman jerks back, visibly affronted, as though a kindness has been rebuffed. She doesn't retort but moves away. The way she presses her lips together and the sideways glance she exchanges with another woman standing nearby says enough. Poor Benjamin. So the lost daughter was a monster after all.

Ellery reaches Verona and thrusts the plate of cheese into her sister's hand. She's shaking her head. Ellery is usually so polite that Verona finds her irritation surprisingly refreshing. Snapping at a bystander is much more the sort of thing she would do rather than Ellery. Maybe there is some common ground between them after all.

'Cheers,' Verona says, and plucks a wedge of cheddar from the edge of the plate.

# chapter twenty

THE GROWN-UP THINGS still remain: the eerie scattering of ashes—Gertrude will take them to Shorncliffe Pier—and the reading of Dad's will. Both are due to occur in private over the next couple of weeks. Unlike Mum and Ellery, Verona is not superstitious; she believes too much in logic. Yet she finds herself remembering those childhood tales once again as she thinks of these final funeral rites, and especially the *bhoot*. Dad's ashes billowing from an urn conjures the image of him as a ghostly figure, hovering over the pier and looking back to the world he has departed and the daughters he has left behind. Verona wishes she could believe that things don't really end.

Gertrude had pulled Verona aside at the wake just before they left.

'Would you like to stay in Brisbane an extra day or two?'

'I don't think so. Unless you need some help cleaning up the house?'

'No, no, it's fine. I'm not moving anything yet.'

Verona isn't interested in Dad's possessions. Most of his stuff will stay with Gertrude, of course, and the only things Verona really wants are his books—they've got his spidery writing in the margins and his name in blockish capitals. Reading one of his books with his thoughts annotating every page is almost like having him in the room: wry little observations of characters and scribbled asides. It's how she first encountered *Pride and Prejudice*, reading Dad's old high school copy. ('Bingley: what an idiot') and *The Weirdstone of Brisingamen* ('less schmaltzy version of Narnia'). Verona also expects to receive his *Oxford English Dictionary*. This is not the condensed version, but the full dictionary in its glorious entirety—a twenty-volume set. Books are a fitting gift from a linguist to his daughter.

The day after the wake passes in easy companionable silence—something she has never felt with Ellery before—and on Sunday the girls board a plane back to Melbourne. They don't talk much on the flight home. The plane banks to the right. More people are killed by sharks, one in 1.2 million, Verona repeats to herself, feeling two rows of molars scrape against each other as she grinds them. Verona wonders whether this strange camaraderie she and Ellery have felt in Brisbane will last or simply ebb away as soon as they touch down in Tullamarine, like ashes scattered from a pier.

'How are we getting home?' Verona asks as the aircraft descends. 'Mum?'

Ellery called their mother yesterday and again this morning, handing her mobile to Verona afterwards for the cursory hello. She never has much to say to Mum—it's with some difficulty that she avoids monosyllables.

'No, Josh is picking us up,' Ellery tells her.

In testament to their truce, Verona avoids rolling her eyes. But she knows just how the scene will unfold: like Ellery is a movie heroine, returned from a decade of exile in a foreign land. She will not be able to avoid rolling her eyes then.

After Brisbane's mildness, the cold air blasts them and makes them scramble for their cardigans. Ellery eyes Verona's outfit.

'Black conducts the heat—maybe you were wiser after all!'

And, as Verona expects, there is a bit of a display when they meet Josh outside the terminal. They see him coming—his floppy brown hair and wide grin is visible from the moment they step outside. Josh has pulled his dented station wagon up to the kerb to avoid the airport parking fees, so they've got all of two minutes to get their bags into the boot and scoot away. Somehow—sure enough—he and Ellery still manage to wrap their arms around each other and kiss like it's 1918. Josh's hands press into the G-shaped hollow of Ellery's back and she runs her fingertips over his ears, nose and cheek, which seems like a peculiarly intimate gesture. Verona, glancing at her watch, allows this to continue for exactly one minute and forty-five seconds before she starts to applaud.

'Bravo, what a lovely performance—always give the crowds what they want. Can we move this along? We've now got fifteen seconds to get out of here.'

The amorphous blob of entwined limbs becomes two discrete people once more. Briefly letting his hand fall from Ellery's back, Josh gives Verona a quick hug too. His hugs are firm.

'Welcome home, both of you,' he says as they clamber into the car, which smells of fried rice and gym clothes.

Josh sticks precisely to the speed limit. As they drive, he wants to hear about Brisbane and asks, almost urgently, whether they're feeling okay. 'You'll both need a good night's sleep. It must have been emotionally exhausting,' he says.

'Not at all. It was great fun,' Verona retorts before she can stop herself, and Ellery turns around from the front seat to give her a look.

Josh looks abashed rather than offended. His face colours and he shakes his head. 'Sorry, I'm stating the obvious, huh? I've never lost a parent—I can't imagine what it's like.'

'It's fine,' Verona mutters. 'I was just being sarcastic. Yeah, I'm pretty tired.'

But when he starts to ask about the funeral, Ellery halts the conversation.

'Later,' she tells him and, with a half-glance at Verona in the rear-view mirror, he falls silent.

Even though, like Ellery, he falls somewhere on the tiny spectrum between straitlaced and boring, Josh is an easygoing conversationalist and manages to keep chatting all the way to the house. He's inclusive too—doesn't just talk to Ellery sitting beside him in the passenger seat but tries to draw Verona in as well. He swivels his head towards the back seat, making sure she knows he is talking to her too. And when Ellery turns the conversation to university and their law classes, he immediately turns it back to something that might interest all of them: books, movies and new cafes. Subjects the baby sister can discuss too. Totally proper and classically Josh.

When they finally reach home, Verona feels a rush of affection for the familiarity of the driveway. Mum's car isn't there, which means that she must be at work. Ellery and Josh disappear upstairs to her room, holding hands, and not long after Verona goes to her own room, aware of the mountain of schoolwork she has to catch up on. She reminds herself sternly that exams are coming up in a few months, but it all feels distant somehow. It's like her mental voice is hungover; rather than its usual hectoring tone, it just sounds vague and lethargic. All year she has driven herself hard to do well and achieve top grades, but today she feels only apathy. There's a chemistry prac tomorrow and she knows she has to study, but she lies on her bed instead and re-reads *Harry Potter and the Prisoner of Azkaban*. When she hears Mum's footsteps on the stairs in the early evening, she quickly switches out the light and pretends to be asleep. Mum's shadow blocks the light from under the doorway as she pauses outside.

'Verona, darling? Are you awake?' Mum calls softly through the door, but Verona makes no noise. When the footsteps retreat downstairs, Verona switches the light back on and keeps reading.

---

Hunger eventually drives her downstairs. Ellery and Josh have migrated to the television, and Mum is in her study, but there are leftovers from dinner in the kitchen. Verona spoons the lukewarm fish stew into a bowl and eats it standing at the sink. She can barely taste what she's eating but it eases some of the hollow feeling in her stomach. When the phone rings, Mum answers it from the other room. From the way she exclaims and the happy note in her voice, Verona knows that it must be Uncle Erik on the other end. Verona never liked phone calls much—they always felt awkward without any body language cues to read—but she likes them even less now. She has barely touched her mobile since Gertrude's phone call the previous week.

It was getting on for five o'clock on Friday afternoon and Verona was in a cafe. She should have been at home studying—those final, insurmountable exams always looming—but she couldn't concentrate. So she had left her textbooks at home and come to sit and eat slightly dry carrot cake while staring out the window at the traffic on Beach Road. When her mobile rang and Gertrude's name flashed up onto the screen, Verona felt everything inside her constrict: she had had this reaction since April, when things started looking serious. A phone call always meant news—and that day Verona thought she almost knew what might be coming. She hurried outside before answering.

'He's gone, Verona,' said her stepmother, in her scratchy chain-smoker's voice. 'At three forty-six pm. It was peaceful. He'd been in and out of consciousness all day. He just drifted off to sleep in the morning and never woke up.'

Verona said nothing. Even though the news was expected and inevitable, she nonetheless felt the emptiness of shock resounding within her, its hollow drumbeat echoing through her torso. The gentle drift to endless sleep, the so-called perfect way to die: peaceful and painless. Yet the image of her father drifting so passively into oblivion was somehow disturbing. *Rage, rage against the dying of the light.*

'When's the . . . funeral?' Verona asked eventually into the silence at the other end, disliking every syllable of the word—cutting it down to two, rather than three.

'Next Friday,' Gertrude said. 'I'll call you back with the details when I've made the arrangements. Will you tell your sister?'

Gertrude rarely called Ellery by name.

'Yes,' Verona said. 'We'll both be there.' But she had wondered whether this would turn out to be a lie.

The call ended and Verona had stared sightlessly at her phone. Last call: three and a half minutes the screen told her. She was just outside the cafe window. Inside, laughter belled out and the overhead lights were bright. A baby in a pram shook his rattle and the milk steamer hissed. She could see her leftover carrot cake on the table, largely uneaten, the buttercream smeared all around the elegant painted flowers of the porcelain. That sickly sweetness was now rolled up in her throat and she turned away from the window, walking home along Beach Road, her thoughts as smudged as the icing.

When she got to the house, Mum was still at work, but Ellery's car was in the driveway. She let herself in and wandered through the living room. This place was the same as ever. And yet so much had changed in the brief hours since she came home and threw down her schoolbag. Her mind kept replaying Gertrude's hoarse voice and the words *he's gone*, but Verona felt oddly detached. The chest-crushing pressure of anguish lay within her somewhere, but it was hovering out of sight. I should cry, she thought vaguely, but no tears came.

Verona searched the ground floor for her sister, but the sofa was empty and the rooms had an undisturbed feel—not just quiet, but still. Yet when she got to the kitchen, the kettle was warm and Ellery's canvas satchel was lying on a chair. Verona headed upstairs for the bedroom and, as she reached the carpeted landing, she heard the low hum of talk through the open sliver beneath the door. It was too indistinct to make out words, but Verona recognised Josh's voice by now. She knocked.

'Come in,' said Ellery, some private laughter still lingering in her voice. 'Oh, hello!' she said when she saw Verona's face appear around the door. Ellery and Josh were sitting on the floor together, mugs of tea cupped in their hands, surrounded by a stack of law textbooks and open notebooks that they did not seem to be reading. They were both fully dressed, but with bare feet. Verona always thought that feet, in their ugliness, were somehow such an intimate part of a person to see—she averted her eyes from Josh's pale instep and long toes.

'Hey there, Verona.' Josh smiled at her.

'Hi. Ellery, can I talk to you for a sec?' Verona kept her eyes on her sister. Her face felt tight and aching, stretched like cling wrap.

'Sure.' Ellery got to her feet and followed Verona out of the room.

They walked back downstairs to the kitchen and hovered at the table, facing one another.

'What's up?' Ellery asked. Her lips had fallen out of their usual upwards curve and there was a faint crease between her eyebrows.

Verona hesitated. What should she say? She had never been the bearer of this sort of news before. And this was someone important—not a friend or an acquaintance, but their own father. The words, when they came, slammed into the air.

'Dad died,' she said.

Ellery exhaled, slow and deep. It was strange seeing the news on Ellery's face—Verona couldn't help wondering if she had looked like that too. Probably not. She had felt airless, breathless, like all the oxygen had instantly been siphoned from her body. Ellery just looked suddenly tired. She pressed the palm of her hand to her forehead.

'Today?'

'This afternoon.'

'Oh, Verona, I'm sorry.'

'He was your dad too.'

'Yeah, but we had a different relationship.'

At once, the tears were there—behind Verona's eyes and then overflowing. Ellery made a small sound and came closer to throw an arm around Verona's shoulders.

'I'm sorry,' Ellery said again and this time, choked by a sadness that she suddenly could not stem, Verona simply nodded. Verona had never been a crier. This hot rush of water and emotion surprised her. The whole time, Ellery kept squeezing her shoulders tight.

After a minute, Verona pushed her away and scrubbed the back of her hand over her nose and eyes.

'I should go look at flights to Brisbane,' she said.

'Just leave it, V. We'll look at it together tomorrow.'

'You'll come?'

'Yes, I'll come.'

'Okay, we'll figure it out tomorrow.'

'Hey, do you want to join me and Josh this evening?'

'Looks like you're busy.'

'Not at all, we're just chatting and talking nonsense, but we might play a game of Scrabble later?'

'I don't think so, but thanks all the same. I'll see you later.'

Ellery was frowning, but she nodded. 'We're here if you change your mind.'

The sisters left the kitchen in silence and parted company at the top of the stairs. Ellery squeezed the bony edge of Verona's shoulder once more before returning to her room and Josh. Verona could not catch the words, but muffled voices carried dully through the closed door. She listened for a moment, half-hoping to catch a strain of the conversation, then stopped herself and walked to her empty bedroom. There, she lay on the bed's patchwork quilt cover and tried to make it all real in her mind.

Forty minutes later, Mum had been knocking on her door—Ellery must've called her. Who knew knuckles rapped against wood could sound so gentle?

Mum called her name through the door. 'May I come in?'

'If you want to.'

Mum sat on the bed, her eyes fixed on Verona's face.

'How are you feeling, sweetheart?' she asked, so unfailingly maternal. It was hard sometimes to even see Mum as a real person anymore. To Verona, she was often an entity, a presence: Mother. Dad, with his quirks and flaws, had been the easier parent to be around. Mum was mostly just irritating.

'I feel like my father just died.'

Mum reached out a hand and tucked one of the short wavy strands of Verona's hair back from her face and behind her ear.

'He loved you very much,' she said quietly to her youngest daughter. 'It's going to be a challenging time. Always remember that it's okay not to be okay.'

'How insightful,' Verona snapped. 'If you don't have anything more useful than fortune cookie wisdom, you should go. I'd prefer to be alone.' Her voice quavered on the last word and suddenly those tears were back and overflowing. First with her sister and now with her mother. Until today, they'd probably only seen her cry twice between them in the last ten years. But Mum didn't leave. 'Please,' Verona said, and this time her voice was thick. 'Please go away.'

But Mum didn't go anywhere. She half-scooped Verona's thin frame off the bed like a toddler and wrapped her in a big hug. And Verona, sickened with sadness and shame, gave over and really cried.

In the morning, the tears seemed to be gone—she was dry-eyed and determined to remain that way. Josh was still in the house. He padded into the kitchen in pyjama bottoms and a white t-shirt while Verona was spreading Nutella on her toast. He flicked the little red switch on the kettle with a familiarity which grated on Verona.

He turned to her. 'How are you doing?' His voice was slightly raised to be audible above the kettle, but sympathetic, and his face was twisted into an appropriate expression.

'Fine,' she replied, shrugging.

'I was really sorry to hear the news.'

'Thanks.'

'I can't imagine what you must be feeling—I'd be a mess if it was my old man,' he tried again.

'Well, I'm not a mess,' she said.

The repressive tone made its point, but Josh didn't seem offended. He simply nodded, his eyes soft and understanding, and set about making coffee.

'You take extra care of yourself, okay?' Josh called over his shoulder as he went back upstairs with two mugs.

Verona stared after him, frowning. Mum quite liked him, but Verona was underwhelmed. He wore plaid shirts and used highlighter in his textbooks. He had a part-time job as a bartender and took Ellery out for dinner on the weekends when he wasn't rostered to work. Ellery had had boyfriends since she was fifteen, but there was something different about the way she was behaving around Josh. They had only been together for a few months, since meeting in their first torts class, but there was the halo of potential burning brightly around them. *He's a good guy*, Ellery liked to say, but Verona wondered whether that was really enough. Shouldn't interesting be more important than good?

Unlike Josh, still in his night clothes, Verona was already fully dressed. When she'd finished her toast, she left the house. In the middle of the night she had remembered not paying for her coffee and cake in the cafe—she had not gone back inside after Gertrude's call. She made a blushing return to the cafe now.

'I'm sorry about yesterday,' she muttered as she handed over the money she owed. She recognised the girl at the till from the day before; she was only a year or two older than Verona. 'I wasn't thinking clearly—I'd just found out my father died.'

Verona had wondered whether they would even believe her explanation, but she needn't have worried. The eyes of the girl behind the counter widened in shock and sympathy. She dropped Verona's coins on the counter like they were scalding her.

'Oh, sweetie!' she exclaimed. 'I'm so sorry to hear that. Don't worry about yesterday at all. It's on the house. In fact . . .' The girl ducked sideways to the cake counter and pulled out a fat golden muffin with raspberries studding the top. She cast a nervous glance over her shoulder, but the manager was out the back in the kitchen. 'From me,' she whispered. She waved away Verona's protest. 'My mother died three years ago and it broke my heart. A muffin won't help, but it won't hurt either.'

'Thank you,' Verona muttered.

But the girl's eyes were out of focus. 'I miss my mum every fucking day,' she whispered.

This was Verona's first experience of the way death draws out hidden stories—a moment of strange authenticity with a stranger.

The kitchen swims back into view, with Verona clutching an empty bowl of stew. She looks around at the familiar mugs on the dishrack and inhales the lemongrass scent of a candle Ellery must be burning. She can hear Mum in the other room, still chatting to Uncle Erik. This place feels the same as ever, yet everything is completely different. This is a world without Dad.

# chapter twenty-one

BUT NOW NORMALITY must resume. After the weekend in Brisbane, it's straight back into daily life for everyone.

On Monday morning, Ellery and Josh have an early lecture. They leave the house around the same time as Verona, except they're in jeans and driving a car. Verona tugs at the hem of her tartan skirt: Next year I'll be at uni too. But for now she catches the bus to school, arriving just before the bell for first classes. The students she passes in the hallways wouldn't usually pay her much attention, but today most of them smile at her. Above their curved mouths, their eyes are nervous and unsure. How do the grief-stricken act? Will she suddenly fall to pieces on the way to trigonometry? The teachers also look apprehensive. She feels them staring at her when she bends her head to take notes, but no words are forthcoming. Except from Mr Caine, the maths teacher, who pulls her aside at the end of the morning's class. Mr Caine is her favourite teacher. He wears knitted sweaters in geometric patterns and commands the class in such a way that nobody ever whispers an aside or passes a note.

'Are you okay?' he asks.

Verona finds she doesn't mind the question. He meets her eyes squarely and, rather than being steeped in the kind of sympathy she finds cloying, the question is toneless.

'I'm fine. Thanks.'

'Do you need any extensions with your work?'

'No.'

'Then hop to it.'

He ushers her out the door.

At lunch Verona sits with her friends at the picnic table by the east entry, in their usual horseshoe shape. Her friends, too, are hesitant. They do not meet her eyes, but glance at each other instead. They're a mixed bunch—a ragtag group of people who didn't quite fit anywhere else. Tommy is into theatre and Claire likes art. Charlie and Luke are maths people, like Verona, while Yumiko is passionate about history. Misfits and oddballs, but somehow the dynamic seems to work okay. There are no drunken parties, only orderly gatherings to play board games or trips to the cinema. Good eggs, to the teachers. Fucking weirdos, to the other kids.

'How was, um, you know—Brisbane?'

An entire world of meaning contained within that word. Brisbane, no longer just a city—now a euphemism for her dead father.

'It was okay.' Verona shrugs, not knowing how to explain or what parts of the trip to discuss. The dead face in the coffin? The tinny sound of bad eulogies trying to be funny? None of these things can really be shared. In the space of a weekend, she has acquired a new knowledge that the others do not yet have. Maybe if she had Dad's gift for storytelling she might be able to recount the funeral parlour scenes. But, then, not even Dad has Dad's gift as a raconteur anymore. That ability is in a million particles of dust, to be scattered across Moreton Bay with the rest of him.

The others look at her with the soft eyes she associates with pity and silence snuffs the group's usual chatter. Eventually, however, conversation reignites as Charlie starts talking about his French essay. The conversation drifts onwards and Verona's sad story is forgotten. Everyone has their own worlds to be dipping back into—their minds turning to crushes walking across the quadrangle, Friday night plans and the pluperfect conjugations of être. Verona nibbles at the edge of her cheese sandwich, half-listening to the conversation which has flowed into a discussion of a comedy show the others saw on the weekend. They retell jokes that aren't funny out of context. Tommy mentions that his father picked him up from the station before breaking off mid-sentence with a horrified look in Verona's direction.

'I'm so sorry, V,' he stammers. 'I shouldn't have said that.'

The word 'father' has suddenly become taboo.

'Don't worry about it,' Verona assures him. 'I wasn't really listening anyway.'

The others laugh, unsure whether or not she's joking. They all belong to wholesome nuclear units, Kmart catalogue families with beach balls, deck chairs and perfect orthodontia. Only Claire's parents are divorced too. And Verona knows just two other people at school who have lost parents—one guy in her year and a girl two years below. She thinks she can see some kinship in their eyes when they pass her in the corridors later that day. Verona had always felt slightly awkward around them: they had known something she hadn't, something unimaginable. But now she knows too.

—

She mentions this to Ellery when they both raid the pantry for a pre-dinner snack that afternoon. Peanut butter and banana on corn thins. Mum and Conner won't be home for another hour or two and there's an ice-cream container of dhal defrosting on the counter. Verona gets excited by the caramel swirl label for a second, but recoils when she lifts the lid and peers inside. Yuck. How boring.

Ellery listens sympathetically, but she doesn't really understand—it's easier for her on campus, where the anonymity of three hundred people in a law lecture means that nobody knows enough to feel sorry for her. Ellery's tutors at uni have been advised of the circumstances, but her classmates don't know anything. She can simply slide into the gentle slipstream of anonymity.

'Uni is so much better than school,' she says with a sigh, and Verona feels the familiar prickle of envy. 'Don't worry about your friends, V. They won't understand or know how to act, but that's okay. You just have to recognise that they're trying their best and that they care about you.'

---

Her friends' strange behaviour continues for the rest of the week, with sudden pauses in conversation and glances at Verona whenever someone mentions their father.

But, then, Verona isn't quite sure how to behave either.

Aunty Maeve calls to invite her to the movies on the weekend. Verona agrees, even though she knows it's a ploy to distract her and get her out of the house. On the car ride to the cinema, she stares out the window, struggling to focus on the thread of conversation that swims in and out of her hearing.

'Do you agree, Verona?' she hears Aunty Maeve ask from the driver's seat and flounders to find her voice.

'Yeah, of course,' she mumbles, with no idea what she is agreeing to.

And in the darkened theatre she shares a box of popcorn with Aunty Maeve's twelve-year-old son, only realising at the end of the movie that she has snatched the entire box from the armrest onto her lap and eaten all the popcorn herself. 'Sorry,' she mutters to the boy, brushing popcorn salt off her fingers as Maeve's son watches with crossed arms.

Uncle Erik also calls to check in. Verona sees the Sydney number flash on her screen and feels a rush of gladness.

'How are you doing, kiddo?' His voice is deep and steady. Like Maeve, he has maintained separate relationships with Verona and Ellery since they were kids. He's more avuncular with them than their real uncles—Verona prefers him to Patrick. Erik gives better presents too—generally Apple products.

'Corporate law has its upsides,' Mum observed dryly when Verona unwrapped a brand new iPod last birthday.

'I've been better,' Verona tells Erik now.

'You'll miss him terribly.'

'Yeah.'

'He was an interesting man. I wish we'd been better friends—he never liked me much, you know.'

'Really?' She already knew this. Dad always referred to Erik as 'the Suit'.

'Benjamin always saw my job as selling out.'

'Law?'

'Working in the corporate sector.'

'Well, I want to do public law,' Verona says and, even through the telephone, she can hear that Erik is smiling.

'Remember that I'm here anytime you need.'

---

On Saturday night, Claire hosts a small gathering at her house. Verona's group doesn't use the word 'party'—it's only ever a gathering. Verona is managing to be cheerful and light-hearted, until she spots a painting of purple irises hanging on one cream wall. It's a twenty-dollar Van Gogh poster produced en masse by the National Gallery of Victoria for one of their exhibitions many years ago, and bought by hundreds of people all around

Melbourne. And yet those stupid purple flowers and cursed green stalks bring the immediate memory of Dad, who had that exact same print hanging in a hallway of his home—a present from their mother, she suspects. Verona can almost feel the industrial-type carpet of Gertrude's place under bare feet and hear Dad grinding coffee in the kitchen, cigarette smoke curling through the house. She stops, ragdoll limp, staring at the undulating shapes she can almost see in the air. Around her, her friends laugh and push the speaker volume to the max so they can sing loud, but she has been left behind.

Back at home, she tells this to Ellery. They've been talking a bit more in the week since their trip to Brisbane. Ellery has poked her head around the doorway to Verona's room a couple of times in the past few days. When she tried to do this in the past, somehow it never worked; they'd chat uncomfortably for a few minutes until Ellery gave up and left or Verona shooed her away, insisting that she needed her space. But twice now Ellery has sat cross-legged on Verona's shaggy rug and somehow Verona doesn't mind having her there so much.

Her sister would never freak out over that picture of irises. When Verona first mentions it, Ellery's eyes go hazy for a second—memory straining—and although she nods again a second later, Verona realises that her sister doesn't remember the picture at all. Nonetheless, Ellery nods and makes her face sympathetic. Ellery tends not to say much when Verona talks about Dad; she just listens. Occasionally her lips part and she looks like she is drawing breath to speak, but a moment later she always shuts her mouth again.

'Go easy on yourself,' Ellery says when Verona is finished. 'Grief affects everyone differently and you're allowed to behave a bit strangely.'

It sounds like something Ellery is repeating from Mum, and Verona looks askance at her sister. Have they been talking about her behind her back? Then again, Ellery tends naturally towards pompous sweeping statements. Adults have always called her 'wise beyond her years', but Verona thinks it simply sounds like pop psychology. Still, as the flicker of irritation passes through her, she remembers the feeling of Ellery's fingers squeezing her arm on a spindly chair in a funeral parlour, and she finds herself opening and then closing her mouth against the instinctive retort.

Drifting downstairs later that evening to get a glass of water from the kitchen when she wakes in the night, Verona overhears Mum's voice as she passes her mother's bedroom. She's whispering, but excitement makes it audible even from the foot of the stairs.

'. . . actually spending time together . . . I know, I don't believe it either, Maeve. My girls, actually friends! . . . What? . . . No, I don't want to push it too much. If they think I'm interfering . . . Yes, they seem to be figuring it out themselves . . .'

In the darkened hallway, Verona shakes her head. Mum thinks they don't see the smile she hides every time she sees her daughters together. Ah, Mum, thinks Verona.

—

Yet there have been other moments when Ellery and Verona are united. Sure, they've never been friends exactly, but flashes of connection occur between them at times.

Last summer holidays, Mum made an announcement. She insisted that the three of them sit down for brunch together. There was a fresh loaf of pumpkin seed bread and hard-boiled eggs on the table and everyone helped themselves. Mum and Ellery both like to sprinkle curry powder on their eggs, which Verona finds nauseatingly bizarre. Her taste in food has never quite aligned with theirs.

'How are you feeling about year twelve coming up?' Mum asked her.

'Fine.'

'It's normal to be nervous—all you can do is prepare as much as you can.'

'I'm already studying hard.'

'Yes, I know you are. But make sure you're also studying smart, rather than hard. It's really easy to put in hours that aren't necessarily effective. It's about the way you study as much as anything.'

'Thanks, but I don't need a lecture on academic study skills. Honestly, I don't even want to talk about it.'

Mum sighed. 'Very well—you know what you're doing.' There was a pause in which Verona had toyed with the crumbs on her plate and Ellery sipped her water. Then: 'There's something I'd like to discuss with you both.'

'What's that?' Ellery supplied the polite response while Verona stayed silent.

'I've decided that it's time to sell the house. In the next year or two, I'll be putting it on the market.'

Even Ellery was struck dumb by that. She gaped at their mother with her mouth in a tiny goldfish circle. 'This house?' she said eventually, her voice incredulous.

'Yes.'

'But why?'

'It's time,' Mum said. 'Places are like people—some aren't forever. I've loved our years here, but it's time for a change. Somewhere smaller, I think. This place is a bit big, especially with you girls growing up and moving on.'

'Is this because of Conner?' Verona demanded.

'No,' said their mother coolly. 'It's got nothing to do with him.'

'But what other reason could there be?' Verona asked. 'We don't want a change.'

For once, Ellery seemed to be in complete agreement, though she still wasn't saying anything, just gazing at their mother as if dumbfounded.

'What if we don't want to move?' Verona persisted.

'Think of it as an adventure,' Mum said after a pause.

'Where would we live instead?'

'I'm not sure yet. Somewhere in this vicinity.'

'If we're going to stay in the same area, why bother moving at all?'

But Mum just smiled. 'Change is a good thing.' She looked unsurprised by her daughters' reactions; they were not reaching her. She seemed unworried, as though she knew how the story ended.

'It's time to move forwards. Don't worry, nothing will happen until after Verona's exams. I'm expecting we'll be here for the next eighteen months or so, but I wanted to tell you now so that you can get used to the idea. This has been several years coming.'

'It isn't a good time,' Verona agreed.

The girls were both sitting with their arms crossed, united.

'It's never a good time. I'm sorry, girls, but it isn't up to you.'

And it dawned on them: Mum wasn't asking—she was telling them.

---

Is life ultimately a matter of surrender? This year keeps taunting Verona with how little she can control. But she is fine.

About everything.

At least, that's what she tells people. People still ask her about Dad from time to time—grave, solicitous and gentle.

'How are you doing? Are you okay?'

Of course, they don't expect her to say anything other than, *Yeah, I'm fine*. Asking is just protocol, it's etiquette, and she would be breaching the conventions herself if she said how she was actually feeling.

Heartache is physical, not metaphorical. She has never realised until now how sadness and anguish are born in the flesh itself. The mind is a mere conduit. The pain itself lives, breathes and writhes in the body: not thought, but felt. And about thirty different feelings layer her body:

The concavity of grief.

The desperate longing to talk to Dad again, which leads her to whisper to him sometimes in the middle of the night.

The hollow playback of his voice and the last things he said to her.

The padlocked treasure chest of childhood memories, locked up tight lest a memory slip away or become dulled from overuse, used sparingly like the good china.

The other memories that threaten to creep in—the missed birthdays and unreturned phone calls. *No*, she mustn't think of those now.

And in the night she thinks of the *bhoot* and wishes she truly believed that the dead could return to haunt the living; better to have Dad as a *bhoot* than to have no Dad at all.

But all she says to the people who ask is, *Yes, thanks for asking, I'm fine*. She is focusing on her studies and Getting On With Things. People look at her with admiration when she changes the subject and talks about schoolwork and clarinet lessons.

'You trooper!' they say with approval in their voices.

Trooper, so typically Australian. The highest compliment, and the antipodean equivalent of the stiff upper lip. We do not talk about feelings here.

At least her mind has returned.

Her period came a few days after Dad died and she'd forgotten to wear a pad. She had noticed the redness in the toilet bowl in the morning vacantly, but not as something that required action. Observed the blood like it was someone else's. She had left the house for the day. When she got home in the afternoon and saw her ruined underwear (thank goodness she'd worn dark pants), she'd been surprised. *What is happening to me?*

And now Verona is fine.

---

Life seems to go on as usual for Ellery, who maintains her ordered routine. She washes her hair every three days and changes her sheets weekly. Verona watches her bringing them in from the clothesline, trailing the scent of Omo. Josh's car is parked in the driveway most days, his shoes by the door. They have joined the French club this semester; Verona can hear them conjugating verbs out loud through Ellery's door. They rarely seem to be reading their legal texts.

Ellery never looks sad, though sometimes she looks tired; the area around her eyes is darker—though maybe that's the mascara she has taken to wearing this year. Does she, too, shed tears in the night for their lost parent? No, Verona cannot picture that.

Even though Verona is lost in a labyrinth of her own study, she looks at Ellery's blockish textbooks wistfully. Their titles convey a whole world of knowledge that remains out of reach. Verona's middling English grades still aren't there. But they will be. They must be. Her notebooks are webbed with perfect quadratic equations and essays with no topic sentence. Dad never read the school reports, but he laughed at how easily she could keep track of the total bill when they went grocery shopping.

'Are you sure law is the right choice for you?' Mum dared to ask her once at the beginning of the year.

Verona didn't talk to her for two days after that.

Verona is taking history, English, legal studies, maths, chemistry and physics. And every time she sits down at her desk to study, she thinks of next year and getting into the course she wants. Dad had been as surprised as Mum when she announced that she was intending to study law at university. He shook his head when she reeled off her subjects.

'Why don't you try for a Bachelor of Science? That sounds like something you'd be better suited to.'

'I don't think so.'

But now that the all-important final exams are drawing closer, she feels the weight of her own ambitions. Three months in which to bolster her flagging grades, to turn Bs into As and water into wine. The thought of failing to get into law when Ellery made the grade the year before turns her cold almost as much as Dad's coffin.

Each night after dinner, Verona studies downstairs at the kitchen table. The TV is usually on in the front room and noise floats out from it as Ellery and Josh watch movies. Every so often, Verona sighs pointedly, but no-one ever turns the volume down unless she specifically asks.

Ellery comes into the kitchen periodically to brew a pot of tea for herself and Josh.

'How's it going?' she asks Verona.

'Don't ask,' Verona replies.

'You'll get special consideration because of Dad,' Ellery reminds her. 'That'll make a difference. You don't need to burn yourself out; you've been here for hours.'

'I don't want to take any chances and I don't want to just scrape in,' Verona says. 'I want to do it on my own terms. I know I can do it.'

The kettle bubbles in the background. Ellery turns away and doesn't say anything.

---

Everyone in year twelve is being forced to sit down with the careers counsellor to ensure their dreams are bite-sized enough to swallow. No-one knows what to make of the word 'counsellor' and there is an outbreak of eye-rolling. Over the course of five days, the students are booked into fifteen-minute slots in alphabetical order based on their surnames. Verona doesn't have long to wait (compared to the Thompsons, Wallaces and Yangs), but she watches those with earlier appointments return from their consultations closely, looking for a clue. No-one says much—but, then, not many dare to voice their career ambitions aloud.

Mrs Royce turns out not to be the lady of cardigans and tissue boxes that everyone had expected. She has a spare face—all utilitarian lines and not a single frivolous curve—and conducts the consultations more like interviews. On Tuesday morning Verona sits outside Mrs Royce's small office, using the time to keep annotating her history textbook. Thinking of her patchwork transcript, Verona takes slow breaths. The counsellor cannot stop them enrolling in the university course of their choice, but she can frown, discourage and make doomsday predictions.

Thirty seconds before the consult is scheduled to begin, the door opens and Mrs Royce ushers Verona into her office. Verona takes the proffered seat and stares at her own unshined shoes.

'Law,' Mrs Royce says thoughtfully, thumbing through the Statement of Purpose Verona had to write in preparation for the meeting.

'Yes.' Verona is defiant. Here comes the lecture she has planned for and the chance to recite the answer she has already rehearsed in her mind. *Who cares what the transcript says? Just watch me—I'll get there.*

Verona has half-opened her mouth to retort, but Mrs Royce does not follow the script.

'Why?' the woman asks, putting the statement aside and looking squarely at Verona.

'Huh?'

'Why law?'

'I think it'd suit me. I've always wanted to do it.'

Mrs Royce considers this. 'Why does someone with excellent maths grades and an aptitude for science want to enter a profession which is all about language?'

'I—I think it would suit me.'

'Why?'

But that question causes only a dizzying emptiness in Verona's mind.

'I believe in the legal system and justice for all,' she stammers out. 'I think the law can—can do amazing things for those who need it. I mean, not just need it, but for people who might want it. I mean—'

Mrs Royce raises a hand to stop her. 'Just something to think about. You don't need to justify it to me, but I suggest getting your motivations clear in your head. Especially if you want to write a convincing application.'

'I'm very clear about why I—'

'Your grades aren't up to scratch,' Mrs Royce says bluntly, interrupting. 'But you know that already. I don't need to tell you how hard you'll need to work in the lead-up to exams to get what you want.' She gives a little speech on alternative pathways that Verona has heard before. *Start off in arts, transfer across, not the end of the world.* Verona nods politely and mentally discards the advice. When her fifteen minutes is up she stands and walks to the door.

'Thanks,' she says.

'And I also recommend you think about what you'll do,' Mrs Royce finishes.

'If I don't get in?'

'Yes. And if you *do* get in. Are you prepared to spend five years of your life reading cases and legislation?'

'I see,' says Verona. But she doesn't at all.

Her friends do not understand. When she returns from the meeting limp and wilting, they look at her in surprise.

'What are you so worried about? You'll get special consideration,' they tell her, echoing Ellery.

Yes, but special consideration still won't be enough to get her into the course she wants if her English grade isn't high. And this isn't how she wants to do things, anyway. She must get into law under her own steam, like everybody else before her.

But no-one at school has time for anyone else's angst—everyone has their own worries.

It's easier for Ellery, who has already applied for an extension on her mid-semester exams. They've been moved back a fortnight—a paltry kind of special consideration. But does Ellery even deserve it? She didn't have a relationship with Dad, so why does she get to benefit from his death? Ellery, with her picture-perfect life. She's always been the 'nice one'—Ellery tries to please, while Verona speaks her mind. Except when it comes to Dad, where their roles get reversed. Verona doesn't care that most people like her sister best. Though it hurt that Dad was so fixated on connecting with his eldest daughter, even while Verona sat beside him in the flesh. Besides, Ellery has always fit so very easily into this family of wordsmiths. It's been much harder for Verona. How come nobody seems to see that? It isn't fair.

# chapter twenty-two

THE MONDAY MORNING maths class is soothing as always. It's a knitted blanket around her shoulders, a lavender-scented candle, the colour aquamarine. She can lose herself in the rhythm of her pencil on the page and the tapping of her calculator. Clarinet is the only other thing that makes her feel so relaxed.

When the bell rings, the others hurry out of the classroom to their lunch boxes, but Verona always takes time to pack her things. As she struggles with the zip on her pencil case, Mr Caine walks over to her and sits on the next bench.

'I hear you're applying for law,' he says.

Verona frowns. 'Where did you hear that?'

'These things get around.'

'The careers counselling sessions are private.'

Mr Caine ignores this. 'I don't give career advice, of course. It isn't my place. But I will say that I was surprised. You're very talented, Verona. You have a gift with numbers.'

'Thanks.'

'And I know it's not just in my classes—I hear you're doing very well in physics and chemistry too. Have you considered a degree that's more orientated towards maths? A Bachelor of Science might be something to look into.'

'You sound like my mother.'

This too is ignored. 'There's beauty in maths,' he insists. 'And value in numbers. Law isn't the only way to do something meaningful.'

'I'm not doing it because it's meaningful.'

The lines on his face are pronounced now, especially between his eyebrows. 'Then why?'

Verona opens her mouth and, as she does, realises once again she has nothing to say.

Apparently encouraged by her silence, Mr Caine hands her a flier. The background is lolly pink and the lettering is fuchsia. 'There's this event next week that I thought might interest you.'

'*Women in STEM,*' Verona reads aloud. 'What's this?'

'It's a breakfast. It's meant to encourage more women to participate in the hard sciences. There's still a gender imbalance. We've arranged for some guest speakers to come in—a physio and a pharmacist.'

'You just need a physicist and you'll have all the makings of a dad joke.'

'I think you should come along. You'll get a free breakfast and hear some interesting perspectives. At the very least, there will be croissants.'

'Why do they even call it the hard sciences anyway? Doesn't that imply a value judgement or some kind of hierarchy?'

'Just come and listen.'

'Okay.'

Verona folds the flyer into a square and tucks it into her books. But she doesn't write the event in her diary and when next week comes around, she forgets all about it. It's only when she sees the posters being taken down around school the next day that she remembers. She feels a flush of guilt and cannot meet Mr Caine's eyes.

---

There is another gathering on Friday, at Claire's place again. After a week of studying, the group is keen to relax over salt and vinegar chips and Vanilla Coke. When Mum drops Verona off, music is playing and most people have already arrived.

Claire's parents are out and the lack of supervision has created its own atmosphere that diffuses through every room. It's a slightly bigger group tonight and there are a few new faces, including a boy in black jeans and green jumper. He is sitting with Tommy on the sofa. From the moment Verona arrives, his eyes swivel to her and she feels a small thrill. Boys don't usually look at her that way. Without realising, she brings her fingers up to tuck a wayward curl behind her ear and she can feel how her walk is more swaying. She moves around the room, greeting her friends and grabbing a drink. All the while he watches her and she feigns indifference while observing him from the corner of her eye.

Half an hour later, she hears him ask, 'Who's the brown girl?'

Verona freezes. The adjective sounds surreal said out loud. Me? Verona looks down at her hands with their caramel hue. Oh yeah.

Nobody else seems perturbed. None of her friends' expressions change.

'That's Verona,' says Tommy.

'Hey there, brown girl,' the new boy calls to her. 'Come talk to me.'

'No, thank you.' Verona crosses her arms. She draws herself up taller and feels her body stiffen. 'And don't call me that.'

'Why not?'

'Because I don't like it.'

'But it's true.'

*It's not,* Verona wants to argue back. *I don't look any different to anyone else.* But as she looks once again at her hands curled around her can of Coke, the retort falls away.

'I'm not insulting you,' the boy tries to clarify. 'I like it. I'm just stating a fact.'

Verona turns on her heel and does not look at him again.

At home later that night, she scrutinises her face in the bedroom mirror. Black hair, dark eyes and, yes, brown skin. She is not as dark as their mother, but she does not share the pale pink colouring of her school friends. The mixed heritage of Mum and Dad, their union, is built into her face. How has she not realised this before now? She feels the heat of shame on her cheeks like she has been caught pretending—an imposter sprung in the act. But could she really not have known? Unlike Ellery, who has always embraced Mum's history, Verona has only ever thought of herself as an Aussie girl. Maybe it isn't that she never realised—maybe it's that she didn't want to accept it.

'It's part of your heritage, V,' Mum had always told Verona. 'You might find that it matters to you one day—it's the other half of who you are.'

But things only seem to be getting less clear as she gets older.

—

In September, a package comes in the mail. Large and too heavy to lift, it needs to be wheeled inside the front door by the courier on a little red trolley. It's late in the afternoon and Verona and Ellery are home. They hover around the box like kids, exchanging glances charged with excitement. Ellery peers at the sender.

'West End,' she says. 'Gertrude's address. Well, that'll be for you. Open it!' She moves out of the way and Verona places her own hands on the box. Yes, those are Gertrude's blockish letters. Verona starts tearing at the flaps of the cardboard impatiently, but her fingers scrabble fruitlessly against layers of masking tape. She cannot find an edge to slide her nails underneath.

'Calm,' says Ellery, with a laugh that sounds slightly alarmed. She ducks out of the room and returns with a Stanley knife. 'Here.'

Verona snatches it, slits the opaque tape and opens the top flaps of the box. Both girls peer into it. At the top are a few books—naval histories and science fiction novels, which Verona remembers seeing on Dad's shelf at various times—and underneath them is the *Oxford English Dictionary* in all its glory.

'Oh, wow.' Verona is breathless. She is already picturing them on her bookshelf—a little piece of Dad to stay with her forever. As she reaches to pick up the first volume, a small white envelope flutters to the floor.

Verona picks it up. But it isn't addressed to her. It's for Ellery. Puzzled, she holds it out to her sister. Ellery looks surprised; her eyes widen and she looks apprehensive. She opens the envelope, pulls out a note, reads it and then hands it to Verona, who reads it too.

> Ellery—
>
> Your father wanted you to have the dictionary. He thought that you might find it useful in your legal studies. I've included a few of his novels for Verona.

There is a long silence which congeals around them.

'There must be some mistake,' Verona says.

'Yeah, maybe,' Ellery agrees. Her voice is beige and neutral.

'Gertrude must've got it wrong. Dad wouldn't do that—he knew those books meant something to me.'

'Did you ever actually tell him that?' asks Ellery hesitantly.

'Yes! Several times.'

'Maybe he didn't remember.'

'He definitely would've remembered!'

'Benjamin's memory wasn't always the most reliable. Don't you think it's possible that he just . . . forgot?'

'No! This is Gertrude's fault!' Verona shouts. 'And now you've got the books. And you didn't even like him. You don't deserve them.'

These are the kind of words that can be felt as soon as they are spoken—the kind with a physical presence, that hang jaggedly and change the very air around them. Corrosive words, vinegar words. But Verona feels only bitterness and fire. And whatever Ellery feels she isn't showing.

'You can have the books—take them, they're yours,' Ellery says, her voice conciliatory. She drops Gertrude's note back into the box. She begins to walk away, but then pauses at the foot of the stairs. 'Verona,' she says, looking back, 'sooner or later you'll have to face the real Benjamin.'

With that, Ellery walks back upstairs to her room, leaving Verona standing in the hallway, with a coil of used masking tape at her feet and a stack of books she no longer feels entitled to.

---

Fuming in her room, having abandoned the box in the hallway, Verona finds herself thinking back to Uncle Patrick's wedding.

He'd got remarried a few years ago—sent out lilac invitations, calligraphic and edged in gold. Both girls were invited to the wedding ceremony and reception. Granny Agnes did not at all approve of the estrangement between Ellery and their dad, making her displeasure known in discordant tones. She calls her son irresponsible and her granddaughter callous.

'I would like to clunk their heads together,' Verona had heard Granny Agnes say.

Patrick was more measured and tried to keep in touch with both his nieces, scrupulously not taking sides.

'There's enough room for everyone,' he liked to say.

The wedding was being held at Uncle Patrick's house, and when Verona and Ellery stood on the nature strip outside, looking at the low-slung gate and front door beyond it, there was a thrum in the air. Maybe it was because they knew that the house was full of people, but it was as if they could sense the presence of a crowd within.

Uncle Patrick had answered the door when they knocked. 'Hello, girls—glad you could come,' he said.

'Uncle Patrick! It's your big day.' Verona leaned forwards to hug him.

'Congratulations,' Ellery murmured. 'We're glad we could be here.' Her voice was so formal that Verona stared at her, but Uncle Patrick's smile was gentle and understanding.

They followed Patrick down the hallway to the party. As they entered the living room, they heard many called-out greetings and exclamations. A few people raised their eyebrows in surprise at seeing Ellery—she had long avoided events that their father would be attending.

Dad was already there, standing by one of the long windows and looking out to Patrick's small garden, with its English lavender and lime trees. Verona had rushed towards him for a hug. He looked up when she came near and let out a whoop of delight, squeezing her tight.

'How's my Monkey?'

She could feel the Marlboro pack in his breast pocket when she hugged him and see his fingers moving restlessly, obviously itching for a cigarette. Probably why he was standing next to the window pane.

'I'm good,' Verona told him. 'Where's Gertrude?'

'Getting a glass of wine.'

'Hmm. Better hope she doesn't run into Ellery.'

'Elly's here?' Dad's voice was surprised.

'Yeah, didn't you know?'

'I knew Patrick had invited her, but I didn't think she'd come.' He scanned the crowd. 'Where is she?'

'Over there.' Verona nodded in Ellery's direction and Dad looked over.

Across the room, Ellery turned pointedly away and began talking to one of their cousins.

'Wonder if she'll come over.'

'I wouldn't count on it, Dad,' Verona muttered apologetically. But she also felt a hot prickle sweeping her cheeks. Like kiwifruit skin.

*I'm here*, she wanted to say. But she didn't.

Dad seemed to sense some of this. 'Ah, well.' Shrugging, he put an arm around her and squeezed her sideways. 'At least I've got one of you.'

When Aunty Martha came over to talk to Dad, Verona slipped away to her sister. Ellery had finished with cousin small talk and was filling a paper plate with salmon blinis.

'Can't you just make nice?' Verona asked. 'He'd love it if you went and said hello.'

'I'm sure he would. But no and no.'

Across the room, Aunty Martha moved on and Dad took a few steps in his daughters' direction. Ellery, noticing this, grabbed Verona's hand and dragged her outside through a crush of people. Dad stopped, his face crestfallen, and Verona wondered which way she ought to be walking.

For the entire afternoon, Dad and Ellery performed a slow dance around the room—Dad always moving closer and Ellery marching away. Their movements may as well have been choreographed: they wound one by one around the platters of blue cheese and Waterford crackers, past the mantelpiece with its row of family photos, and circled the L-shaped sofa. It was Ellery first and then Dad, five minutes later, slowly tracing her steps. She never stopped moving, never let him catch her.

Except Dad had never played by the rules. Ellery wove ceaselessly through uncles, aunts, cousins, family friends, but did not appear to expect their father to suddenly emerge right in front of her.

'Hello, Benjamin,' Ellery said.

'Ellery, it's so nice to see you. Look at you, all grown up.'

The words were wistful. Even watching from a few metres away, Verona could see how hard he was trying, but Ellery just stared at him. She didn't say a word, just stood silently with closed lips and narrowed eyes.

Dad tried again. 'I think about you often, you know. You and your sister are always with me. I've got a photo of your first day at school on my bedside table.'

And he did—Verona had seen it. But Ellery had nothing to say to that either.

'Excuse me,' she said and walked away.

Dad just watched her go. And Verona watched Dad.

'He doesn't look good, does he?' Ellery whispered to Verona later, distaste on her face. 'He looks melted.'

Dad might be carrying a bit more weight than when they were kids, and his skin was more mottled, but Verona couldn't see what Ellery saw. His face was ruined and red, according to Ellery—each cheek, a bouquet of capillaries—with browned smoker's teeth.

The wedding ceremony itself had been nice. Ellery stood on the other side of the room to their father but he did not try to approach her again.

At the reception, Dad and Gertrude smoked outside, while Ellery stayed inside nibbling on the canapés. Verona mostly stayed with Dad. And nobody said anything more about it.

Now, pacing in her room, the memory of that day fills her with rage. Why had she bothered trying to smooth things over? Ellery hadn't cared and Dad hadn't noticed. But this time the hot rush isn't just centred on her sister—it is spreading outwards and beyond.

---

Verona hasn't raised the subject of the house with Mum again, but she intends to. She can't quite believe that Mum will go through with it. It therefore comes as quite a surprise when she returns home from school one afternoon to find a man in an expensive suit finishing a cup of coffee in their living room. He wears a silver watch and has the kind of salesman's smile she generally associates with the lawyers in her mother's office: shiny and full of teeth. Verona nods an uneasy hello and skulks in the corridor, listening as he tells Mum he'll be in touch. When he leaves, Verona comes back into the room. The man's half-drunk black coffee is on the table, along with a sheaf of brochures and documents. Mum closes the front door behind the man and comes back into the room. She is humming to herself and smiles when she sees her youngest daughter.

'How was school?' she asks.

'Fine. Who was the guy?'

'A real estate agent having a look at the property. I'm just starting to make some enquiries—nothing is happening yet.'

Verona opens her mouth to object, but it's somehow hard to interrupt Mum's humming. It sounds like 'Chiquitita'.

'Feel like a cup of tea?' Mum asks. She's smiling and Verona can see plans behind her eyes.

'No,' Verona snaps, but she doesn't say all the things she's been thinking. Instead, she goes upstairs. It feels good to slam her door closed.

---

The sisters haven't crossed paths much at home the past week or so. Not since Gertrude's package. It's almost a pity. It had been kind of nice having Ellery knock on her bedroom door to say hello and getting a lift to clarinet lessons with her. Weirdly, Ellery is the only one with whom Verona has felt genuinely comfortable discussing

Dad lately. She doesn't know where to start with anybody else and their discomfort and confusion is too apparent to her, written on their face: *Should I ask? Should I not?* But Ellery gets it.

Ellery has been mostly in her bedroom with Josh when Verona gets home from school. Dinnertimes are no longer always a family affair—Ellery and Josh cook together and sit on the couch eating. There is a world of whispered words and private jokes, with only room for two. Josh is almost living at their place—he's around nearly as much as Conner. Sometimes their mother can talk the couple into joining the dinner table like civilised adults, but mostly it's just Verona, Mum and Conner. Mum often cooks curries, which Ellery loves and Verona hates.

But on Sunday afternoon, ten days after Gertrude's parcel arrived, Verona knocks on her sister's door. This is rare.

'Come in,' Ellery calls.

When Verona's head appears around the doorframe, Ellery's inflection goes up in the middle.

'Verona? What are you doing here? Is everything okay?'

Ellery is sitting at her desk but has swivelled around in her chair to face her sister. She is alone, but Josh's clothes are folded on the pillow and his tennis racquet is beside the door.

'Yeah. Where's your boyfriend?'

'At work. Come in.' Ellery turns back to her computer and finishes off a sentence of what looks like an essay. She knows better than to make a big deal of this visit. Verona sinks down into the lime green beanbag in the corner of the room and studies Ellery's books. She shrugs off the satchel still slung over her shoulder.

'How are you doing?' Ellery asks, as she hits the full stop button and turns back around.

'I'm okay,' Verona says. Somehow it's a more honest answer than *I'm fine*.

Ellery nods. 'Yeah, me too.'

'Ellery?'

'Mm?'

'I'm sorry.'

When Ellery doesn't say anything, Verona tries again.

'I'm sorry,' she repeats. 'I was really unfair. I've been thinking about it.' She takes a deep breath and fishes a heavy book out of her bag. The first volume of the dictionary. 'These belong to you. I've got the others waiting in my room for you and you should take them.'

Ellery glances at the book and shakes her head. 'I don't want them, Verona; they don't mean anything to me. They're yours—keep them.'

Verona puts the book on her sister's carpet and they both stare at the glossy cover.

'I keep thinking about Dad,' Verona whispers. 'Do you?'

Ellery fiddles with the edge of her seat cushion, plucking at the fraying fabric.

'It's confusing for me,' she says eventually. 'But it's more difficult for you. We haven't lost the same parent.'

Verona considers this. 'Have you heard from Granny Agnes?' she asks. She herself has had a couple of text messages. Granny Agnes has never shied away from technology—she got dial-up early and has read up on a new product called Kindle which is meant to be released next year. Imagine having a whole library in your pocket!

'No, I just saw Agnes from afar at Benjamin's funeral.' And even then, their grandmother had avoided Ellery.

But that isn't what troubles Verona.

'I wish you wouldn't call him that,' she hisses.

'Benjamin? I've called him that for years.'

'Why can't you just call him Dad? It's so contrived.'

'No, it's honest.'

And there goes that temper, flaring to life. Verona remembers watching Dad light a fire once when they went camping overnight—she can recall the whoosh of kindling catching flame and the sudden inferno, not red, orange or gold but some coppery melange of all those shades. That is Verona's anger.

'And you were such a sweet kid.' Unusually for Ellery, the tone is sarcastic. Words hurled in anger many years ago suddenly flood into Verona's mind: *That's because you're a puppy dog.*

'He wasn't a father to me and I'm not going to call him that,' Ellery says.

'So he missed a couple of school concerts.' Verona is defensive. 'So what?'

'Come on, he wasn't available at all.'

'Well, who cares if he didn't call us every night? He was a wonderful father.'

But Ellery simply looks at her and there's pity in her sister's face. There's sadness there too, but a distant sort of sadness—like the kind you'd feel reading a history book about people who died two hundred years ago. A shallow sadness which cannot grow roots inside your belly.

'No, V. No he wasn't.' Ellery doesn't say it angrily—she says it so gently—but Verona wants to slap her face. 'He was an interesting guy and might've had the best intentions, but he could never actually live up to them. My memories are all broken promises. Oh, Verona. Don't you see it?'

Verona feels her mouth flatline into a hard horizontal dash.

'You know what? Forget it. Forget I even came in here.' It's hard to storm out of a beanbag, but Verona manages it.

Back in her bedroom, she remembers lying on the floor of the breakfast room as a kid. Dad would go to such trouble to stock the Ferntree Gully house with food they might like and prepare their breakfasts. He would sit and talk to them at the table, not even bothering to read his morning newspaper while they were there.

She doesn't talk to Ellery for the rest of the week. But she leaves the other volumes of the *Oxford English Dictionary* outside Ellery's door.

# chapter twenty-three

VERONA IS STANDING in line at the tuckshop to buy a vegetable pastie. As the most senior grade in the school, the year twelve students have the right to jump the queue. Verona has waited five years for the chance to cut in front of the others—to push to the front like staff members are allowed to do and be served first—and she has used that privilege a lot this year. But this time there are three other year twelves in front of her and she is stuck waiting at the end of a line anyway.

She drums her fingers on the thick metal railing. She is thinking about Mr Caine's face when he spoke to her all those weeks ago, serious and urgent. There had been genuine concern behind his words to her and a desire for his star maths pupil to shine. Now that the irritation has settled, Verona wonders if she misjudged him, mistaking his advice for interference. It surprised her that he'd remembered her subjects. He'd seemed paternal, sitting on the bench with his arms folded and a frown, trying to understand—a very different paternal from Dad, who wouldn't have known what subjects she was taking or ever offered her career advice. The hands-off approach, she thinks approvingly. I like it much better that way.

---

Yet Dad's casualness had a few different sides. Verona remembers him promising to attend her clarinet recital. She had been working hard in the primary school ensemble and she was to perform three pieces on stage, including her first-ever solo. The night arrived and Verona was convinced that he was in the audience, never once wavering even when Ellery made sceptical faces beside her. Verona asked the other kids which family members had come to see them perform, just so she could say that her mum *and* her dad had come to watch her. Mum was always in attendance, but this would be the first time Dad had come to a concert. Verona's solo had been perfect: clear notes and timing. She'd let herself fall into the melody and, for once, let her body sway as she blew. Verona had raced out from the change rooms at the end of the recital, flushed with triumph. Mum and Ellery were waiting for her in the theatre.

'My darling, you were wonderful!' Mum exclaimed as she kissed Verona's forehead and smoothed her hair. 'Absolutely wonderful.'

'Thanks, Mum. Where's Dad?' Verona was scanning the crowd.

Mum's face went suddenly tight, but her voice remained gentle. 'His meeting finished late and he couldn't get here in time. He's coming to visit tomorrow instead.'

'Oh. It doesn't matter.' Verona shrugged and her eyes stopped skimming the room.

The next day, Verona received a call from Dad, still in Brisbane, apologetic but blithe.

'Sorry, Monkey, my meeting yesterday ran overtime. I got to the airport late and missed my flight. I'll be there tonight, though. How about I take you out for a late gelato to make up for it? You can even have three scoops if you want.'

Verona paused, considering his words uncertainly.

'Okay, Dad. Sure thing.'

'Good girl. You're so easygoing—I love that about you. I can always depend on you to understand.'

Those words had spun around in her head in the lead-up to his death. When she knew the extent of the diagnosis, she arranged with Mum to fly to Brisbane every three weeks.

'Come as often as you want,' Dad said. 'I won't be flying to Melbourne anytime soon.'

Gertrude was more reticent. 'That's very frequent, Verona. He and I need time alone together too.'

'I'm his daughter,' Verona reminded her indignantly.

'One of his daughters,' Gertrude replied. 'Your sister isn't showing her face, I assume?'

'What's Ellery got to do with this?'

'I know your father would like to see her. Maybe the two of you could come together. A trip every six weeks might be more realistic.'

'He's my father and I'll see him as often as I want.'

Dad had been distracted the first time she'd flown up. He had weekly appointments for his treatments and was taking what seemed like fistfuls of medication, all in different colours and sizes.

'It's a good thing I like drugs,' he joked. 'I'm living the dream.'

Dad's face was grey-tinged and his eyes looked drawn and small.

Verona had brought her clarinet up with her, so she said, 'I thought you might want to hear me play—I've got a solo coming up in a few months.'

But Dad declined. 'I'll be there to see it in person, Monkey. There's no need to start making contingency plans.'

'You don't want a preview?'

'Too much of a good thing, you know? You can play for me at your recital.'

Except he'd never actually managed to attend a recital.

Conversations with Dad had changed as well. He wanted to talk about events from his boyhood years and his time at university. Rather than the usual jaunty passage through endless new topics, discussion had become firmly anchored in the past. And on Ellery. Her name had started creeping into the conversation. Dad didn't ask Verona questions about her sister, but he wondered aloud whether Ellery could be persuaded to visit.

'Do you think she might come if I asked her, V?'

Verona was perplexed. 'Maybe,' she told Dad. 'But can't you and I just enjoy our time together right now?'

As she answered, Verona heard old words in her head: easygoing, dependable, understanding. Dad's words. Adjectives he used for Verona long ago that had become badges of honour. Except that she was here and her sister was far away. Verona was sitting in the same room as Dad, making him tea and listening to him talk—but not about her, and his eyes did not focus on her face. *I'm the one who has come to see you*, she wanted to say.

'Yes, of course, Monkey,' Dad said.

The subsequent trips to Brisbane had been much the same. Again, he'd talked about Ellery, this time wanting to know what kind of girl she had become. With the demands of year twelve, managing trips every three weeks had proved tricky after all—Verona only flew up once each month, six times in total. Sitting in the living room with Dad asking about her sister was not what she had envisaged for their time together. She answered his questions as quickly as possible and tried to steer the conversation back to their favourite topics.

'Should I put on Phil Ochs?' she asked and Dad had smiled.

'That's a great idea.'

But in June, to everyone's surprise, Ellery announced that she would be accompanying Verona.

'Why?' Verona had been shocked.

'People keep telling me that there won't be any second chances after this and maybe they're right. We're out of opportunities with Benjamin now—this is our only chance for resolution.'

'Is this a reconciliation?' Verona asked. She knew she should want this for Ellery and Dad, but all she felt was a serpentine twisting in her gut that she could not define.

'No,' said Ellery firmly. 'It's a goodbye.'

Mum had a conference in Brisbane and decided to come with them. The three of them stayed in a hotel room together in the CBD. The next day, the sisters caught a bus to West End. Verona had been taken aback when she saw the ramp heading up to the house and, inside, saw her father in a wheelchair. She bent to hug Dad, for the first time in her life not standing on her tiptoes to reach. Even though she'd been as gentle as she could, he still winced in pain.

'Sorry, V, you got a tender spot.'

His face was thinner than last time, cheeks concave.

Ellery didn't look at him. 'Hi Benjamin,' she said, her gaze slightly over his head.

'Ah, Elly, it's so good to see you.' Benjamin scrutinised her face and outfit. 'Boots and those earrings.' He sighed. 'You look just like your mother did at your age. She was beautiful.'

Dad led them from the front door down a specially constructed ramp, one wheel of the chair squeaking. He turned to Verona. 'V, do you mind waiting in the kitchen for a little while? Pop the kettle on and we'll all have a cuppa. I'd like to catch up with Ellery first.'

'Sure,' Verona said, 'I'll leave you to it.'

She flicked on the kettle and took down the teapot, but when Dad turned away to lead Ellery into the small sitting room, Verona crept after them.

'Please,' she heard Dad say, gesturing at the sofa which had Gertrude's crocheted blanket draped over the back. Ellery had sunk down awkwardly, arranging her skirt and delaying the time until she had to look up at his face again. Except for those few stilted pleasantries at Uncle Patrick's wedding, Ellery and Dad hadn't had any contact for six years.

'What did you want to talk to me about?' she asked after a couple of minutes of silence.

'Nothing,' Dad said. 'I just wanted to see you.'

'There's nothing you want to say to me?'

'No,' Dad said again. 'What can I say?' He shrugged.

'You could try something. How many more chances do you think you'll have?'

But Dad just looked at her, his eyes huge and his mouth falling open like she had struck him. Even from her vantage point at the doorway, Verona could see how those words had hurt.

'I'm sorry,' Ellery muttered.

'I know you and your mother are very close. Malti's done a great job with you and your sister. But in many ways, I think you're mostly my daughter. You and I, we're alike.'

Compliment or insult? Flattery and offence warred on Ellery's face. In the end, she just looked at him and Dad's next words came out so haltingly that they were barely coherent and so quiet that Verona had to strain to hear.

'I wish I'd known you, Ferret.'

And Verona, having heard enough, walked silently back to the kitchen.

Dad and Ellery reappeared twenty minutes later.

'I'm heading back to the hotel,' Ellery told Verona. 'I'll see you there later.'

Now it was just her and Dad.

'What's the update?' Verona asked with some trepidation as they sat in the living room with mugs in hand. They didn't discuss medical things over the phone.

'Secondaries in the bone,' Dad said, his voice clipped.

'Oh my God, Dad.'

'None of that, Monkey. I'll be just fine.'

'Don't you want to talk? Don't you think we should discuss things?'

That undulating feeling in her stomach was back. It wasn't quite nausea or pain, but it made Verona recoil.

'Ah, Monkey, let's just hang out and enjoy the time we have.'

'But—'

'Did you know the etymology of "cancer" can be traced back to the Latin word for crab?'

---

*You're so easygoing, Verona, I love that about you. I can always depend on you to understand.*

*Yes, Dad, it's okay.*

But what if it won't be okay forever? Will she one day stop saying that?

---

As the weeks pass, the questions about Dad are more sporadic. People expect her to be over it now and they themselves have started to forget. No, perhaps they haven't quite forgotten—Verona can see the remembrance flash back into their eyes on occasions when she is near and the topic of conversation tumbles its spinifex route towards fathers. But her loss is not foremost in their minds anymore. Too many losses of their own cloud their minds: everyone has their own pain to worry about and a collection of bruises which throb and ache perennially.

It is also the end of year twelve. The final week of classes is a mix of feverish eleventh-hour questions and bittersweet excitement. There will be a few weeks of study break and then they will return to the school for the exam period, but it won't be the same—they will no longer be students. Most of the cohort look sad to be leaving, their faces already nostalgic, but Verona and her friends have spent years waiting for high school to end.

On the final day there are no classes, just an assembly in the morning—the principal and the student captains give pleasant, orderly speeches. It's all over by lunchtime but everyone mills about in the quadrangle, chatting and hugging people they didn't like.

The teachers hang around too, shaking hands with the school leavers. In case there are last-minute questions during revision they give out their mobile numbers, which the students take, not entirely aware of the kindness that these gestures represent.

Mr Caine is standing against the wall and Verona wanders over to say hello.

'Hey, Mr Caine.'

He smiles. 'Call me Albert.'

Verona, alarmed, shakes her head. All the teachers are reintroducing themselves to the students by their first names today, but nobody has the nerve to actually use them. Mr Caine will always be Mr Caine.

Verona fumbles in her pocket and hands him a small paper bag. Mr Caine looks surprised, but takes it nonetheless. He reaches inside and pulls out a metal keyring ornamented with miniatures of a calculator, compass and protractor.

'I found it at the Acland Street market,' Verona tells him. 'I thought you might like it.'

She shuffles from one foot to the other— she has never bought a present for a teacher before and it feels a bit weird. But Mr Caine is smiling.

'Verona, I'm touched. Thank you.'

Verona finds herself dropping her eyes to the ground. 'No,' she shakes her head, talking to her shoes. 'Thank *you*. For everything.'

'You've been a pleasure to teach. Do keep in touch and let me know what adventures you get up to.'

She nods, and they shake hands.

And, just like that, it's over. Verona, Tommy, Claire, Charlie, Luke and Yumiko walk out through the school gates for one last time as a group. None of them knows what the future holds but, right now, they have each other.

---

In October, Mum reads the newspapers with her forehead creased. A spindly-legged fifteen-year-old on a bike throws the furled-up scroll over the wall each day and Mum goes out in her dressing-gown to fish it out of the dewy garden bed. She doesn't usually sit over the paper in the mornings—that was more Dad's thing. She only gets absorbed in news if it's bad.

'What's up?' Ellery asks the first morning this happens. Mum sits with the newsprint like a placemat underneath her coffee mug and a taut expression on her face.

'Oh, nothing,' Mum says, looking up from the paper and frowning. 'Just problems in Fiji as always.'

'Like what?' Ellery asks.

'History repeating itself,' Mum replies. She sounds tired rather than sad. She shakes her head and folds the paper roughly, so the edges no longer line up. Verona is surprised—she had assumed that Mum was following the passage of a case. Mum does that from time to time and calls the High Court judges names under her breath.

'Another coup?' asks Ellery.

'A third coup seems likely,' Mum confirms.

Ellery and Verona exchange a glance, trying to take clues from the other as to how to act. How much care are they supposed to show for Mum's homeland? It does not belong to them, after all.

'That's really sad,' Ellery says. She at least has been to Fiji and has some frame of reference.

'Yes, it is, but not really surprising,' Mum says. She gives the paper a little shake and leaves it on the bench, heading upstairs to get ready for work. Ellery picks it up and flicks through it, while Verona tries to locate the island geographically in her mind. Is it near New Zealand or out towards the east? Come to think of it, maybe New Zealand is eastwards. She constructs the shadowy, misshapen globe in her mind and lets it spin. Half of who she is. But what does that actually mean?

Things just get worse in coming weeks and Mum keeps reading the paper at the breakfast table. Both the girls have taken to flipping through it when she's done—Ellery first and then Verona—becoming familiar with new concepts and names neither of them dare to attempt to pronounce aloud. Bainimarama and Qarase. Calls for resignation. Ellery seems less mystified by the whole thing, but Verona suspects that this is a bluff. None of it makes a lot of sense to the girls, though it seems to mean something to their mother. Even though she says that she never felt at home in Fiji, she seems attached to the country of her birth in a way that cannot be fully excised or surmounted. Mum reads the paper dutifully and, at the end of the day, the papers tumble into the blue recycling bin with the washed-out containers of Pura and empty egg cartons.

---

Ellery is in the kitchen, cupboard-foraging. She pulls out a packet of salted cashews and, seeing Verona hovering in the doorway, pours them into a white ceramic bowl. She carries them to the kitchen table along with a half-drunk glass of milk.

'Not like you to snack between meals,' Verona observes, sitting down at the table too.

'I'm stress eating.'

'Comfort eating I think they call that.'

'Whatever.'

Ellery doesn't volunteer any further information, but Verona is curious now. Ellery's eyes are wide in their sockets and her fingers twist the cashews around in her hands like worry beads, fiddling with them rather than eating. On closer appearance, the roots of her hair are not silky like usual, but clumped into greasy little strands.

'Okay, I'll bite,' Verona says. 'Why are you stressed?'

Ellery flushes. 'I'm not fishing,' she says in a sharp voice more like Verona's than her own.

Verona stares at her, but for once does not snap back. 'Why are you stressed?' she repeats instead.

Ellery shakes her head, looking into the middle distance.

'Well?'

For several minutes, Ellery says nothing—simply rolls the cashews between her fingers. Then she cranes her neck to peer out into the hallway. Verona knows that particular move: checking that their mother is not standing outside. Verona herself does this frequently.

'I sat my end of semester constitutional law exam and I'm sure that I failed.'

Ellery is usually calm about exams—she doesn't jump to assumptions or freak out over an unexpected question. She has never failed an exam before, never even hypothesised about it. Verona is the one who goes in for post-mortems and funeral rites, but Ellery never has.

'You'll be fine,' Verona says. 'You always are.' Her sympathy is limited when her own exams are mere weeks away and will, she suspects, decide the rest of her entire life—her whole future happiness and fate for eternity. But whenever she says things like this, Ellery rolls her eyes and their mother gives the kind of considered, thoughtful advice which, if possible, is even more frustrating. Verona will decapitate the next person who uses the phrase 'alternative pathways' in her presence. It's the educational equivalent to there being many more fish in the sea: totally unhelpful.

'Not this time I won't be.' Ellery shakes her head miserably. She holds up her fingers, flecked with salt. 'The first hypothetical was impossible, and even though I'd read the case law carefully all I could think of in the second one was Mabo. I have no idea what response they wanted . . .' The pitch of her voice is rising, like a wayward recorder being played in primary school music class.

'So? Just take the exam again.'

'I can't! If I fail I have to repeat the unit—it's a core subject.'

Ellery's eyes are button-bright and her throat twitches as she swallows. And, okay, there might be one horrible moment when Verona feels a dark rush of pleasure at seeing her sister unspooling. Verona can make out the forked pathway ahead of her; does she offer a prickly retort or murmur sympathetically? She hesitates.

'I'm sure that it'll be fine,' Verona says after a long pause. 'What did Josh say?' She's a bit surprised that he isn't here now to hold her sister's hand and fuss.

But at this Ellery twists in her seat and won't meet Verona's eyes. 'Josh doesn't know.'

'Wasn't he at the same exam?'

'Yes, but I didn't talk to him.'

'You two haven't broken up, have you?'

And though she has kind of been hoping for this, speaking the words splashes a chilly wave of sadness over Verona. It's almost too weird to think of Josh no longer being in the house with them—trying to engage Verona in conversation, and his deep laugh when he and Ellery sit on the sofa watching movies.

'No,' Ellery mutters. 'But I don't know what to say to him.'

'What's the matter with you? Of course he'll understand.'

Ellery eats another couple of cashews. 'No, I mean he asked me to move out with him and I don't know what to say.'

'Move out? Just the two of you?'

'Yeah.'

'Wow. Well, that's a big step.'

'Exactly.'

Verona pictures being in the house with just their mother and grimaces; it would be very quiet around the dinner table.

'Well, you've been dating all year.'

'Seven months.'

'Whatever. If it doesn't work, you just move somewhere else or come back home.'

'I still don't know how serious I am about him.'

Ellery's forehead is drawn up towards her hair—creased—and for a moment, Verona can see an image of her sister in thirty years' time.

Maybe Ellery too is lost and flailing. Again, Verona perceives that fork in the road and one part of her is so tempted to antagonise her sister. But today she channels their mother.

'Don't worry, Elly,' Verona says. (Ellery raises her eyebrows at the seldom-used nickname.) 'You'll figure it out.' And she takes a few of the cashews from the half-full bowl.

---

Josh turns up later that evening. Mum is working late and the girls are fending for themselves. When Josh comes over, the two lovebirds usually like to cook: spicy bean homemade pizza, jalapeño fish tacos, sage and mushroom pies, Portuguese feijoada—their menus are endless and varied. Tonight, however, the kitchen has the cold, loveless look of a place that hasn't been occupied all day. It'll be scrambled eggs on freezer toast for Verona, while Ellery looks like she is skipping dinner altogether. She has been upstairs in her room all afternoon. Verona refuses to go and knock on the door to ask if she is okay—that would be patronising. But tonight Josh arrives without the usual shopping bags of ingredients; his hands are in his pockets rather than clutching plastic handles.

'Is Ellery here?' he asks when Verona opens the door.

'Didn't she invite you over?'

'No, I haven't seen her all day. She was five desks away in the exam room, but didn't talk to me beforehand and pretty much scarpered afterwards.'

Verona shrugs. 'She's weird today.'

But Josh looks upset. 'She's avoiding me. Do you know what's going on?'

'Maybe you should ask her.'

'I would, but she hasn't responded to my messages.'

Verona hesitates. *She doesn't want to move in with you.* 'She thinks she failed the exam.'

'Everybody thinks they failed the exam! She'd know that if she'd stuck around for more than ten seconds afterwards.'

'So go and tell her that.'

Josh disappears upstairs and Verona puts the frozen sourdough in the toaster. Three times she lowers the lever: once to defrost, the second to get hot, the third for some colour. She is peering into its metallic grille, monitoring for the precise shade of gold that she requires, when Josh reappears at the foot of the staircase.

'All good in paradise?' she asks. She's going for comedic, but it just sounds snarky. 'How is she?'

'Maybe I shouldn't have come over tonight,' Josh says uneasily, rubbing his palm on the nape of his neck. He looks tired and pale. 'Maybe she needs some time alone.'

'What did she say?'

'Nothing—that's the weird thing. She just seems kind of . . . distant. I came to make us a cup of tea and then maybe I'll just go home.'

Verona has not been watching her toast and it pops up now, heavily bronzed, almost blackened. She wants to throw it out, but Josh is watching and her conscience—or maybe pride—has pricked its ears: think of the starving children in Africa. She sighs and begins buttering it reluctantly.

'I wouldn't worry about it,' she says to Josh. 'Ellery has strange reactions to things sometimes.'

'What do you mean?' He has flicked the switch on the kettle and is fishing teabags out of the cupboard.

'She always had strange responses to Dad.'

'Ah.'

'She never let him do something right, she always had to find fault with him.' Verona's mind is so ready to drift on this tangent, memories already hammering at the door to be let in. She knows she ought to steer the conversation back to the topic at hand.

'Really?'

'Yeah, and he was such a good man. Good to us.'

'Is that really how it was?' Josh asks quietly.

'What are you saying?' Hackles raise immediately and Verona hears her voice go all tough. 'You're just listening to Ellery.'

Josh nods like he's thinking about this, like she has presented a well-reasoned argument which he must now consider. He always takes her seriously, never treats her like just the kid sister.

'Ellery sees things her way, you see things yours. I'm guessing reality is somewhere in the middle. Well, it usually is.'

'Not always,' Verona retorts.

'No,' Josh agrees. 'But maybe it's possible to love dearly someone who might still be flawed, don't you think? Maybe it's okay to see people for who they truly are and love them anyway.'

'What are you saying?'

'It's easy to love idols, but it's not a very true form of love. You've got to remember all of him—not just some parts. If you're keeping him alive, keep all of him. Ghosts have warts and flaws, just like the rest of us.'

He adds milk to the tea and carries it away upstairs.

---

As it turns out, Josh leaves after breakfast the next day. He and Ellery emerge from her room around 11 am. They're not holding hands or stroking each other with private little caresses when they think nobody is watching, but Ellery seems calm and at least smiles when Josh makes a joke. Apparently there's nothing a bit of sex won't resolve, Verona thinks, sour and envious.

They're all on swot vac, so the three of them sit in the kitchen making idle small talk. But when Josh's station wagon puffs its way out of the driveway, Verona's curiosity gets the better of her.

'Did you patch it up?'

Ellery sighs. 'Not really. It's okay for now, I guess. But I still don't know if I want to move in with him.'

'Why? Josh is alright.'

Ellery stares at her. 'What makes you say that? You hate him.'

'I don't.'

'You always say he's boring and proper and predictable.'

'Well, he is.'

'So then?'

'He is all those things, but isn't that what you want in a boyfriend? He's a good guy.'

'Did I miss something?'

'We had a chat last night. Move in with him or not, it's your choice, but don't discount what you'd be giving up.' Verona pauses, and then: 'If it were me, I'd go for it. Why not?'

'And leave you and Mum here alone together?' There's amusement in Ellery's voice.

'Yeah, well. Maybe we'll be okay too.'

# chapter twenty-four

THE NOVEMBER PAPERS bring tidings of negotiations in Fiji.

'That's promising,' Verona comments.

Mum's laugh has a bitter resonance. 'It won't last.'

But Verona has more important things to worry about. The year has crept by and she has been preoccupied with ghosts and tissue boxes, trying to juggle her studies with the endless flow of grief.

Most of her exams take place in the small classrooms in which they usually have lessons. The teachers push open the dividing walls between four or five rooms, and measure the distance of the desks from one another. Their faces are set into humourless lines lest the formality of the situation be forgotten, but it's still somehow different sitting these all-important exams with a row of windows to her right and the periwinkle sky all too visible. Six exams are spread over two weeks in polite intervals which force her to sell her soul to study timetables and keep a meticulous diary.

She juggles memorising the Krebs cycle with re-reading her notes on the caesura. She recites legal terminology and does so many algebra problems that she dreams about the bottom of the alphabet when she closes her eyes.

Doubts lurk on the sidelines and pour their poison into her ears. She swore that she would come to the end of her final year of school with no regrets and nothing half-done, but now that it is here she wonders if maybe she could have worked harder. Mum's favourite little saying keeps occurring to her—she's worked hard, yes, but has she worked smart? Why do all the most insidious questions come at her in other people's voices?

She comes out of the maths paper—her first exam—with an internal smile that she tries not to show. Chemistry and physics go well too. But English is as difficult as she feared, as are the other humanities subjects. Her last exam is history. She has gone over all the papers in her head a hundred times and now can't even remember the questions.

'That was good, I thought,' says Yumiko, walking out with her.

'Yeah,' Verona says quietly. 'And who cares anyway? We're done.'

She comes home with a hot sickly feeling in her belly.

'You can never really know how you did,' Mum says when Verona shares her fears at the dinner table that evening.

'Don't count your chickens,' Ellery agrees.

They both look so earnest and adamant, but Verona can't help thinking that their voices sound overly hearty. She knows that they don't expect her to get the grades she needs, and this polite encouragement is irritating. But she is too sad and tired to be snappish.

'Maybe' she says.

But a new plan is forming in her mind, where Mr Caine's words reverberate. Late at night on her laptop, she researches university courses, trying to find a contingency plan in case her fears are confirmed when her results are mailed out to her later in the month. She doesn't quite know how she comes across Roman Jakobson—she spirals down a rabbit hole where one search term leads to another until she is deeply embedded—but when she comes across a passage he has written, she feels her breath stop in her chest: *One cannot but agree with the mathematician J. Hadamard, who in 1943 acknowledged the progress of the structural trend in the science of language by declaring linguistics to be a bridge between mathematics and humanities.*

It turns out mathematical linguistics is its own discipline—a whole area of study she never knew about. Why has nobody told her? Skimming through the terminology Jakobson uses—recursion, automata, theories of communication and probabilistic models—Verona feels something illuminate within. Yes, this is it. Reading these words gives her the same feeling as walking into maths class on a Monday morning—familiarity and confidence. But this is even better, because it will take her forwards in Dad's footsteps. I'll keep you alive, she resolves anew, even if all she can offer is imitation. He'd be proud, she thinks. I'm going to be just like him.

Verona is not superstitious enough to think that the *bhoot* is hovering at her shoulder—she will not entertain such thoughts—but all the same there's a chill on her skin and she finds herself peering into the corners of the room and eyeing the gap beneath her built-in robes. The *bhoot* leaves when unfinished business is resolved, so why does the air still feel so charged with melancholy rather than celebration?

---

That Friday night, Mum insists on a dinner in the CBD to commemorate the end of Verona's exams. Ellery, Josh and Mum are there, and Conner comes too, carrying a small bunch of freesias for Verona. The others seem to find this sweeter than Verona, who can't help seeing it as for Mum's benefit. Still, Conner is alright. He's more conventional than Dad was but at least has the good sense not to try to step into the girls' lives as some kind of watered-down replacement father. He's distantly paternal and that'll do just fine.

The city is crackling and coming to life. The wind sweeps the streets, making her shiver. The buskers, performers and artists have staked their street corners. A man in a brown fedora has a line of saucepans in front of him and he is going at them with wooden drumsticks—an artsy twist on the toddler game of kitchenware percussion. One block down, another man paints his half-remembered dream onto the concrete Mary Poppins–style. There is pastel on his fingertips and fervour in his eyes. And just up from the train station, a woman sits on an upended milk crate. She is smoking a cigarette and watching the screen of her phone, but she's fixed a cardboard sign to the table in front of her: *I'll write a free poem for you on any subject. Come say hello.* Nobody approaches her.

In the restaurant, Josh and Ellery hold hands under the table, obviously under the impression that nobody can see. They cannot help putting their hands on each other when they are together, little strokes and pats. Ellery rubs Josh's wrist and he swirls his fingers under the crease of her knee. Verona refrains from snark with difficulty. She looks down at the list of dumplings instead. And, now that her final year of school is officially behind her, there is the hope unfurling—the one she can barely admit to herself and will never speak aloud: And next year, there will be someone for me. So she keeps her snorts and eye rolls to herself. They seem happy, Ellery and Josh. They are sharing a plate of dumplings and using the same bowl of dipping sauce. Ellery's eyes are clear and she does not pause or hesitate before she places her fingers on the back of her boyfriend's neck. They have not made any announcements about their living arrangements, but they have been stealing the rental sections of the newspapers, squirrelling them away to Ellery's bedroom. Sooner or later they will find a shitty little bedsit somewhere and disappear. In the past week, Mum has officially listed the house on the market, but Verona can't even bring herself to get worked up. Whatever Mum and Ellery say, she knows she has not got the marks for law. But all she is thinking about is being out here tonight—the way Melbourne sparkles and the company of her family. And the fact that Dad won't be there to watch her graduate. Everything else seems far away, like a hazy, cloud-tinged horizon. A far-off fairy tale.

---

Soon afterwards, in early December, Mum reads the story below the fold and throws the paper down on the table.

'Well,' she says. 'So that's that.'

Verona glances at the headline. 'Another coup?' She can say the word properly now and spell it too. She knows to sound incredulous but not astonished.

'Another coup. The second one this year.' Mum leaves the kitchen without looking back at the paper. She continues to follow the goings-on for a few days more, but it looks like she is just skimming, and when Fiji drops from the headlines she does not go out of her way to hunt down news. George Speight will go on trial in coming months and Mum will pick up the paper again, watching afar in resignation. Homeland is unchangeable, but home is a choice.

Yet there are still pictures on the walls of Mum growing up in Nadi, a skinny teenager with plaited hair and a pale skirt past her knees. Also a picture that Dad took of her on their honeymoon, standing on the beach, head thrown back to catch the wind and hair streaming like squid ink. And if they were to look in the photo albums tucked away in the brown wicker basket that was once a toy box, there would be pictures from Mum's trips to Fiji. The island won't be escaped so easily.

---

There's never any garish sign out the front, but there are house inspections by appointment in the coming weeks before the Christmas period kicks off. Mum doesn't ask the girls for help—just tells them to keep their rooms tidy on those days—but they see her scrubbing the benches and sweeping the floors. The house gleams for the well-dressed strangers who walk through it, who see the house as a property rather than a home. Verona wonders what they will think of her tessellated doona covers and the Neil deGrasse Tyson books on her shelf. Will they invent a character for the house-dwellers as they pass through the rooms? Will they judge her on her reading taste? The imprint of these strangers lingers in the house long after they have passed through; Verona can smell strange cologne in her room and sense the tread of clean runners on the stairs.

Verona keeps her reservations to herself, bites back all the counterarguments, and sees Ellery look at her approvingly one evening over dinner when she lets an opening go by and doesn't bring up how much she doesn't want to leave.

So this is growing up.

---

Dad haunts Verona daily. But she will take a ghost—a *bhoot* even—over complete absence. A world without him is unthinkable.

She will keep playing Phil Ochs for him and reading his weird fantasy novels. *The Weirdstone of Brisingamen*, wreathed in marginalia, sits on her shelf. She has left his dog-eared pages as they came.

Sometimes she thinks back to the day she heard the news of his passing. She can't decide whether it feels like two weeks or two years ago.

But the Dad drifting in and out of her mind looks a bit different now. Small, forgotten memories keep creeping and it's harder to dismiss them. Maybe their father was somewhere between her Dad and Ellery's Benjamin.

Josh's words ring in her mind. *Remember all of him—not just some parts.*

# coda

# 2007

THE FURNITURE HAS been spirited away, the round table and heavy bookshelves lifted from their rooms for the first time in twenty years. Left behind on the floors are stencils of dark polished wood. Sunlight and footfall have dulled the rest of the boards, but these circles and rectangles are a time capsule back to when this house was in its infancy. In the front garden, the hydrangeas are in full bloom and the flowerbeds are flushed with colour from petals and kumquats. The hinges of the back door no longer squeal and the walls have been freshly painted. Malti has tried to erase the wear and tear of two decades as much as possible with small renovations: the skirting boards have been wiped clean of the bruises from school shoes and the venetian blinds cured of the greenstick fractures which had bent their edges. The house is both better and yet inevitably more careworn—clean and repaired, but without the aura of newness.

Once again, the books were the first things to be packed—Malti's legal textbooks and classics—but this time there were no naval biographies to place alongside them in the boxes.

Once again, the removalists had worked efficiently as they moved through the house, but this time Conner and the girls had joined her to help arrange all the belongings for the trucks.

And now, once again, Malti stands alone under the high ceilings of the house, but this time because she has asked for it to be this way.

---

Malti's friends responded to the news with frowns.

'You actually went through with selling the house? But why?'

'Keen for something new.'

She kept her response light, devoid of the bittersweetness of saying goodbye. Only Erik and Maeve seemed to understand.

'It's time,' they agreed when Malti told them she had accepted an offer.

The girls were both living out of home, but had clothes and books stored in their childhood bedrooms. They returned on weekends to help their mother pack. Grown children. *Empty nester* was the phrase they used for women like Malti in the Sunday papers, as though her whole life was defined by her kids.

The girls had not said anything, but Malti saw their downturned mouths and crossed arms. They exchanged glances with each other when they thought she was not looking and she could hear the words they did not speak in their silences.

She was grateful for the long settlement—it had taken months to sort through all the small fragments of domesticity: old bank statements, rubber bands, cloudy Tupperware and missing socks. Despite her attempts at curation, in the end there was still a full truckload of accumulated debris and paraphernalia leaving the house.

The removalists were due on Saturday afternoon, so Conner and the girls convened at the house in the morning.

'Right,' Malti said. 'This is the list of things we need to do.'

The girls' phones weren't far away from their hands and they carried the boxes more slowly than Malti would like, but they were there. When Conner and Malti's cars were full with boxes, Ellery took a bucket and detergent to clean the bathrooms while Verona scrubbed the oven and kitchen countertops. It was just a rudimentary clean—professional cleaners would come through on Monday. They set up an iPod and speakers downstairs which blared guitar and drums.

'What about some nice clarinet music?' Malti suggested.

'This is Kings of Leon, Mum,' they replied in disgust.

At lunchtime, Josh turned up with ham sandwiches and vanilla slice. There was enough for everyone.

'You shouldn't have,' Malti told him.

'It was no trouble,' he said. 'I got them from work. We were catering an event and had leftovers. If you want, we could put some boxes in my car too? I emptied the boot.'

Nice young man, Malti thought, not for the first time. He and Ellery shared secret smiles and gentle touches, looking at each other in a way that made Malti remember blue eyes, draughty lecture halls and red-and-gold saris.

Malti and Conner ate quickly and returned to the boxes, but the kids took their time over lunch. The dining room chairs were piled in the hallway ready to be moved, so the three of them sat cross-legged on the floor. There was no friction between the sisters today—the girls were united in their disappointment, heads tilted towards one another conspiratorially. Still, disappointment was better than antipathy. When they'd finished eating, both girls walked through every room, trailing their hands over the walls and whispering quietly. *Bye, house.*

Malti could still see the babies that they were in her daughters' faces—bone structures still partway between one world and the other. They were legally adults now, all grown up, but still so young and on the cusp of so much. *Women children.*

And look at them—look at who they were. Ellery, with her easy sunny smiles and caring disposition. Verona, fiery, independent and entirely comfortable in her own skin. Malti felt a fierce rush of warmth for both of them.

'You did well,' people often told her. 'They're wonderful girls.'

'Yes, but that's just who they are—I didn't have much to do with it,' was her usual demurral. But not today. Today she saved a secret piece of the warmth spreading up from inside for herself. She savoured the sight of her daughters sitting together in the house they lived in as a trio for so many years. This was her handiwork.

The removal trucks came after lunch and the boxes and furniture were whisked away. Malti, the girls, Conner and Josh watched from inside. But Verona's eyes were on the sky.

'Rain coming,' she predicted, pointing to the encroaching greyness.

'Damn,' said Ellery to Josh. 'I just hung out the towels.'

The removalists followed Malti and Conner to his place two suburbs over in St Kilda, where they unloaded everything with their trolleys. Josh and the girls arrived just behind, bringing the final boxes in Josh's car. Both Malti and Conner had carefully rationalised their belongings to merge two houses into one—everything would fit, Malti had to reassure herself as she surveyed the cardboard chaos around them.

The kids were done. They stood in the hallway of Conner's house with bags slung over their shoulders and vague references to house parties. Josh and Ellery were off to Brunswick and Verona was headed to Prahran.

'I'll call you tomorrow, Mum,' said Ellery, with a hug and a kiss.

'See you, Mum.' Verona's hugs were more grudging and dutiful, but she nonetheless allowed Malti to give her shoulders a quick squeeze and kiss her cheek.

'We'll drop you off,' Josh said to Verona, who muttered a thank you.

The long process of unpacking would start later; for now, Malti and Connor headed back to the Beach Road house for the final clean-up. Conner drove as Malti stifled a yawn in the passenger seat. By the time they arrived, the sun had moved further across the sky and the grey clouds were gathering, as Verona predicted.

The driveway was just as empty as the house. Inside, the rooms were bare and hollow and, looking around, Malti felt a tightening somewhere between her stomach and chest.

Conner reached for the vacuum cleaner.

'Should we do a quick spruce ahead of the cleaners? I'll take the upstairs. Do you want to sweep downstairs?'

But Malti hesitated. 'Actually, do you mind if I finish out the day by myself? There's not much more to do.'

'I'm happy to help. Many hands and whatnot.'

'It's not that. I just want a bit of time alone today.'

'Are you sure?'

'Yeah.'

Conner wasn't taciturn, but he used words sparingly. He'd take her in his arms rather than wrapping her in words. He'd cook a meal he knew she liked and forgo the lavish compliments. He did not follow words down rabbit holes, get lost in verbal eddies or hurl them like blades in anger. Words were merely incidental. A small crease had formed between Conner's eyebrows, like the turned-down corner of a page, but he just kissed her. 'Then I'll see you a bit later. Give me a call for a lift when you're done.'

The day had been dry and hot, but now came the rain. It burst from above and fell hard—Conner had to sprint to his car through a deluge, arms curled ineffectually over his head.

---

When Conner has left, Malti stands alone in the entrance hall. Without the gentle electric hum of the fridge and the stereo, the house is preternaturally silent—all the appliances are at Conner's and even the pipes are still and quiescent this afternoon. The road outside is the only source of noise, but even the rush of cars is muffled by the fall of raindrops—and Malti's ears are turned inwards anyhow.

The home she has worked so hard to build is drawing its final breath—a gasping inhalation which will be released when she passes through the front door one last time and the heartbeat of domesticity is laid to rest. She flashes unexpectedly on William Wordsworth, who once admired the quietened city of the early morning, a fragment long-forgotten from high school English: *The very houses seem asleep; And all that mighty heart is lying still!* This house will not die, but simply lie dormant—a new life cycle emerging for the next owners in an eternal reincarnation.

She supposes she should give the floors a final sweep and flit over the surfaces with a duster before she loses the light, but the broomstick falls from her hand. In the silence of the house, so many memories collide in her mind: Ellery gazing longingly as gulab jamun cools on a round silver tray on the dining table; the uneven stair to the laundry where Verona fell and chipped her tooth; the cupboard under the stairs where the girls would burrow in games of hide-and-seek; a balmy Boxing Day evening with Erik and Maeve drinking port on the balcony; and Conner whistling to himself as he planted marigolds in the garden bed last year.

But there is also the absence of memories too. The memories that never came to pass—the ones that never got to be memories at all, but remained simply as fermented wishes and lost hopes—like the child that was never born and the uneaten dinners packed away in Tupperware in the fridge. Today these lie thick and heavy over the house. This house was salvaged from sadness—the husband returning home to a darkened house and a wife feigning sleep.

The visions playing across her mind are not hologram memories; they are somehow more robust and animate. From the corner of her eye, Malti can make out slight movements. There's a faint shimmer to her left, an interplay of water and light on the window. Perhaps these memories are really spirits, appearing one final time. Not Udre Udre, the figure she had so badly misunderstood, or Ellery's Kuttichathan, the mischief maker. No, this is a ghost—Verona's *bhoot*, come to visit. Benjamin is the conspicuous memory at the fringes of all the others. Does he still exist in this house? He only lived here for a few years, but he is the reason she is standing in this place; the house had been bought for a life with him. Malti suspects that even now there are yellow-tinged books hidden away unnoticed in those boxes with Benjamin's name scrawled in the front, just as he lingers on in the shape of Ellery's eyes and Verona's tempestuous moods.

And, suddenly, the scene is conjured in the empty room, figures so real she could touch them: herself and Benjamin clinking glasses in a bare kitchen, surrounded by the boxes and debris of arrival. Their faces are clear and unlined, lips curved upwards and eyes shining with excitement. That young woman in the kitchen is looking at Benjamin with desire that fumes in the air. Malti, for a moment seeing back in time, can discern so much hope on her own face that she closes her eyelids tight against the apparition.

She had been driven not even by love, but by hope—the dream of what she wanted—which was somehow more powerful and dangerous. Hope, she had realised far too late, will make a person do anything. Perhaps wooden structures could never have supported the weight of so much expectation.

Almost concurrently, the future that never came to pass emerges, bright and blazing. The thirty-something couple fades away to be replaced by her and Benjamin packing up the house together, grey streaks at their temples and mouths bracketed with slight lines from years of smiling. When Benjamin seals the final box shut with brown masking tape, they fish out a pair of plastic cups and a bottle of champagne. This time, they can both drink the alcohol as they toast, once again, to new beginnings. *Here's to the next chapter, my love. Here's to freedom.* Or would she have been left with dustpan and brush, and an apology on voicemail as Benjamin worked late once again?

The fragments of regret she feels in her chest are not sharp-edged anymore, but dull and fuzzy. Yet, still, they are there.

The rain is really coming down now—slanting onto the windows, the drops splintering into triple shards on the glass. The rush of cars on Beach Road sounds wet and sibilant, the tyres kicking up a sea spray of their own.

Every moment here brings frissons of finality. As she moves through each room of the house the awareness resounds in her mind: this is the last time. And although she knows that change doesn't have to mean loss, sometimes it feels as if the two are helplessly entwined.

She stood alone on this doorstep almost twenty years ago to enter this house for the first time, and she will pull the door shut alone too. Was this full circle inevitable? Was this always a square dance back to the beginning? Maybe, in the end, it's all been choreographed to precision: begin and end in the same place and circle back again. Orchestral, played to a score.

Then again, maybe not. Malti knows the malleability of home more than most.

Fiji had become home for her ancestor—an adolescent girl who had been taken from her village in India and carried across the waters to grow up on foreign soil and harvest sugar for white men. The woman's children had grown up thinking those lands were their home, but the land was never really theirs, and her children's children and their families had ultimately been displaced from their adopted homeland.

Home is where the heart is: a proverb turned cliché which, like most clichés, turns out to be deeply true.

Home is your safe harbour, with all its pleasures.

Home is belonging. Even when Australia offered a prickly, ambivalent welcome, Malti has always belonged in this house.

Home is the kids eating lunch on the floor together and Conner busying himself packing the cars.

---

The rain has finally stopped. Through the window, Malti can see dappled light and patches of sun—the caramelised shade of late afternoon. Her girls are out in the city, while Conner will be cooking fajitas in his lemon-coloured kitchen.

'We should get married,' he says from time to time. 'If I asked, would you say yes?'

'Don't ask,' Malti always advises. 'If you need to pre-empt the question, you already know the answer.'

'They say it's different the second time around.'

He looks wistful in a way she cannot understand. Her mind flashes to empty driveways and silent dinners. Some experiences do not bear repeating.

'We'll make our own way forwards,' she likes to tell him, reaching for his hand.

Malti ties the strings on the plastic bags of rubbish they left in the front room and slings her handbag over her shoulder. The key is in the palm of her hand—she will drop it to the estate agent tomorrow for the cleaners and, after them, the new owners. She passes through the front door. Outside, the scent of damp earth and newness hangs in the air, thick and fecund. Fecundity, a word Benjamin would've plucked from the air to play with. But there's a better word for it—petrichor. Another one of Benjamin's words.

She remembers the rise and fall of Benjamin's chest through his cotton t-shirt as he inhaled, head thrown back and mouth slightly open. The air was thick with remnants of dampness, but everything had looked particularly clear and washed clean. Campus was deserted and entirely theirs—everyone else had retreated to the dry safety of lecture halls or the library, unaware that the rain had ceased. Benjamin had stepped off the concrete walkway onto the grass itself, mottled from too many stray feet.

'Can you smell that?' he asked.

'Yes,' she replied, pausing to tilt her nose to the sky. 'There's a scent in the air.'

'Exactly. There's a word for it, you know.' He gave her the requisite etymology lesson as they walked, their shoes sliding slightly in the damp soil. 'It was coined by Australian scientists in the sixties,' he told her.

'Is that right?' she murmured, more focused on him than his words.

'Petrichor. The smell of hot dry earth after the rain.'

'It's not a pretty word,' she observed.

'Not phonetically, perhaps,' he agreed. 'But the semantics are pretty wonderful, don't you think?'

'Yes,' she said. 'They are.'

He took her hand, and from that moment on she had always remembered the word in the aftermath of rain when the earth came alive. Petrichor: possibility and renewal. A Benjamin word, perhaps, but a Malti concept—something that, of the two of them, only she had lived.

---

Malti pulls the front door to number 112 shut. She feels the heaviness in her hand as the wood thuds and, as it does, she feels something heavy release within her chest.

She does not linger on the doorstep, but steps onto the pathway, bordered by sodden grass. The rain is still at bay and for a moment she toys with the idea of walking, keen to breathe in the scent and feel it washing through her alveoli. The sky is pale apricot and cloud-marbled, making promises of the sunset ahead and, after all, Conner's place is only half an hour away. But her feet ache dully from being on the move all day and she doesn't want to wait to see his face.

As always, when she rings, Conner answers immediately.

'How's it going over there?' There's some hesitancy in his voice. Perhaps he, too, has been wrestling with the ghosts.

'Can you come and get me?' she asks. 'I'm ready.'

# Acknowledgements

I WOULDN'T BE writing this at all if it wasn't for the opportunity that the Richell Prize for Emerging Writers offered me, so thank you first and foremost to the Richell family and the 2020 judges. Some experiences are genuinely life-changing (which isn't a word I use lightly)—and winning the award certainly was for me.

Thank you to the entire team at Hachette Australia and especially to the incredible editors who have worked with me on this novel. To Vanessa Radnidge—editor extraordinaire and all around lovely human being—I've felt so lucky to have your warmth, empathy, and care during this process. The amazing Karen Ward was also tireless in her work on this book and Ali Lavau's thoughtful edits and insights smoothed out my draft into an actual novel.

Thank you to both the Dylan Thomas Foundation and to the Allen Ginsberg estate, for kindly allowing me to quote from two of my favourite poems.

Thank you to my mother, Ranjani Ratnam, and to Satya Nandam for all their love and encouragement, and patiently providing feedback on early drafts. To Saroj Nandam for answering my obstetrics questions. To Judith Smith for being such a constant and supportive part of my life. To Heather Yelland for her encouragement and generosity. To Will.

Thank you to Evan Smith. Malti's experiences as lawyer draw inspiration from his accounts of life at the Victorian Bar.

Thank you also to Joel Friedlaender and Liora Dafner-Beach for running Red Guava in a way that gives me flexibility to write and introducing me to a wonderful bunch of people at the company.

**Aisling Smith** is a Melbourne-based writer. She was the winner of the 2020 Richell Prize for Emerging Writers and holds a PhD in Literary Studies.